You Think You Know Me

You Think You Know Me

Clare Chase

A delicious selection of fiction!

Published 2015 by Choc Lit Limited
Penrose House, Crawley Drive, Camberley, Surrey GU15 2AB, UK
www.choc-lit.com

A CIP catalogue record for this book is available
from the British Library

ISBN 978-1-78189-254-1

Printed and bound by Clays Ltd

To Charlie, Georgie and Ros,
with very much love.

Acknowledgements

Huge thanks to my family for the amazing support they've given me, especially Charlie, Georgie and Ros for their steadfast encouragement, and Mum for acting as a one-woman PR agency. (I haven't forgotten the photocopied Bookseller article at the family party…!) Also to Dad, Phil, David, Pat, Warty and my wider family. Massive thanks to my friends too, the Cambridge ones, the Westfield gang, the Portland ones and all elsewhere.

Before signing with Choc Lit, I received invaluable advice from the RNA's New Writers' Scheme. It's also been great to get to know fellow RNA members. And in those pre-signed days, thanks also to Novelicious for shortlisting *You Think You Know Me* (then called *Anna in the Works*) for their Undiscovered prize.

And so to Choc Lit, and heartfelt thanks to the Tasting panel who gave my book the thumbs up (Sarah C, Leanne, Sandra F, Rebecca, Linda Sy, Liz G, Betty, Jane O and Margaret J). And thanks also, very much, to the entire Choc Lit team who have been truly great to work with: friendly, professional and supportive. And last but definitely not least, thanks to my fellow Chocliteers, who've made me feel instantly welcome.

Chapter One

It was 8 p.m. when I walked into Sebastian Rice's gallery that Halloween. I'd come late for the event, hoping I could lose myself in the crowd.

Given the option, I would have avoided the private view altogether, but there was no wriggling out of it. The exhibition was opening in just over a week and I needed to get my article written in advance. I was meant to be whetting people's appetites. Radley Summers, Seb's exhibitions manager, had been enthusiastic. 'It'll be a whole different experience to coming along later, with the hordes,' she'd said.

I knew that. It would be a nastier experience, where I would be expected to strut around making intelligent comments about Zachariah Shakespeare's paintings. I'd seen a photograph of one of them beforehand and had been instantly struck dumb.

The work showed a woman and man, standing partly entwined, but where they touched there was decay. He'd painted both whole and rotting flesh perfectly, the peach and cocoa skin tones giving way to sickening blood-red, creeping with the browns and blacks of gangrene. It was horribly graphic. He certainly had talent but, with his taste in subject matter, that wasn't a plus. Still, I would just have to make the best of it.

I was wearing a woollen mini dress – green, to match my eyes – and knee-high boots so I wouldn't feel too much like me. Instead, I hoped the costume would instil confidence. I just had to play a part for the evening and then I could escape again. Unfortunately the boots had to have towering heels, to bring me up to normal adult height, which meant I'd be in agony before home time. It was always the same; my mother used to call me her little fairy child. Having that sort of stature was all well and good when I was eight, but less than ideal now I'd reached maturity.

I waited in the queue for the cloakroom, my coat slung over one arm. In front of me, a tall woman with spiked blonde hair was rattling on to a tiny woman in leather and four-inch stiletto heels. Watching her mouth open and close at such a speed was mesmeric.

The effect of my own clothes was ebbing away already; the brief feeling of alrightness seeping out of me as though I'd sprung a small but definite leak. The stupid thing was, I didn't really need to talk to anyone if I didn't want to. I could just soak up the atmosphere and then leave again. I had my interview with Shakespeare booked for the following week, so I could probably even avoid him, for now.

But the mad flurry of conversation in the room left me feeling conspicuous: a small isolated pool of silence in amongst the carrying, confident voices that filled the air.

The man after me in the line had just met a friend. They embraced, with lots of kissing on both cheeks: 'Haven't seen you since that awful do of Simeon's', 'God! Don't talk about it. Been looking forward to this for ages though ... Did you see Désirée's here? We'll catch up with her in a moment. I did hear she was at that party Shakespeare threw a week ago ... you know, the one that made the nationals?'

A woman with a nose ring, black mini dress and fishnets took my coat and gave me a skull and crossbones tag with the number ninety-four on it. There was no more queuing to do, and barring a sneaky spot of loitering in the ladies' loos there was nothing for it but to go and join the melee.

A waiter put a tray of red fizzy drinks under my nose.

I raised an eyebrow and he leant forward. 'It's just Cava with food dye in it. The purple ones have got Pernod in, if you want something stronger.'

'This'll do fine thanks.' All the same, I decided to keep an eye out for the purple ones, just in case.

I paused next to a group by one of the canvases and listened to their talk.

'... epitomises the relationship between love and death,' a man was saying, indicating the painting with an outstretched hand. It was the same one I'd seen in the photograph before I came.

Seb had been right to have the private view on Halloween. Zachariah Shakespeare's paintings fitted the occasion perfectly. Each picture was lit from above by a clear, white light, but around the artworks lamps glowed dark red and orange. Some of the bulbs had been embedded in a false floor and everywhere they cast strange shadows, making the faces of the visitors almost as sinister as the paintings. Wherever I looked shapes distorted, heads seemed to elongate and lights danced. I made my way round the room, taking in canvases with titles such as *Road Kill* and *Autopsy*. Another, *For All Time*, was created entirely in shades of white and grey and stood out all the more because it left the gore behind. It showed a woman encased in ice, her face devoid of expression.

Not all of the guests were repelled. One man was so enthusiastic his companion seemed almost flattened by the force of what he had to say. I grinned in her direction but she didn't notice.

Then, looking just over her shoulder, I realised someone else was watching the scene too: a dark-haired man, tall and broad, lounging against a pillar. After a moment he raised his eyes, caught mine and cocked an eyebrow. He held my gaze for a moment before moving off to another part of the room.

A waiter darted past with a plate of crudités. He looked edgy. At least I was having a better time than he was. It would be tense downstairs in the kitchens where Alicia was no doubt in full flow, spitting out orders. My cousin was scary enough at the best of times, and if I ever found myself quailing at the prospect of my own work, I could console myself that it couldn't be as bad as working for her. Lodging with her was enough of a challenge to the nerves.

The gallery was stifling. The windows had been covered with reflective film – almost entirely opaque – which increased the claustrophobic atmosphere. Over at one end of the room I could see a way out. Time to investigate.

The swing doors closed quietly behind me, though they didn't do much to keep out the din beyond. The bliss of finding myself on a landing was almost overwhelming, and would have been complete if I hadn't known I'd have to go back in again.

My green dress contrasted my auburn hair nicely, but it was way too hot. I could feel myself becoming auburn in the face as well.

I glanced over my shoulder to check for onlookers and then rubbed at the wool where it was irritating my neck. The gentle scratching gave some relief, so I scrabbled away some more, aware I was probably leaving a mark. Never mind. I would let it fade before I faced anyone again.

I leant against the landing windowsill, bending my head forwards until it touched the cool glass. The smell of gloss paint filled my nostrils; Seb had spent a fortune recently, doing the place up. Or at least a fortune to anyone else. Small change to him.

Outside, a patch of the Thames glittered in the lights that ran along a jetty. Nearer, in the square just below, some party-goers straggled by, leaning in against each other and stumbling sideways. One was wearing some kind of monster mask. From a distance, the face looked like molten wax, reminding me of the people I'd just left in the exhibition hall, with their freakishly up-lit cheekbones.

'Had enough?'

The voice made me jump so badly I knocked my head against the glass. Turning, I saw the man who'd caught my eye earlier. The light of the landing revealed a five o'clock shadow. His ruffled hair contrasted with his suit, but fitted with the sleep-deprived look. Still, there was a twinkle in his blue eyes.

I suddenly realised I'd been sizing him up so thoroughly I'd forgotten to speak. My embarrassment must have shown, but luckily he misread it.

'You look guilty,' he said. 'Are you meant to be in there for work?'

I nodded. 'I'm interviewing the artist in a couple of days.'

'And you don't fancy chatting to someone you suspect might be a latent serial killer? Don't worry. His publicist will have the answers you need. Contact with Shakespeare should be minimal.'

I noticed he had a small scar just by his left eye, but pulled my attention back to the matter in hand. 'You've met him?'

'Lawrence has, my brother. He's an art dealer, but he

had to be with a client tonight so I'm here in his place. What will you write about the paintings, do you think?'

I shook my head. 'God knows. They're brilliantly done of course, but I can't wait to get away from them.'

'Sounds like a fair comment. Shakespeare will probably love it. I get the impression he enjoys repulsing people.'

He moved closer to me.

I was very conscious of his nearness and it took me a moment to think of something to say. 'I still haven't met him. I assumed he'd be in evidence.'

'Word is he decked a man outside a restaurant at lunchtime and is helping the police with their enquiries.'

'Blimey. And you still reckon it's usually minimal contact as far as he's concerned? One punch and he's off?'

He laughed. 'It's probably just a publicity stunt. It all boosts the hype and avoids the risk of him turning up and demystifying himself. Do you always write about art?'

I shook my head. 'I'm a generalist. I'm cashing in on the fact that I know Sebastian Rice. Shakespeare's his discovery. Unfortunately, I can't seem to work up the required enthusiasm.'

'Hang on a moment.' He disappeared through the swing doors into the gallery and returned with a couple of the purple drinks. 'Here.' He handed one to me, his fingers touching mine for a second. 'I met someone earlier who told me that after four of these, the paintings seem quite appealing.'

'Sure they didn't say appalling?'

He laughed again and raised his glass to me. 'I'm Max by the way, Max Conran.'

'Anna Morris.'

'So, have you known Sebastian long?'

'Since university. Do you know him?'

'Hardly at all. What's he like?'

'A charmer …' God, after all these years that was still the first thing to come to mind. 'Intelligent … single-minded. I guess you can just about imagine. It's harder to catch up with him now he's such a hotshot, but we were quite close once. I mostly deal with his publicity people these days.'

He had drained his glass and so had I, despite the knowledge of the Pernod. I had a feeling he'd be able to cope with a lot more purple drinks than I would.

Now he moved next to me, his elbow on the windowsill.

I felt light-headed and a familiar warm and unreliable sensation lit up somewhere inside me. I couldn't put it all down to the cocktails.

His blue eyes were the sort you found yourself staring into; lulling you into a false sense of security. He smiled and I realised I'd been looking into them for slightly too long.

'I'm glad I came now,' he said and I turned to look outside again, my cheeks feeling hot.

As he shifted position his shoulder brushed against mine. It had a disturbing effect, as though the patch was newly sensitised. What on earth was happening to me?

He pointed down to the square below. 'There's a bar just off Tanner's Yard. Let me buy you a drink?'

'Anna Morris?'

I jumped almost as much as I had the first time. The doors from the gallery were far too quiet on their hinges. When I turned my head, a woman I didn't recognise was looking at me, her eyebrows raised. Her smile revealed very white, but uneven, teeth. She had slanting cheekbones, a wide mouth and long eyelashes.

'Yes?'

'Radley Summers, Sebastian's exhibitions manager. We've been speaking on the phone.' She held out a hand and I shook it, noticing the silver ring she wore on her thumb and her neat, unvarnished nails. 'Good to meet you,' she went on. 'Seb pointed you out to me earlier. Look, I'm sorry to butt in, but could I have a quick word? I've got a bit more background for you.'

She turned to Max and he looked over towards me. 'Come and find me when you're ready,' he said and disappeared, back into the orange glow of the gallery.

I spoke into the silence he'd left: 'It's good to meet you face to face. So, you had more information for me?'

'Sorry,' said Radley, 'but that was just an excuse. I thought you might need rescuing.'

'Rescuing?'

'I don't want to freak you out, but Seb has several of us watching the CCTV cameras, looking out for social wheels that need oiling, that kind of thing. It helps this sort of event go off smoothly.'

'And you were watching me and Max Conran?' I suddenly wondered about the scratching earlier. Radley was just the kind of woman I particularly wouldn't like to scratch in front of.

She nodded. 'Seb pointed you out to me quite early on. I wasn't keeping an eye on you specifically of course, but I noticed when you nipped out here for a break. I switched screens and I could see you were just cooling off. All fine. But I'd already seen that man watching you when you were inside the exhibition.'

'Watching me?'

'It made me uneasy. I mean, it wasn't as though he was just eyeing you up. It was as if … well, as if he was taking notice of what you did. Do you see what I mean?'

I thought it was a pretty fine distinction. Perhaps she just found it unbelievable that someone like Max would be interested in me.

'And then I saw him follow you out here. He stood behind you for ages before he said anything.' She paused. 'I even wondered if he was going to try to steal your bag.'

I must have looked incredulous.

'I know,' she said, 'it's pretty weird. Well, the next bit's even weirder. At that point he took out his phone. And I'd swear he took your photograph.'

'That doesn't make any sense.' I tried to keep the hostility out of my tone.

'I know. I think it's as odd as you do. And in many ways I'd rather not have had to tell you. But given that your safety might be in question, I hope you can see I had no choice.'

I sighed. 'Then what happened?'

'You moved your head and I think he thought you'd seen him. It was only then that he spoke to you.'

'You can't hear what everyone's saying from your control room as well, can you?' I said.

Radley shook her head. 'But what I saw was enough to make Seb think I ought to intervene.'

'I was actually having quite a nice time.' I was finding it hard to match Radley's version of Max Conran with the one I thought I'd experienced. I looked over her shoulder, wondering if he might come back onto the landing if I didn't appear.

'I sent one of the marketing guys off to talk to him,' she said, spotting the direction of my gaze. 'You don't need to worry. He won't bother you again.' She looked at me, her expression intense. 'He's after something, Anna. I don't know what but, well, there's a bit more to it than I've told you.'

9

'Go on,' I said.

'When I saw him acting oddly I was particularly disturbed because of who he is. Or rather, who he isn't.'

She wasn't making any sense. 'I know who he is,' I said. 'He introduced himself. He's Max Conran; he said he came in place of his brother.'

'Lawrence Conran, the art dealer?'

I nodded.

She looked back at me, her gaze steady. 'Yes, that's the information he gave when he arrived too. We have cameras recording everyone coming through the doors.'

'You *are* well organised,' I said. It was slightly hard to take.

'We have to be tight on security.' She sighed and then went on: 'And it's handy for Jane too. She's a consultant, working on sales and marketing for us at the moment. She was watching as people came in, so she could see who to target.'

She glanced at me for a second and I'm sure she guessed I disapproved. I found it hard to stop my mouth from taking on a thin, lemon-sucking appearance.

Radley paused for a moment before she said: 'When Jane saw Max Conran's name come up against that guy you were just talking to, she knew at once we'd got an imposter.'

'I'm sorry?'

'He's not Max Conran, Anna. Jane dated Max at the tail end of last year and she was quite positive about it. Whoever he is, he's lied to us. And to you.'

'But you let him stay,' I said eventually.

She nodded. 'There was some question over whether Lawrence Conran was in on the deception. He's very valuable to the gallery; he spends a lot of money with us. You can imagine Seb didn't want to create a scene unnecessarily. But at the same time, you'll understand why I was monitoring the situation.'

The silence seemed to expand between us. At that point I suppose I ought to have been unnerved, but in fact I mainly felt humiliated. She must have seen how I was behaving around Max, taking his approach at face value.

'I don't know what his game is,' Radley said at last, 'but I'd be inclined to take a cab home tonight, rather than the tube.'

Chapter Two

Ten pounds poorer, I slammed the taxi door shut after me and let myself into Alicia's place. It was one of a row of large town houses in a wide, leafy road. Goodness knows what it would be worth if she ever decided to sell it. It was much too big for her alone, but it had belonged to her parents and I suppose it must have felt too familiar for her to want to leave it. Instead she installed a series of lodgers, or paying guests as she called us, to help fill it up. My quarters were up in the attic and a girl called Sally was occupying the basement.

I paused momentarily to switch on the upstairs landing light and unzip my boots, which were killing me, as anticipated.

'It's not James bloody Bond,' I said aloud, still thinking of the man who wasn't Max and the photograph.

I don't normally talk out loud to myself in public, but I was confident I was alone. Alicia wouldn't be done with the gallery catering for hours, I knew. And as for Sally, well, I'd hardly seen her since I'd moved in, but she definitely didn't seem the sort to be in on a Friday night, least of all on Halloween.

Consequently, I jumped out of my skin when a voice said: 'What's not James Bond?'

I turned to see a glamorous witch with slightly damp hair at the top of the basement stairs. She held a towel in one hand and was wearing the traditional black dress, together with fishnets and purple nail varnish. Sally.

It now occurred to me that it was too early for her

to have left to start her evening. Mine had been such a washout that I'd made it home before ten.

I wished I'd kept quiet and got safely back to my room.

'D'you fancy a drink?' she said, with a smile that suddenly made her seem very young and not at all witch-like. 'I'm having one – just to get into the party spirit. It's always a bit freaky going into a room full of monsters and ghosts without a drink inside you.'

I paused for just a second.

'I've got gin,' she added, as though I might make up my mind according to the quality of refreshments on offer.

'Thanks,' I said, putting my boots back on again and feeling all grown-up and un-Halloweeny.

It was the first time I'd been into her room. In terms of mess, it was spectacular. I pushed two or three pairs of tights, a pair of knickers, a paperback and a packet of cotton wool to one side so I could perch on her sofa. It was only when I took the drink she held out that I realised I'd sat on an open tube of foundation.

'Oh God,' I said, leaping up again. My green dress was safe, but the make-up was oozing out onto a red cotton cushion.

'Oh don't worry about that!' Sally said, rubbing at it with a tissue, making the smear thinner, but more widely spread. 'I get that stuff half-price anyway.'

'Really?'

She nodded. 'I work at Farquharson's. I'm a pedicurist.'

That explained it. Farquharson's: the most exclusive health and beauty spa in London. It was the kind of place where you could spend three hundred pounds to have someone place pebbles down your spine for an afternoon whilst you lay on a couch. Each to their own.

I hoped the cushion belonged to Sally and not Alicia.

I reckoned my cousin couldn't have been down to Sally's room, at least, not when I'd been in the house. I'd have definitely heard the screech if she had.

Sally looked at me for a moment, her head on one side. 'I've got a colleague who could sort you out with some great make-up,' she said. 'I love your colouring; auburn hair and honey-coloured freckles are to die for at the moment.'

I was pleased that she thought this, as someone in the know, although, from what she said, they were only enjoying temporary popularity, which meant I couldn't relax.

'How do you find it, living here?' I asked.

She grinned. 'I thought you might be after the low-down, given that you've only just moved in. Well, I've been here for six months. My uncle knows Alicia and he got it all arranged for me.' She reached for some blusher and started applying it, facing the mirror as she spoke. 'I mean it's a great house, isn't it? All those antiques! And I've never seen so many books ... but I guess Alicia and me, we don't quite see eye to eye.'

I was willing to bet that was an understatement.

'She does like everything to be just so, doesn't she?' Sally said.

I nodded. 'At least I was forewarned about that though. She's my cousin, so I've known her since I was tiny. I can remember her coming upstairs to tidy my bedroom with me when I was about six. She must have been around sixteen. She was completely obsessive about order even then.'

'Pretty weird,' said Sally. She had reached the eyeshadow and mascara stage now. 'Sorry – no offence – she is your cousin after all. So where were you living before?'

'With a friend just outside London,' I said. 'But I really needed to move down here for my work.'

And that was how we got on to my so-called career, as well as my evening at the gallery. It was only after the second gin and tonic that she persuaded me to explain the James Bond comment. Once I had, she was delighted; I suppose to an onlooker it was like something out of a soap opera.

'He took your photo?' she said. 'Wow!'

'That's what this woman, Radley Summers, reckons. I can't help feeling she's mistaken though. I mean, why would he?'

'Freaky!' said Sally, as though it was the highlight of her week. 'And, I mean, who is this guy? Why would he be lying to everyone? It's like something out of film or something.'

'First really sexy bloke I've met in ages, and it looks as though he's a stalker with criminal intent.'

'You haven't got a boyfriend then?' said Sally, turning to the mirror to apply some scarlet lipstick. 'It must be hard getting to meet many people when you're older.'

At that moment there was the sound of a text coming in. Sally lifted up layers of black skirt, rummaging amongst lace and velvet. 'I had to sew in a pocket for my phone and cash. I mean, whoever heard of a witch carrying a handbag?' She found the phone at last and checked the message. 'Greg! He's outside. I'd better shoot.' She grabbed a set of keys and tucked them into the hidden pouch.

As we walked up the stairs to the entrance hall she carried on chatting. 'I can't believe you were actually at Zachariah Shakespeare's do!'

'You know about him then?'

'God! Who doesn't? He's as popular as a rock star. Everyone at Farquharson's is talking about him.'

So Seb had done his job well, I thought. Zachariah Shakespeare was hot property. And the people at Farquharson's had lots of money.

Before she let herself out, Sally glanced round at me. 'You will tell me what happens next, won't you?'

'I'm sorry?'

'With the mystery man from the gallery!'

'Oh!' I paused for a second. 'Yes.'

But nothing would happen, I was quite sure of that. Either 'Max' had made a mistake about who I was, or Radley had got it wrong about the photo, or, or … well, something. Weird things didn't happen to me.

I watched as Sally closed the front door behind her and then pulled off my boots again, ready to climb the stairs.

It was the smell of baking pastry that woke me on the morning of my interview with Zachariah Shakespeare. It had woven its way up two flights of stairs and was playing with my senses, so that hunger was my first conscious thought. This made a change from coming to with vague images in my head of the man who wasn't Max.

I'd successfully avoided Alicia all weekend. She'd headed off to give herself a break after the gallery do, but I could smell that she was back in work mode now.

As I showered in the attic bathroom I thought there was a good chance I could give her the slip again if she was busy cooking. She had a separate kitchen on the ground floor where she prepared for her catering jobs: all gleaming hobs and granite. I'd only seen it once; it was definitely her own private domain, to be left well alone.

Sally and I had the use of a smaller, communal kitchen instead, which was a very different affair.

It turned out I was to be disappointed. The moment I'd opened the fridge to get the butter, Alicia's cropped head poked round the kitchen door.

'Oh, it's you,' she said. 'I thought it be might Sally. I wanted a word.'

Seeing the look in her sharp grey eyes I was immediately glad I wasn't the one in the dog house. 'Good weekend?'

She put her head on one side. 'So, so. I went to Bridget's, you know? She took me to an awful restaurant on Saturday night. Horrible food, dirty cutlery and the waitress had a cold.'

It must be such fun having Alicia to stay. Bridget would probably need a week in bed to get over it.

She moved to leave the room, but then suddenly dashed my hopes by changing her mind and reaching for the kettle instead. 'I'll pause for a break.'

She stood there, tapping her fingers on the work surface as she waited for the kettle to boil. She was wearing a black ribbed polo neck sweater and chocolate coloured trousers. If I'd been cooking in an outfit like that it would have been flecked with flour by now, but – Alicia being Alicia – there wasn't a mark on it.

'Smells as though you've been hard at work.'

She nodded. 'Food for a do at Number Eleven.'

She meant number eleven Downing Street, I knew. It sounded intimidating to me but, of course, Alicia had had years of experience and, in any case, it wasn't in her nature to get intimidated.

She brought the cafetière and a couple of cups over and came to join me at the table where I'd settled myself down with a brown roll stuffed with thick-cut marmalade.

'Don't you ever eat properly?' she said, peering at my breakfast and shuddering slightly.

'There's nothing more proper than marmalade.'

'It's what you do with it that worries me,' she said. 'I don't know why you can't have it on toast like anybody else.'

She poured me a coffee and pushed it across the scrubbed oak. 'You don't look very together for someone who's meant to be interviewing the biggest rising star in the art world this afternoon.'

I instantly stopped feeling hungry.

'You do have to make the effort you know,' she went on.

I tried to open my eyes wider so that I would look more alert and she would leave me alone. It wasn't working.

She leant towards me. 'So, what was Shakespeare like when you met him on Friday?'

I shook my head, swallowing my mouthful of coffee. 'I didn't get to meet him.' I could see she was about to boil over with indignation, so I added quickly, 'I couldn't. He wasn't there. Something about having beaten someone up earlier in the day. He was meant to be in a police cell or something.' I could hear myself sounding incoherent. She always had this effect on me.

'Or something? Really, Anna, you could at least have ascertained the precise facts. And anyway,' she said, swigging more coffee, 'I don't believe a word of it. Clearly a publicity stunt. You really should use your connections. If Sebastian won't let you see Shakespeare then who will? You should make it clear from the outset what you expect of him. After all, you'll be providing the gallery with excellent publicity.'

'Yes, Alicia,' I said, sighing and leaning back in my

chair in an attempt to distance myself, 'and that's all been arranged by Seb himself. He's got a friend on The Enquirer, and that's why they're taking my article in the first place. It's a great break for me. I'm not in a position to go haranguing Seb and having tantrums about the place.'

'Tantrums!' Alicia snorted.

'Doesn't any of your food need checking on, next door?'

'No it doesn't! I'm not suggesting you have a tantrum. You just need to be a bit more professional and assertive. Until it's you that's calling the shots you can't steer where you're going.'

Like I didn't know that. In a minute she would start on the well-worn tale of her humble beginnings in business.

'It was the same for me you know, when I started out.' Here it came. 'And there have been obstacles along the way too. You may remember that Sebastian was very much against me taking on the gallery contract at first, for instance.'

Yes, I remembered. It was very easy to recall things when someone kept repeating them every few days. And in any case, I had been involved. 'I seem to remember I put that business your way, Alicia,' I said.

'You did. You used your contacts to help me and I'm grateful, but all the same, Sebastian didn't want me to do the work. I had to take control of the situation. I went to Mel, because she was in charge of operations, and I got her along to one of my soirées. It was my plan to get her hooked and I did.' She looked at me and went on, 'Because I was professional, and because I didn't take no for an answer.' She tapped the table each time she said "because" for emphasis.

'It's lucky that he kept you on, even when he and Mel split up,' I said.

She sat back in her chair at last, her hands wrapped round her coffee mug. 'By that time he'd realised what an asset I was.'

'Why didn't Seb want you, anyway?' I had the ungenerous urge to focus attention on her shortcomings. The opportunity rejuvenated me, and I got to work on the marmalade roll. I was sure I could feel its bittersweet flavour giving me a new strength of purpose.

Alicia sighed. 'Oh some stupid sentimental nonsense from what Mel said. I only remember because I thought it was so ridiculous. It was something to do with associations. Because I was your cousin he associated me, indirectly, with his university days and he couldn't bear to be reminded. I mean, honestly, did you ever hear anything like it?' She got up and took her coffee cup to the dishwasher. 'It's a wonder he's made such a success of himself if that's the kind of thing he gets bogged down with.'

'He did have an awful time,' I said, getting up to make myself a second roll.

She looked at me over her shoulder as she took a cloth and wiped invisible marks off the working surface. 'We've all had awful times, Anna. Both my parents were killed in a car crash the night before I did my first catering job at Lord Buckeridge's place. That contract's earned me tens of thousands of pounds since. Where would I be if I hadn't kept my head together?'

'More of a human being?' I muttered under my breath.

'What?' But she didn't wait for an answer. 'What about Sebastian on Friday anyway? How was he?'

I told her I hadn't seen him either, but I didn't say

anything about the other goings-on that evening. I was in no mood to extend the conversation.

As she left the room, Alicia said: 'It seems to me that Sebastian's avoiding you. And there have been a number of times, over the years, when he could have been more helpful than he has.'

'It's the old associations at work again,' I said. 'He's been keeping his distance.'

She fixed me with a look. 'What he went through happened a long while ago now, Anna.'

But she didn't know the half of it.

Chapter Three

Up in my room I went through my notes again, ready for the interview. After Alicia had left the kitchen I hadn't felt much like my second roll; I was too nervous. I hated meeting big stars. Sometimes, it felt like I was in the wrong job.

As well as writing the straight piece for The Enquirer, I was charged with writing a feature for the rather more accessible magazine, Epic. The slant for that was quite different, so the questions I needed to cover spanned a bizarre range of issues. I also had a nasty shock mid-morning when Helena, the features editor of Epic, called me.

'All set?' she asked.

'Yes thanks,' I lied.

'Great,' she said. 'I just wanted to throw in an extra question. Maeve, the editor, wants you to ask about underwear.'

I was silent for a moment.

Helena went on: 'You know, whether he's a boxer shorts or a briefs man, where he buys them, that kind of thing.'

Well, I was glad she'd called because I have to admit, pants hadn't been on my original list of questions. Now she mentioned it, it was obvious of course. I wrote "Weave in pants" next to my list of topics for Epic.

I then spent the next half hour wondering how to slot them in. I mean, I'd got what I hoped were some fairly searching questions for The Enquirer, and then lots of more informal ones for Epic, but pants didn't sit easily with either set.

I'd been asked to submit my questions to Shakespeare's publicity person, Miranda, just as 'Max' had said I would be. He wouldn't be expecting the pants one, although obviously I'd be adding in extra questions as they came to me anyway; that was bound to happen.

I dithered about the whole thing for a bit longer, and then ended up calling Miranda, even though I knew her schedule for the day was probably manic.

'Pants?' she said. 'I'm not sure. Just a moment though. I might be able to get you an answer right now, if you don't want to bring it up at the interview.' The line went quiet, but a few seconds later she was back. 'Just caught him between his eleven o'clock and his eleven thirty,' she said. 'Apparently he doesn't wear any.'

'Really?'

'He's one on his own.'

Which was something of a relief. I wondered if ditching my underwear would make me seem truly original too. Somehow I didn't think it would work; aside from the fact that no one would notice. 'The readers of Epic will love it anyway,' I said, hating myself for being such a sycophant. Deep down, I was willing to bet he really wore M&S, but didn't like to admit it.

At eleven forty-five Alicia came in without knocking. I had given up on my questions; going over them was just making me jittery. Instead, I'd taken out some sewing: a clutch bag I was making my mother for Christmas. I was embroidering tiny birds over a sunset in pink and orange silks.

'I must say,' she said, peering over at me, 'you're very self-confident, just sitting there sewing like that. Shouldn't you be swotting up?' She handed me a parcel. 'Delivery for you.'

I peered at a label on the package, which said Tillsbury Silks.

Alicia was peering at it too. 'More material for your sewing?' she said. 'You know, Anna, it's a very good thing you came to live here. I do think perhaps you were allowing yourself to get a little unfocused, stuck out in the sticks with Terry.'

'St Albans is hardly the sticks.'

She made a noise like a horse coughing up a fly, which I took to indicate disapproval. 'You know what I mean. After all, it must be, what, fourteen years since you graduated? Time's getting on. Terry's got his career sorted, but I always felt you were rather dragging along in his wake, just enjoying life.'

She left the room again and I stowed the sewing away. It was time to go in any case.

Zachariah Shakespeare had long, dark wavy hair and wore sunglasses, despite the fact that it wasn't sunny and we were sitting inside The Prestwick Hotel. Periodically, he sipped from a can of Coke, and I noticed that his hand shook slightly each time he gripped the drink.

He sat on a dove-grey sofa, reclining as though he had a physical need to be in that position. I was on some kind of mock-Regency chair with lots of red velvet and gilt paint. I had a digital recorder between us, so I could forget all about having to note anything down, or argue the toss later about what he had said.

Miranda sat with us the whole time, in a dark suit with a mini skirt that revealed bony knees. She had a clipboard and a mobile on her lap.

It wasn't the most comfortable interview I'd ever done. Throughout, he behaved as though he was there under duress. And 'Max' had been right: he certainly wasn't chatty. Remembering what he'd said brought back his image, very vividly. Well, whoever he was, his knowledge of Zachariah Shakespeare seemed genuine enough.

Zachariah's voice, when he did speak, was surprisingly high and mockney. The questions for Epic were the worst. The pants theme was typical of the long list of areas I'd been asked to investigate. I had to go through relations with siblings, love life (of course), preferred holiday getaway, and so it went on. At least they hadn't asked me to find out what his favourite colour was or how he liked to have sex. The questions I'd come up with myself weren't much better though. He looked bored and I decided something had to be done.

'What do you think of Mary Poppins?' I said at random.

He raised an eyebrow.

'That wasn't on your list of questions,' said Miranda, scribbling something onto her notepad.

I gave her a look. She had already been constraining the proceedings as far as I was concerned. 'I didn't realise I was straying into dangerous territory.'

Shakespeare grinned suddenly and I saw Miranda give him a repressive glance, but he took no notice.

'I was in love with Mary Poppins when I was little,' he said. 'You've no idea the emotional depths you're plumbing. But Chitty Chitty Bang Bang was better.'

'Did you like the child catcher?' said Miranda hopefully.

Shakespeare gave her a look and shook his head slowly, draining the last of his Coke. 'He used to creep me out. My favourite character was Grandpa Potts.'

Miranda actually followed me out of the interview room to take me to task over the additional question.

I could see why: there was a danger that Shakespeare's answer might make him sound quite human. I wondered how many thousands that could knock off the value of one of his masterpieces.

'I'll be sure to mention any family movie topics beforehand next time,' I said over my shoulder as I dashed towards the hotel foyer. 'I just hadn't thought of it being at all controversial. Thank you very much for having me.'

I was so busy trying to escape from her that I suddenly realised I was about to leave without my coat. I waited to one side, hovering in the shadows until she was safely out of the way again, and then went back to get it from the cloakroom.

It had been oddly mild earlier, but with rain in the air. I peered out of a corridor window to see what the weather was like now and was brought up short.

'Max' was there, standing just outside. I would already have run into him if I hadn't had to come back for my coat.

When I saw him I felt the same strength of reaction I'd had when we'd met at the gallery. I wanted to run outside and join him. There was an urgency in the pit of my stomach, as though I'd been fancying him in a pent up way for years, not just a couple of days.

But Radley's words came back to me, together with a nagging voice that asked why it was that he'd come to look for me. Always assuming it *was* me he was looking for. After all, he could be there for any number of reasons … But then he did know I'd be interviewing Shakespeare. It wouldn't take much to find out where he was staying and what day he'd set aside for dealing with the press.

I waited, just standing there holding my coat, peering out of the window. No one else rushed up into his arms.

No business contact emerged from the doorway, striding up to shake his hand. He walked a couple of paces forward, past one of the pillars, so that he could look into the foyer, then stepped back again and continued his wait. He didn't look at his watch. Did that mean he hadn't got a pre-arranged appointment to meet someone? Could he really just be there in case he managed to catch up with me?

More people left the building and still he waited. Then at last he came right inside the hotel.

I paused, undecided. Eventually, I walked very slowly down the corridor back towards the reception area. 'Max', or whoever he really was, was leaning on the counter of the front desk, his dark hair hanging down over one eye.

I could just hear the receptionist's words: '... didn't see her go past, but I think she must have left already.'

My stomach muscles tightened. He was looking for me, I was sure of it, but what did he want? He was standing in that characteristic pose, leaning forward, the touch of a smile on his lips; that powerful, confident stance. And suddenly I was afraid. Cutting through the feeling he stirred up inside me came the reality I'd been trying to ignore: he could be absolutely anyone, wanting any number of things.

I backed away, retreating up the corridor, and found a side door that opened onto New Row. Looking over my shoulder, half running, I took the fastest route to Leicester Square tube station.

Chapter Four

Sally had the next day off and decided to spend half of it at work, introducing me to the delights of Farquharson's. I must admit I was quite wary about the idea, feeling it might be too new-agey for my tastes and too expensive for my wallet.

'They won't make me lie down for two hours wrapped in seaweed, or anything like that, will they?' I asked as we neared the tube station. Sally just laughed and I took the lack of straight denial as confirmation that that was probably just what they would do.

But I needn't have worried. We spent all morning in the relaxation pool, which was like being on a film set. The lighting was low and there were archways everywhere, rather like those I'd seen at the Roman baths in Bath. You could swim (or float if you didn't feel that energetic) under arches and between pillars, looking up at a ceiling dotted with pinpricks of silvery light. There was even a swing, though I felt I might be too self-conscious to sway back and forwards in front of everyone so ostentatiously.

The trip gave me a chance to regale her with a blow-by-blow account of my time at The Prestwick the previous day.

'I'm feeling like a prat now,' I said, as a large lady in a blue floral costume drifted past us.

'Why?'

'Because I was so melodramatic about the whole thing. I mean honestly, it's not as though he's been stalking me down dark alleys or anything, is it? He chatted to me in a gallery stuffed full of people and waited for me outside a hotel that was swarming with journalists.'

'True,' said Sally. She paused a moment, then added, 'But, hey, he still lied about his name. There's definitely an aura of mystery and potential danger about him.' I could tell she wasn't going to let go of this satisfying thought. 'Anyway,' she went on, 'for all you know he might be itching to pursue you down dark alleys, only he doesn't have enough information to go on. He can't follow you very easily if you keep giving him the slip.' She gave me an accusing look.

We got out and put on bathrobes.

'And now you can come and see my rivals,' Sally said, leading me into a tiled room with granite footbaths.

'What's in the water?' I asked. The women dangling their feet into the baths seemed to be wriggling rather oddly.

'Tiny fish,' Sally said. 'It's a popular exfoliating treatment. They nibble away at your dead skin.'

'I can't think of anything more revolting.'

'A lot of people claim to like it. But,' she added, 'I think my job's safe. There are still plenty of clients who prefer the human touch. And in any case, the fish are absolutely crap when it comes to applying nail varnish.'

After that we went for a boozy lunch in the restaurant.

Back at the house, Alicia caught me bowling into the hall and seemed to sense that I'd been relaxing and enjoying myself. Perhaps she could smell the wine. Whatever gave the game away, she looked very disapproving.

'What work have you got coming up next?' she said, as I hovered, one foot on the stairs, hoping to make my escape.

'Well, I've still got to finish the Shakespeare articles and get them off.'

'That won't take you all week.'

'I know it won't, but I've got to go in and meet Seb's exhibitions manager about some more press work on Thursday, and I've got a backlog of copywriting to get on with. In fact,' I looked at my watch, 'I really ought to dash up and get cracking on that now.'

'Well, if you're going to go for long lunches you will need to put the hours in later to make up for it I suppose. What copywriting have you got, anyway?'

My task for the afternoon was to write a piece about the expansion of a potato processing factory for a company magazine, but I was damned if I was going to tell her that. 'Oh, there's too much to go through it all now,' I said, waving a hand. 'It's just the usual corporate stuff, you know.'

'No other significant work's come in then? I mean interviews and the like, with people that count?'

'I don't know what will result from the meeting with Radley.'

'Hmm.' She paused for a moment, as though debating something inwardly. 'Look, I'm very busy, but what the hell, why don't you interview me? I'd pretty much guarantee you a slot in Observer Food Monthly or somewhere like that.' She frowned. 'You'll need a day or two to research and prepare, I suppose.' She took out her diary. 'Let's book it in for Friday. First thing in the morning.'

I confess I was speechless, which wasn't usual for me. I think my mouth might have been hanging open, because I swear she was about to tell me to close it when Sally unwisely appeared at the top of the basement stairs. It was a slip-up on her part, having escaped so successfully on our return from lunch. Her mind must have been elsewhere, because she started when she saw us, and then appeared to try to creep round behind Alicia towards the kitchen.

'Ah, Sally!' my cousin said, rounding on her. 'I've been wanting a word. One of your boyfriends was knocking on the door at three in the morning on Sunday. I want your assurance that nothing like that will ever happen again.'

I made sympathetic grimaces over Alicia's shoulder, causing Sally to laugh, which didn't help the situation at all. I turned quickly to limit the damage and dragged myself upstairs. Thank goodness I'd at least got a kettle in my room; I could stoke up on black coffee before trying to get imaginative about spuds.

In the end I decided to make potato processing my only job for the afternoon. It was much more manageable than writing up the feature for Epic and I'd already done the work for The Enquirer. The lunchtime wine was sure to help me get nice and creative, which would be necessary if I was going to make the topic sound interesting.

I had hardly started when my mobile rang. It was Terry.

'How's it going?' he said.

'Arggggh! Why did I ever move out of your place?' It was fun letting off steam.

'Well why did you? I did say you shouldn't. We loved having you here.'

'Even when I left pins on the sofa and hogged all the marmalade? Anyway, it wouldn't have done really. I needed to come to London for work.'

'I know you moved out to give us some space when Steve moved in, so don't think I don't, little miss tactful.'

'Well, that and because the extra queuing time for the bathroom was getting to be a pain.'

He laughed. 'Naturally.'

'How are things at the restaurants?'

'Hectic, but going well. We got three reviews in national Sundays in September you know. It's busy as hell, but I couldn't live without it. I'm thinking of opening up a third venue.'

'Wow, that's great. Where are you looking at?'

'Maybe London.' He paused. 'It does help to have a presence in the smoke, I must admit. It means I'll pick up reviews from some of the lazier critics and get in with the in crowd. Anyway, enough about me, how are you?'

'Oh you know,' I said, staring at my potato text on the computer screen, 'still wildly unsuccessful and lying to others about the glamour of my everyday life.'

'Ah, I don't believe it! What about that interview you were going to do for Seb?'

'I didn't exactly excel myself. Besides, I'm going to run out of famous contacts I can sponge off one day soon. Just think what a non-starter I'd have been if I hadn't known you guys.' I'd already done a piece on Terry for one of the Hertfordshire papers. He was national territory now though, I knew. Maybe he'd let me do another if he opened up this new venue.

'Using your contacts isn't wrong you know.'

'It makes me feel like a cheat. Anyway, the latest news is that Alicia's condescended to let me add her to my repertoire, so that's one more celebrity piece. After that I think I'll have used all the eggs I so unwisely put into one basket.'

'Seb might push some more work your way.'

'He might, but he's still avoiding me – or avoiding personal contact at least. If he does give me more, I'll bet it's through other members of staff.'

There was a pause on the other end of the line. Then

32

Terry said: 'I always used to think you were sweet on him, you know.'

'I was only ever sweet on you Terry, and what a waste of time that was.'

He laughed. 'Seriously though, weren't you? Just a little bit?'

'Do you think that's what he thinks now? And that's why he's distanced himself?'

He must have heard my tone. 'Oh good lord no.' Another pause, during which he was no doubt trying to think of how to make himself sound more convincing. 'No. Apart from anything else, it's not just you he's distanced himself from. I don't know when I last heard from him. I think he's pulled back from all the university gang. I spoke to Jez the other day, and I mentioned you were doing this interview for Seb. He was interested. Like you and me, he said he'd been pretty much cut off.'

'He put it like that: cut off?'

'Uh-huh. Apparently he'd emailed Seb a couple of times when he was going to be in London, tried to get back in touch. Seb had just blanked him, so eventually he gave up.'

'Did it hurt his feelings?'

'Not really. He knows what to expect from Seb by now. What I'm saying is, I'm sure it's nothing to do with you personally. After what happened, I guess we all felt Seb was entitled to a little leeway. It would just be nice if he got past that eventually, that's all.'

When he rang off there was nothing to save me from the article. At least it would help pay the bills. Once I'd got it cracked, I put on the radio to listen to the news and went back to the clutch bag I was working on. I'd embroidered five tiny birds against the sunset, and was planning to add another couple. I was just about to finish up when there was a knock at the door.

'Come on in,' I said, wishing I could add, 'unless you're Alicia.'

It wasn't her. It was Sally. She rushed in and closed the door behind her, leaning against it as though warding off an attack. Then she burst out laughing. 'Can you believe she's been on at me ever since you came upstairs?'

'Good grief. You ought to get a reduction in rent for that.'

She laughed again. 'She's been through everything you can imagine, from my attitude to work, to my style of dress, and does my uncle know how late I stay out? I mean, I had to remind her I was twenty-two.'

I felt older than ever. 'Would you like a drink?' I said.

She nodded.

I glanced at my watch, probably compounding all her ideas about me being far too grown-up, and came to the conclusion that it was wine time. 'Red or white?'

'Red thanks.' She wandered round my room. 'I like it up here. You get a lovely view.'

It was true. It was already dark, but spread out to the rear of Alicia's place the lighted windows of other town houses sparkled back at me through the branches of a willow and a eucalyptus. In the distance a bright light picked out a couple of cranes on a building site.

'I love being in amongst everyone else,' I said.

She nodded. 'Yeah, I like that too. I wonder if that's what Alicia enjoys as well. I mean, I can see I really get on her nerves – in fact, everyone seems to get on her nerves – and yet, she still has us here, doesn't she?'

It wasn't something I'd ever thought about before, but

Sally was right. Alicia could certainly afford to keep the place to herself if she wanted to.

'Do you think she gets lonely on her own?' said Sally.

It was a weird thought. 'That would imply she's capable of human frailty,' I said. 'But on the other hand, I can't actually think why else she would have us.'

'Unless she just loves luring people in here so she can boss them around.'

'That does seem rather more likely.'

'What were her parents like?'

I grinned and sipped my wine. 'Are you wondering whether she's got a good excuse to be the dragon she is?'

She shrugged. 'She needs one.'

'Agreed. Well, her father was just like she is: very exacting, a real perfectionist.'

'He wasn't a sergeant major was he?'

I sniggered. 'He was in the army actually. A Field Marshall no less. He brought her up to despise weakness.'

'And boyfriends.'

'And drinking at lunchtime.' I raised my glass.

'Oh wow!' Sally said suddenly, snatching up her red wine. 'That is gorgeous!'

She went to pick up the bag I'd been working on. It wasn't that I didn't trust her but I did have a momentary flutter at the proximity of her drink to the rather pale silks.

'Did you make it?' she said, looking up at me, her eyes bright.

I nodded. 'It's just something I do to relax when things are a bit stressful.'

Sally grinned. 'Well in that case I guess you'll be making quite a few more whilst you're living here at Alicia's.' She put the bag back down again and had another swig of wine. 'You don't think you could make me one, do you? I mean, I'd pay, obviously.'

'You could just give me the money for the materials.'

'No, no, that wouldn't be fair. The thing is, I've been invited to this party by one of the regulars at Farquharson's. I want to make the right impression, in case I meet the man of my dreams.'

'Greg's not the man of your dreams then?'

She smiled, but didn't comment. Poor Greg.

'Anyway,' she said. 'I've got loads of bags, but they suddenly all seem a bit run of the mill; you know, the kind everyone wants and saves up for and then suddenly everyone has. But something like that,' she waved a hand in the direction of my bag, 'would definitely create the right impression.'

By the time Sally left, I'd had far more wine than I'd meant to, and that was on top of the lunchtime dose. I really needed to get some food inside me, but when I listened from the landing I could hear that Alicia was still in evidence. I waited until she'd gone back into her own lair and then trod lightly down the stairs. I wasn't risking the kitchen, not tonight. Chatting with Sally had been fun, chatting with Alicia hadn't, but now I just wanted peace and quiet. I let myself out of the house and walked towards Heath Street. The cold, damp air seemed to work its way inside my coat, increasing the already strong desire I had for heartening junk food. I went and got myself a burger and chips.

On the way home, I decided to cut along Back Lane. It didn't really qualify as a deserted alley, I reflected. It might be empty of people just at the moment, but it was surrounded by houses, mostly with brightly lit windows.

As I walked along I could hear snippets of other people's lives: someone laughing, a baby crying, a shout of 'You're kidding!' and someone using a vacuum cleaner. The breeze lifted a little and the leaves that had already fallen stirred on the pavement. Ahead of me, a man was just letting himself into his house, a Waitrose bag over one arm.

I was about mid-way down the lane when my phone let out the familiar *pip pip* that told me I had a text. I pulled it out of my jeans pocket and glanced at the screen, then felt my breath catch. It read: 'Are you avoiding me on purpose? Missed seeing more of you at the gallery. Call me. Max.'

Chapter Five

'How did he get your number anyway?'

Sally had invited me in the moment I showed my face, clearly sensing gossip. I'd gone upstairs to eat my burger, and had now taken my indigestion downstairs again, feeling that I needed to talk to someone.

'No real mystery in that. When I started out copywriting, I put my mobile number up on a couple of websites to try to get business. It was so long ago I'd forgotten about it; these days I just rely on word of mouth. But when I Googled, I found my details were still out there.'

'But he was obviously pretty determined to track you down. I mean, he could have just left it, couldn't he?'

'True.' And in fact, finding my number on the internet must have involved some searching. It would have taken more than just a minute of idle browsing time.

'So?'

'So?' I echoed back.

'Don't be like that!' she said. 'So ... what are you going to do?'

'I'm not sure,' I said. 'Maybe I should call him. Otherwise I'll always have this question mark in my head. It's bugging me, not knowing what it's all about.'

'Oh thank God for that. I thought for a moment you were just going to leave it. I don't think I could have coped with the mystery.'

'I'm going to watch out though.'

'Well, of course.' She rolled her eyes. 'Everyone should always watch out.'

'But if we arrange to meet I can make sure it's during

the day, somewhere nice and public.' I was convincing myself as much as her.

'I could come with you.'

I looked over at her long, gleaming hair, perfectly manicured nails and twenty-two-year-old figure. 'It's okay, thanks,' I said. 'Maybe I'd better just go alone. I don't think I can come to much harm. In any case, this whole thing's crazy. He seemed like a nice man.'

'Whatever you say.'

I went back upstairs and stared at my mobile for twenty minutes, then at last I plucked up courage and called him. While the number rang, I played over in my mind what I wanted to say. I needed to get straight in there and tell him I knew he wasn't Max. It didn't make sense to arrange anything until we'd …

'Hello?'

'Max? It's Anna.'

'At last. I thought you were ignoring me. I tried to find you at the hotel where the almighty Shakespeare was doing his interviews, but you gave me the slip.'

'I had to dash off quickly.'

'You did?' Something told me he knew I was lying. I don't know how he'd worked it out.

'So you must be busy then, if you had to dash away so urgently.'

I didn't answer.

'Too busy to come out with me?'

'Not necessarily.' A quivering sensation stirred in the pit of my stomach.

'We never made it to that bar in Tanner's Yard.'

I suddenly remembered the safeguards I'd been itemising to Sally. 'Do they do lunches there?'

'They do.'

'Maybe a lunchtime meet up would be good.'

'What happens in the evenings? Do all your clothes turn into rags or something?'

'I've had too many late nights recently.'

'Okay,' he said, but I was sure he didn't buy my excuse. 'What about tomorrow, 1 p.m., at the bar in Tanner's Yard? It's called The Old Faithful.'

'Okay, and Max?'

'Yes?'

I paused for a moment. It was a great cavernous gap in our conversation, but at the same time it would be so much easier to tackle the identity thing face to face. 'Actually, it doesn't matter.'

Chapter Six

But in fact, of course, it did matter, I reflected as I stood waiting for a tube to St Paul's on the day of our meet up. I could just sit there and chat away without finding out who he really was, and the longer I left it, the more awkward it would be. A rush of warm, rubbery-smelling air heralded the arrival of the train and I stepped on board. It wasn't crowded, and I found somewhere to sit between an unsmiling woman with a recently-acquired perm and an empty seat, smeared with chewing gum.

So, as soon as I got there I would tackle him.

Well, that made me feel nervous enough, and then there was the fact that I actually hated meeting people in bars. What if I got there first and had to wait for ten minutes before he appeared? And then what if he never showed up at all? It would look as though I'd been intending to drink alone all along.

After leaving the train I walked over the Millennium Bridge. I should never have agreed to go to The Old Faithful anyway. It was probably some intimidating place full of old men. I should have suggested a quick coffee in a Starbucks or something like that. What was I thinking of, letting myself in for a boozy meal? Though obviously I could just have a Coke.

'A gin and tonic please,' I said, in reply to 'Max's' question. I was still seeing him in inverted commas.

He had appeared out of the shadows, come straight over and pulled me into a hug. All the bells were ringing again, fireworks going off, the lot; just from that one fairly platonic gesture. Except that it didn't feel platonic.

He turned to the barman. 'And I'll have a pint of Sambrook's please, Dave.'

He knew the people here. I waited for Dave to get our drinks and call him something other than Max.

Instead the barman looked up at him and grinned as he started work on the pint. 'Haven't seen you in a long time.'

'I've been out of the country, otherwise you wouldn't have kept me away.'

'Back for a bit now?'

'There's no knowing for sure, but I hope so, yes.' He handed over a twenty pound note, and took his change and a menu. 'It's quite a pubby pub,' he said, ushering me ahead of him to a table by an open fire, 'which is one of the reasons I like it. When I am at home it's nice to go somewhere that feels like the real thing. The food's great too.'

I sat nearest the flames and gradually peeled off my scarf and layers. It was a pubby pub in a good way, I decided. The warmth didn't just come from the fire. Dave was serving another customer now, beaming and reaching over to pat them on the shoulder. It was somewhere where you were welcomed in, and invited to hole up, away from the cold. Or whatever it was you were trying to escape ... I wondered what had taken 'Max' out of the country.

'Have you decided what you'll have yet?' he asked. We'd been scanning the same menu, his head very close to mine.

I stood up. 'Macaroni cheese with the crusty bread please. I can go.'

'You stay right there,' he said, pressing on my shoulder

so that I sat back down. 'If I let you go up I might turn my back for a moment and find you've disappeared again.'

I gave him a look.

'If you're worried about paying your way I won't stop you,' he said. 'But running away for a third time isn't allowed.'

So I got a tenner out of my purse but stayed where I was. He did know I'd deliberately avoided him at The Prestwick then. He always seemed to be one step ahead of me.

He was talking to Dave again. I tried to hear what they were saying, but the place was filling up with the lunchtime trade and the ambient noise made it impossible.

He came back with another pint and a large glass of red wine for me. And I didn't normally drink at lunchtimes; the wine at Farquharson's had been a special treat. At least I was in training.

'Dave'll bring the food over,' he said.

It was now or never. 'I didn't hear him call you Max.'

He was too quick, I knew, to miss this obvious hint. He paused for a moment, looking at me with one eyebrow raised. 'No,' he said at last. 'He wouldn't.'

'Why not?' I held my breath.

'I don't think I've ever told him my name.'

'Oh.' I looked up and saw that Max was laughing. 'What?' I asked, letting my exasperation show at last.

'Sorry,' he said, recovering himself with an effort. 'But the look on your face just then was a picture.'

I felt uncomfortable and took another sip of the wine, which was already going to my head.

'So you know I'm not Max Conran then?' he said, laughing again, his blue eyes fixed on mine when I looked up.

I nodded, feeling as though it was me who'd been keeping a secret. He didn't seem remotely concerned that I'd found him out.

'I suppose Seb Rice knows as well, does he? Is that why you sneaked off at the gallery?'

I nodded again and had the ridiculous urge to apologise.

He reached out and squeezed my hand until I looked him in the eye. 'I'm sorry I wasn't straight with you,' he said, and some more rockets went off before he let me go.

'So,' he looked at me, 'does Seb know who I really am then? Do you?'

I shook my head. 'I certainly don't know. It's been bugging me a bit. As for Seb, well, I don't think he knew on the night of the private view. He might have found out by now I suppose. Radley – that woman who came and interrupted us – just said one of the team there knew you weren't Max Conran.'

He raised his eyebrows. 'That was unlucky,' he said, taking a sip of his beer. 'How the hell did they know that?'

'The team member in question had been out with him, apparently.'

He roared with laughter again. 'Max Conran mostly lives in France, so I reckoned I'd be totally safe using his persona. Lawrence certainly thought so.'

'He *was* in on it then?'

'Of course. His PA had to ring Radley Summers to change the details on the guest list. I thought it was one of the least risky stunts I'd ever pulled. Not that there's much harm done.'

At that moment Dave appeared, gripping the plates of steaming food, his hands protected by red-striped oven gloves. Even under the current circumstances I noticed how good it smelled.

'Wonderful,' said 'Max', digging into steak and Guinness pie.

'Max ... I mean not-Max!' I hadn't started on my food, in spite of the smell and the fact that I was actually feeling slightly more relaxed now and consequently ravenous.

'What?'

'What do you mean what? You can't just sit there eating like that. I'm still calling you Max. I don't know who you are. I've heard of blind dates, but this is ridiculous!' Oh my God. I'd called it a date. Where had that come from? I was going to have to have a mineral water next.

He looked at me again, with the same twinkle in his blue eyes. 'I'd really rather stay as Max in fact.'

'No way.'

He sighed. 'Oh all right then. You'll regret it though. My real name's Darrick Farron.'

'Darrick?'

'I know. You see, I told you so. Max was much better.'

I thought about it. 'It actually makes me think of Garrick, like the theatre, which seems quite appropriate, given that you're obviously good at acting.'

'Fair comment,' he said, taking a draught of his beer and leaning back in his seat.

'And so I know your name, but who are you? Why were you at Seb's?'

'If I tell you, will you eat up your food and stop looking at me like that?'

'It's a promise.'

'Okay then. I investigate and report on all things arts related.'

'I see,' I said, digesting this. 'Who do you work for?'

'I'm freelance. I went into Seb Rice's gallery under a false name because I did some work on a mate of Seb's a little while back. It was a bit controversial and made me very unpopular. And, as you can imagine, with a name like Darrick I tend to stick in people's minds. On the other hand, although Seb knew my name, he wouldn't know my face, so I figured I'd get away with it.' He looked at me and I opened my mouth. 'Eat,' he said. 'Dave's mild-mannered but he does get cross if people let his food go cold.'

It was only when I'd finished every last bit of macaroni that he answered the question that had been on my lips. Of course, he had already known what it was before I voiced it.

'You want to know what I was nosing into, the night I was at the gallery?'

I nodded.

'Not Seb himself.' He drained the last of his beer. 'It was one of his rich contacts who'd been hauled in, in case he could be persuaded to buy a couple of Shakespeare's paintings. More than that I cannot say, so don't ask. Now, coffee?'

Whilst Darrick returned to the bar I sat back, nursing the last of my wine and thinking about what he'd said. It all sat far more easily with the impression I'd got of him. The whole thing seemed to make perfect sense now, except for one point: it didn't explain the photograph Radley said he'd taken.

I could quite happily accept that Radley had imagined him following me and looking at me in a suspicious way, but now I was faced with what seemed to be the full facts, the photograph was the one thing ruining my new version of events. I'd told myself previously that she must have been mistaken, but now I wondered if that was really possible. If he'd definitely taken out his phone and held it up in front of him, what else could he have been doing?

'Here.' He arrived back at the table and the rich, bitter smell hit my senses as he put the steaming cup down in front of me. 'So we've done me,' he said, although I felt we had barely scratched the surface of that topic. 'What about you?'

'What about me?'

'Tell me more about your work. You said you don't normally write about arts stuff in particular, so what's your field?'

'I'm still deciding,' I said. 'I take whatever's going, and see if it throws up anything interesting. Thanks to my university friends, who've all conveniently made it big, I've had a reasonable source of high-profile interviewees so far.'

'So this is the gang of people you hung around with back in the days when you and Seb were studying together?'

I nodded, counting them off on my fingers: 'Seb, of course, you know about, then there's Terry Mallion.'

'The chef?'

'You're well informed. That's right. He's doing really well now. He's a great cook of course, but he's also good at being outrageous and funny, so they've picked up on him for a couple of TV things, and I expect that will expand.'

'What's he like in real life?'

'Very kind,' I said. 'He'd be hopeless on one of those programmes where you have to be all bolshie and mean to people. He'd keep accidentally patting his victim on the shoulder and making sure they were okay. I'm rather hoping his sort will come back into fashion.'

'You sound fond of him.'

'I am, very. I was living with him until a few weeks ago.' I looked up and caught Darrick's eye. 'I mean, not living with him in that way. He's gay. He was the best flatmate you could have, but I needed to come up to London. It's better for work.'

Though actually of course, I could write articles about potato processing from anywhere. I took a sip of coffee and moved quickly on to the next member of our university group before he could ask me more about my writing.

'So back to the gang from uni days. You might not have heard of Zoë Bannister. She's a very successful businesswoman in New Zealand. I managed to do a feature on her for the Manchester Evening News; it's her home city.'

'Good one.'

I nodded. 'And then there was Terry's boyfriend at the time, Jeremy Ellis, Jez.'

'Well that name's very familiar. I just can't place him for a moment.'

'He's an actor, up and coming, doing very well.' I was surrounded by people who were doing very well. Occasionally I thought they must be over-achieving on purpose to give me a complex. 'I've done a piece on him too. It's possible I could just keep going round and round them all as their careers progress without interviewing anyone else at all.' I drained the last of my coffee.

'Shall we go for a walk?' Darrick asked.

It was just what I felt like. The food and wine had made me dopey, in spite of the coffee. I followed him out of the pub, the cold air making me catch my breath as we left the cosy warmth behind.

We made our way towards the river and walked west in the direction of the National Theatre and the Royal Festival Hall. The wind whipped at our faces, blowing my long hair so that I had to keep pushing it out of my eyes. It was sunny though, and the low angle of the rays caught the ripples in the river, making the water sparkle as we walked by.

'I should think Seb would be a good source of more stories. If he carries on being so quick to spot new talent he could probably serve you up with an artist a quarter. You said you were close.'

I laughed. 'He probably could. But as far as closeness goes, "were" is the operative word.'

A boy whizzed past on rollerblades, narrowly missing me. Darrick put a protective arm around my shoulders for just a second. I found it hard to remember what we'd been talking about and longed for him to put it back again and pull me closer.

'"Were"?' Darrick said, dragging me back to reality. 'I remember you said he was very busy these days and you mainly got to deal with his minions instead. But I presume you could arrange a meet up on purpose.'

'I could,' I said. 'But there's more to it than that, to be honest.'

'Sounds complicated.'

'It is. It all goes back to what happened a little while after we all graduated and Seb was just starting out.' I pushed my hair out of my face for the umpteenth time. 'He had a girlfriend back then, Julia Thorpe. She lived up in Cumbria, where Seb was brought up.'

He glanced at me, his blue eyes on mine.

'They were completely taken up with each other – always on the phone, talking for hours. Then one morning he called her from London, but there was no reply. He didn't know it, but the locals had already found her body – floating in Derwentwater.'

Chapter Seven

I shuddered. It was horrible, remembering. 'There was no note, but Seb knew she'd been depressed. She'd taken a whole load of barbiturates and it was clear from her condition that she'd been in the water since late the night before. The police said she'd probably swum out until she couldn't go any further. Then, in the morning, when the ferry started up again, its wake would have washed her body back towards the shore. It sounds awful, but the rest of us were hardly aware of how low she was at the time.'

'You didn't know her well then?'

'Not really. I feel I should have taken care to get to know her better.'

'I don't suppose there was anything anyone could have done.' He looked down at me. 'And you were all studying in London, weren't you? If Julia was based up in Cumbria it was inevitable that you wouldn't see much of her.'

'That's true.'

We'd reached the Jubilee Gardens now, with the London Eye up ahead of us. A small child was running along, shouting joyously to a dog, his father taking a photograph.

'Seb met her when he went home for the Christmas holidays during his second year. He comes from a tiny village in the Lakes. When he turned up at his parents' place he found that the tenants of the big manor house round the corner had moved out, and Julia had appeared in their place.'

'Just Julia?'

'That's right; she was on her own, and only just

eighteen. Poor girl. Now I look back, I wonder how any of us could have thought she'd be anything other than depressed. Both her parents had been diplomats, killed in an air crash in Kenya. She was at boarding school, taking her A levels, when it happened. Suddenly all that structure went from her life and at the same time she had the responsibility of being an heiress, in charge of a dilapidated old house in the middle of nowhere.'

'Wasn't there anyone to look after her?'

I shook my head. 'Not really. I remember Seb saying there was some old man, but he wasn't much use. I gather he was an army type her parents had nominated to look after her legal rights, and help her with money issues, if they died once she'd reached the age of eighteen. Any earlier than that and she'd have been the ward of some aged aunt in Aberdeen.'

'Which doesn't sound ideal either. So Seb took her under his wing? With the help of his parents maybe?'

As we walked past a gang of pigeons, scrapping over some bread dropped by a toddler, I thought wryly of Seb's parents. 'I don't think they were involved,' I said at last. 'They didn't even go so far as to look after Seb all that much.'

'You met them?'

'Oh just the once, very briefly at some posh drinks do in London. No, I only know because Seb opened up one evening and told me all about it. Their overriding concern was making money, and being successful. It didn't leave much room for family life. But Seb certainly took Julia under *his* wing.' I found myself sighing. 'I think he fell for her as soon as they met. She was very striking.'

'What was she like?'

'She had this silvery quality about her. Her hair

was very blonde and fine, and her eyes were grey, and absolutely huge. It was the first thing you noticed about her. She was tall, very slender, and quietly spoken. You always got the impression she was thinking just what to say before she said it.' I suddenly felt as though I'd been babbling weirdly. 'Not a bit like me,' I added.

'What happened next?'

'For the rest of Seb's time at university, they were besotted. She came to London periodically, but usually he just went to her. Julia couldn't drive, so Seb used to dash up there at every opportunity in his VW. I went up once or twice too. Then Terry and Jez joined them for New Year, just a few months before Julia died. They said she seemed fine then. Quiet, but they assumed that was just her way.'

'Did you see her again?'

'Just the once. She came down to London to look at some of the art schools and we went out for a drink together. She was trying to work out what to do next. And then she invited me up to join them at Easter, but at the last minute Seb put me off. Someone else needed the guest room apparently.' I remembered that, because it had hurt my feelings a bit. I was well aware that they had plenty of spare bedrooms. It seemed childish and self-centred of me now. 'So anyway,' I said. 'That was it.

'I think he preferred it when it was just the two of them anyway. He'd always been a bit of a party animal up until then, but at that point he suddenly seemed more settled. He didn't encourage us to go up there much.'

The sun was getting very low in the sky and the temperature was dropping fast.

'It must have been horrendous for him when it happened,' Darrick said.

I nodded. 'It was a weekend, and he was down here in London. Things were really taking off for him at the time. He'd been planning to go up and see her overnight, but there was pressure of work this end. It was all to do with the gallery.'

'He already had it back then?'

'Not quite, but almost. As a matter of fact I spotted that the building was for let. It's in a prime spot and I didn't think Seb could possibly afford it, but something made me mention it anyway. There was no way his parents would have put up the cash, but Seb always had an air of being able to work miracles when it mattered. When he spoke to the estate agent he found it had already been reserved by a woman called Mel Swann.'

'Was that the woman he ended up going in with? Didn't they get married?'

'That's right,' I said. 'Seb being Seb, he evidently found a way to meet her, and they decided to pool resources. On the day Julia died he was in a business meeting with Mel. They were so excited, and Seb was all set to tell Julia. And maybe she'd come down and do her art degree, and the whole thing would fit perfectly, and this, and that ... He'd got it all worked out. And then the news came.' I shuddered, and felt the hairs on my arms lift. 'It still goes through me when I think about it.'

He put an arm back round my shoulder and pulled me in towards him. 'I'm sorry. I've brought it all back.'

'It's okay. It's been on my mind lately anyway, what with visiting the gallery and everything.'

'So does Seb ever talk about Julia these days?'

'Not as far as I know.' I paused. 'But then I wouldn't know. He keeps all the old university gang at arm's length. It's as though he associates us with a time when everything was as good as it was ever going to get. If he sees us now he sees his past, and the memories are too much for him.'

I suddenly realised how far we'd walked and glanced at my watch. I knew I ought to be heading home. Sally had made me promise to check in with her on my return, just to be on the safe side. We started to make our way back towards Waterloo.

'Where are you headed?' he asked.

'Hampstead.'

'Nice location.'

'I've got a room in my cousin's house. She wanted to help me out with somewhere central to live.'

'So are you making plenty of contacts?'

I paused for a moment too long, trying to think how to keep my end up. 'It's not going too badly. And now my cousin's offered herself up as an interviewee. She's the society caterer, Alicia Greenstock.'

'You do mix with the rich and famous.' I could tell he was laughing at me.

'It's not my fault,' I said huffily. 'And she's a real pain to live with as a matter of fact.'

'And after you've interviewed Alicia? What are your work plans then?'

I wasn't sure if he sensed my insecurity. Did he want me to come right out and say I was floundering? 'I'm going to see Radley again tomorrow,' I said, 'mainly to talk about the Shakespeare stuff, but I might probe and see what else is on the horizon. I'm determined not to give in, now that I've made the move to go into freelance journalism. Even if I do have to sub it by taking on some corporate copywriting ... And you could be right about Seb putting more stuff my way.'

'Maybe he's trying to move on from what happened

before,' Darrick said. 'Even if it's Radley you're meeting, Seb must be behind her approaching you.'

'I suppose so.'

'You might have grown apart,' he went on, 'but people do tend to remember old ...' He paused for a moment. '... friendships.'

There was something about the way he said 'friendships' that made me look up. He had used a slightly questioning note, and I had a feeling he'd mentally put inverted commas around the word.

Without really thinking I said: 'And sometimes old friendships mean ongoing relations can be problematic.' I realised too late that I'd put the same inverted commas round the word myself.

'I see,' he said, and I could tell he was drawing conclusions.

'It was all such a long time ago.'

'Not so very long.'

When we got to Waterloo Station he stood a few feet apart from me. He kissed me on the cheek before I got onto the tube, but didn't mention meeting up again and I felt a stab of disappointment. As the train gathered speed, propelling me back to my ordinary life, the look in his eye stayed with me. I was sure he was judging me in some way, and I didn't know what it meant.

Chapter Eight

The following morning I woke up in a disgruntled mood after a very graphic dream about Darrick that had ended just at the wrong moment and was obviously destined never to come true. Then the instant I poked my nose downstairs I ran into Alicia. She was in bulldozer mode.

'I can't do your interview tomorrow morning after all,' she said. 'So it'll have to be today; say ten o'clock.' She glanced at her watch and sighed. 'That should just about fit okay.' She looked at me as though I was causing her the utmost inconvenience and seemed to have forgotten that the whole idea had been hers in the first place. 'So come and find me at ten then,' she said, and swept out of the room.

Crashing about in the kitchen helped me to let off steam, though my violent actions meant I spilt marmalade on the floor. I went back upstairs feeling bloody-minded. She might have caught me on the hop as regards to the timing of the interview, but I was going to make damn sure everything else about it went my way.

The change in schedule that morning was actually pretty inconvenient. I was due to be with Radley at the gallery by half-past two, and what with the final preparation I had been intending to do, together with the tube journey, I was a bit short of time. I huffed about my room, getting my voice recorder ready and inventing annoying questions to ask Alicia.

When I went downstairs she was in her sitting room.

'I'd like to talk to you in the kitchen,' I said, determined to take control.

'But Sally might interrupt us if we're in there.'

'No. I mean *your* kitchen.'

From her expression, you'd think I'd asked to interview her in the lavatory. 'Why?'

'Because you're a cook.'

She looked at me as though I'd gone crackers.

I sighed. 'I want to describe you in your typical surroundings. I want to be able to tell readers about how you like to work, what kind of set-up you have, you know.'

She sounded exasperated. 'Oh all right then. Come on.' And she went on through to the room of gleaming stainless steel and stark lights.

It occurred to me that it all looked hard: the metal hobs and sink, the granite worktops, the stone floor. I could gear the piece so that the description came across as a metaphor for Alicia's character ... I took a deep breath. I really wasn't going about this the right way.

'Have you got any photographs of yourself down here?' I asked, trying to get back into friendly mode.

'Certainly not,' Alicia said. 'I like to keep this part of my operation private.'

'You did say I could do a piece on you, Alicia, and whichever magazine I approach they will want some pictures. Showing you on home turf would be something new.' I took a seat on one of the high stools by the island unit. 'I'll bring down my equipment in the next day or two and take a few shots.'

Alicia looked as though she was about to say something aggressive, so I quickly turned on the voice recorder, and she shut her mouth again.

'So what were your earliest childhood experiences of cooking?'

The aggressive look was back again; jaw clenched, chin

jutting out. 'I didn't start cooking properly until I was twenty,' she said.

'I know,' I said. 'I read that in the interview you did for Good Food. But I want to know about your experience of cooking informally, before that.'

She was looking at the floor now, which wasn't like her.

'Or, if you like, you can tell me about your early experiences of food. I mean, something must have turned you on to cooking in the first place. Did you have interesting meals when you were little?'

She got up and walked towards one of the tall windows that faced onto the street.

'What is it?' I asked.

'I normally like to talk about my training, and the people I've cooked for.'

'They may be famous but they're not that fascinating. I'm more interested in you.'

'You're my cousin. No one else will want to know about my childhood.' She was still looking outside, her jaw taut.

'I think you're wrong. Go on, Alicia. You were the one who suggested I interview you. I'd like to come up with something fresh, something that no one's read before. An editor can decide if I'm right about what's interesting, and if I'm wrong, you can say I told you so.' I paused for a moment, but couldn't resist it: 'And I know how much you like doing that.'

She turned and, to my surprise, gave me a half smile. It was such a rarity that I felt a sudden rush of fondness for her.

She sighed and walked back to the seat opposite me, next to the recorder. 'Okay,' she said. 'I did have nice food when I was a child. We had plenty of money and a very good cook, Mrs Wallis. Shirley. I liked her and we kept in touch until she died.'

'And were you allowed to hang around in the kitchen?' I said. 'Did Mrs Wallis show you how she made things?'

Alicia leant forward on one elbow and rested her head in her upturned hand. 'I don't know whether I want to go into all this,' she said and I realised that the questions I'd thought were so innocuous had struck a raw nerve. 'It's personal.'

'Do you want me to turn the machine off?' I asked, reaching for the recorder.

She hesitated. 'Just for a moment, please, whilst I think.'

I clicked the stop-recording icon.

'If I don't talk to you, I'm being a coward,' she said. 'But if I do I'm gushing out a load of personal stuff that's no one's business but my own.'

'We can do whatever you want,' I said. 'Would you like me to get you some water while you think it through?' I tried not to look at my watch and pushed thoughts of Radley from my mind.

She looked up at me. 'I think it might help your career as a writer if I go ahead and answer.'

She'd activated my irritant sensor again.

'Put the machine back on,' she said and I did, with a sharp tap to select the record icon.

'So I was asking about you watching Mrs Wallis cooking for your family,' I prompted.

Alicia nodded. 'I did watch, and gradually she started to let me do things for her too. I had a go at icing cakes, and whipping cream – that kind of thing.'

'So that was when you started to enjoy cookery?'

She nodded. 'And then, as time went on, Mrs Wallis let me have a go at more complicated things. By the time I was six I was doing some dishes almost unaided – although obviously I wasn't allowed to use sharp knives or turn on the gas by myself or anything like that.'

'Sounds like good training though.'

'It was excellent. I loved Mrs Wallis, and I loved cooking.'

'But something went wrong?'

She nodded. 'One day we had a fruit tart as part of our dinner. I'd made the pastry, prepared the filling, and then decorated the whole thing with whipped cream. My mother called Mrs Wallis through especially to say how good it was.' She shifted in her seat. 'Well, Mrs Wallis had been dying to tell my parents how promising my cooking was for ages. I think she was embarrassed that I'd been doing so much of it without her ever having consulted my mother.'

'So I'm guessing that seemed like the ideal moment to bring the subject up?'

She nodded. 'And, instead of being pleased or impressed, my mother was absolutely livid. She yelled at Mrs Wallis for not doing her job properly, for taking on the role of my teacher or governess, when that was the responsibility of others. She said that Mrs Wallis had ideas above her station, and that she had no business letting me even sit in the kitchen without her permission.' She blinked as she looked up. 'Mrs Wallis was in tears, standing there at the dinner table. I've never forgotten it. My mother threatened to sack her, and I just sat there and didn't defend her at all.'

She paused then, and went to get herself the glass of water I'd suggested earlier.

'I was forbidden from going into the kitchen again. Do you know,' she said, suddenly looking up at me, her voice bitter, 'I think my mother was jealous of Mrs Wallis? She could never be bothered to spend time with me herself, so *we* weren't close, but she couldn't bear anyone else filling the gap.' She sipped her water and when she spoke again her voice was steadier. 'A real bitch in the manger, that's what she was.'

'So what happened next?'

'A funny thing. An older cousin of mine used to come visiting quite often, and more than once I saw *him* sneaking into the kitchen. He was funny and quite kind to me. He used to put his finger up to his lips if he saw me watch him go in.'

'Don't tell me he was into cooking too?'

She shook her head. 'He was into Daphne, the girl who used to help Mrs Wallis.'

'Ah. I see.'

'Anyway, I don't know what they talked about on his visits, but when I went away to school things changed. During the first set of holidays, I was invited to stay with his younger sister and their parents down near Winchester. They didn't have a cook, or anything like that, and his mother had us in the kitchen, baking and doing all sorts of things. When I first turned up I remember her saying she'd heard I liked cooking, and that was what made me wonder. They did a lot of entertaining, so I got plenty of opportunities to practise.'

After another half hour or so we'd finished and I thanked her.

She smiled. 'I want to help you get a good story if I can,' she said. 'I almost had the career I adored taken away from me. That mustn't happen to you; I want you to be able to carry on doing the job you love.'

It was very kindly meant, of course, though verging on the schmaltzy. It did explain why she was always such a nag though.

Chapter Nine

I dashed up the stairs two at a time to get ready for my meeting with Radley Summers. Within moments I was slinging on what I'd already decided to wear: green suit, matching court shoes (with the obligatory height-enhancing qualities) and an arty necklace I hoped would appeal to gallery types.

There was a healthy stream of people filing through the gallery foyer when I arrived: a couple arm in arm, making me think wistfully of Darrick for a moment, and then a gang of students, loud, cocky and clever, reminding me of bygone university days.

I stood at the front desk while the receptionist dealt with a couple of queries, enjoying the warmth and bright lights. It was good to escape from the grey day outside, where the Thames was the colour of clay. I spent my time browsing the leaflets on display. There was one about some public art in North London, and another about a poetry and short story competition. Then my eye was caught by one advertising a new gallery devoted to textile design. The pictures inside showed pieces that were awash with colour: vivid blues, greens, purples and oranges. Nets overlaid silk, filigrees of threads danced over the fabric. I tucked the leaflet in my pocket and looked up as the receptionist turned her attention to me.

Radley's office was on the fourth floor. The woman on the front desk gave me directions and I took the lift up, emerging on a corridor that smelled of new carpet.

I knew I was meant to turn right, but at that moment

I noticed an office diagonally opposite on the left, with Seb's name on the door. Its walls were glass, but covered by blinds that had been adjusted so no one could look in. I hadn't actually seen him for months, and found myself hovering for a moment. But then a well-dressed man I'd spotted in the foyer appeared, approaching quickly. He must have come up via the stairs whilst I'd been in the lift. He shoved the handle of Seb's office door down without knocking, and I hastily turned to go on my way. Presumably I would see Seb again one day. Now wasn't the moment.

The corridor I walked along was lined with photographs of Seb with some of his discoveries: Seb and William Vagas, Seb and Valerie Turland, Seb and Fiona Webster, and so it went on. Another man appeared in several of them: he always seemed to be wearing a long, dark coat, wherever the shots were taken. It made him look like the character in a movie that you know is meant to be mysterious. Occasionally the photographs showed larger groups – other members of Seb's team, or a gang at a private view – but most·were intimate close-ups of artist, gallery manager and the man in the long coat. I wondered who he was.

'Sir Anthony Peake,' said Radley, when I'd found her room and asked. 'He owns this building and he's also the Chair of our Board.'

'I wondered about the coat.'

'He enjoys meeting all the young starlets,' Radley said, 'but he doesn't really like to get his hands dirty. We think that's the explanation behind the coat. He only stays long enough to say hello, drink the champagne and get his picture taken. After that he's off again. I imagine he doesn't feel removing his outdoor layer is worth the effort.'

I was slightly worried about the way Radley was looking at me. When I'd first gone into her office I'd thought she seemed on the frosty side, so I'd asked straight away about the man in the photos to break the ice. Now she'd told me, but her tone was irritable, and I could tell I was going to be the one driving the conversation. It bothered me that I couldn't guess why.

'You got the draft copy for The Enquirer okay?' I asked, tentatively checking for possible causes of friction.

She nodded. 'Looks good.' She sounded grudging.

'I'll get it off to them later today,' I said. 'And then there's the copy for Epic. I'll have a draft of that with you early next week.'

She bent her head forward in acknowledgement. 'I think Seb would like you to come back and write about some of our other upcoming artists.'

Of course, it was half what I'd wanted to hear, but at the same time it was putting me in the gallery's pocket. I was becoming more and more like a PR person, getting them publicity through my stories, rather than writing proper independent reviews. It felt wrong, but, then again, I didn't really have the luxury of turning down that kind of offer at the moment.

'I'll have to write honestly about what I see,' I said, feeling that I should set the right tone. 'Otherwise the papers won't want my work.'

Radley raised her eyebrows. 'Of course.'

I was about to come out with it and ask if I'd done something to offend her when she said: 'I saw you coming out of The Old Faithful the other day.'

'Oh,' I said. 'Yes, that's right.'

'I go past every day to get my sandwiches from Valerie's in Tanner's Yard.'

'You must have been having a late lunch.'

'I've been rather busy recently. I'd love to be able to keep the hours you do. You looked as though you were having a nice time.'

I sighed. 'Yes, it turns out your mystery man from the gallery is quite all right. He tracked me down and he was perfectly open about the fact that he'd come to the exhibition under false pretences.'

'Oh well, that's just great then. No problem at all.' She sat back in her chair and folded her arms.

'Sorry.' I suddenly realised it was still a bit of a cheek as far as she was concerned, and had probably caused her and Seb a certain amount of worry and inconvenience. 'It was wrong of him, obviously. But you see I'd started to wonder if he was up to something really dodgy, and it seems it was all a bit more low-key than that.'

'So what did he tell you then?'

I sat back in my chair, glancing for a moment out of Radley's window. I wished I was out there. 'That he's a reporter and his real name is Darrick Farron. He was chasing some story about one of your rich art collectors. He wouldn't tell me which one, but I was pleased it was nothing directly to do with the gallery.'

'And were you planning to tell us what you'd found out at any stage? I must admit I expected a call from you, once I saw you'd obviously got to the bottom of the mystery.'

Now she mentioned it, perhaps it did seem like an oversight. I started to feel belated guilt, but it simply hadn't crossed my mind.

'And how did he explain the photograph he took of you?' Radley said.

This was getting worse. 'I didn't actually ask him

about that,' I said. I could feel a red blush creeping up my neck.

Radley rested her elbows on the desk and put her head in her hands. 'For God's sake, Anna,' she said. 'Doesn't that seem like rather a glaring omission from your conversation?'

I carried on saying nothing. It was a bit like being back in the headmaster's office at school. Eventually I said: 'To be honest, I just kept thinking you must have been mistaken. I mean it was such a peculiar thing. Like something out of a second-rate spy movie.'

I could instantly tell I shouldn't have let the phrase "second-rate" slip out in connection with anything she'd thought or done, even at one step removed.

'How could I have been mistaken?' she said. 'I wonder if you didn't ask because you didn't really want to know.' She stood up and walked over to the window for a moment, looking down at the square. 'Look, Anna,' she said. 'We get paid quite a bit of attention. There's a lot of money sloshing around in this business, and that makes some people, jealous people maybe, keen to do anything they can to put a spanner in the works.'

'And you think that's what he's out to do?'

She turned to look at me. 'He says he's a journalist and he took your photo. Well, what if he wants to smear the coverage we're getting for the Shakespeare exhibition? He might use your picture then, mightn't he? Perhaps he's preparing his own article right now, pointing out that one of our glowing reviews was organised by me, and written by an old university friend of Seb's.'

It was an unpleasant thought, and enough to shake me, but I wasn't really convinced. 'It wouldn't make much of a story,' I said.

She walked back to her chair and sat down. 'Maybe not. Perhaps only a paragraph in a gossip column where they like to slag off successful people. Doesn't mean to say that's not what he was up to. It's instinct with people like that. They have a spare evening and they use it to get a story, some extra cash and a kick out of causing trouble.'

She pressed the button on an intercom on her desk. 'Elsie, bring some coffee for me and Anna Morris will you?' She looked up at me again. 'You say he tracked you down. If that's the case, and my theory's right, then he's after something extra.'

I thought of what I had hoped Darrick had been after and looked down at the desk.

'What did he ask you when you had lunch together, can you remember?'

'He didn't spend the whole time firing questions at me. We talked about writing a bit, and the pub, and I explained how I knew Seb, and about the rest of our gang. I was telling him how I'd been interviewing them all in turn because they'd done so well.'

'So let me get this straight. You knew this guy was a journalist, and that he was dishonest enough to have blagged his way into the gallery of one of your oldest friends. And, that being the case, you decided to spend your entire time with him passing on a whole load of personal details about that very same friend and some of his contacts.'

I could feel my heart racing, adrenaline arriving ready to fuel my reply. It was probably just as well that the coffee turned up then, and meant I could take a deep breath before I began.

Once we were alone again, I was reasonably measured. 'I can assure you, Radley, that you're worrying unnecessarily. I didn't say anything that hasn't been written already in umpteen different magazine profiles, to say nothing of Seb's biography. You may know I was asked to contribute to that at the time, with Seb's blessing. In fact, I probably told Darrick pretty much what I told the author of the biography.'

Seb hadn't shied away from us mentioning Julia, or relating the awful events that had unfolded. He'd said not talking about it fully would be like denying her existence. He'd wanted his love for her and the tragedy of her loss to be known and for people to appreciate what she'd had to go through. It seemed to be part of the grieving process for him.

'You might at least have contacted him to let him know what had gone on,' Radley said, breaking in on my thoughts.

'What was there to tell, given what I've just said? And in any case, I've hardly seen Seb for over two years now. He hasn't exactly given me the impression that he wants a blow-by-blow account of my everyday life.'

She just sat there, looking at me. There was a new expression in her eyes now that I found hard to read.

'What do you talk about when you go out on a first date with someone?' I said. 'I'll bet you mention where you grew up, where you studied, what you do and who your friends are. It's not exactly controversial.'

'It is when you're seeing a journalist.' She took another sip of coffee, looking at me with watchful eyes. 'It was a date then?'

Had it been? Probably not so as you'd notice. Perhaps he really had just been pumping me for extra information. I had to admit that he'd seemed pretty interested in what I'd said about the old days. But then again, it was interesting. The story was tragic, the people involved well known, and he was a journalist. He'd be interested by instinct.

Oh to hell with Radley. She wouldn't know one way or the other anyway. 'Yes,' I said. 'It was a date.'

'I see. And are you intending to see him again?'

'I haven't decided.'

On the way home, I came to terms with the fact that I hadn't been properly honest with Radley. Obviously, I'd exaggerated my relationship with Darrick, but that had been a conscious decision and I was quite happy with it. I'd enjoyed winding her up.

What was more disturbing was that, deep down, I knew I had really given away more information than was in any magazine article or biography. I was sure Darrick had read something in my tone when I'd talked about Seb. At least he didn't have anything factual though. But the stuff about his parents wasn't in the public domain either. Seb wouldn't want that used. And then there were bound to be nuances and little details in what I'd prattled on about that amounted to new information.

There had been something about Darrick; for whatever reason he'd had me just where he wanted me. And I had decided that it didn't matter because I felt some kind of weird closeness to him; something that made me relax and told me I had nothing to fear. But then, when we'd parted, I'd been quite sure he was holding something back.

I hoped to goodness that Radley was wrong about him.

Chapter Ten

After the way my meeting with Radley had gone, I felt the extra work she'd hinted at was unlikely to materialise. There wasn't much I could do about that though. I'd gone out of my way to annoy her and, having behaved like a toddler, I would have to take the consequences.

But not everything was going pear-shaped. Alicia had done me a really good turn by opening up. In the last half hour of the interview she'd given me all sorts of gems: how she'd secretly used a candle to melt down some chocolates she'd been given at Christmas to create new ones, and how she'd made friends with one of the cooks at her boarding school.

She even admitted the burning envy she'd felt for one of her classmates, who was good at music and had been hot-housed at every opportunity. In the end, she'd said, she'd decided to hot-house herself if no one else would.

It was a real story of gutsy determination leading to success against the odds. I managed to sell the article nice and quickly. In the end I offered it to The Enquirer again, and they took it for their culture section. It was good to know it was going to appear in a mainstream newspaper rather than a more specialist magazine. I was hoping it would keep me fresh in the editor's mind too.

In my spare time, I worked on Sally's bag. It was still three weeks until the party she was going to, but I wanted to let her see it well in advance, in case she didn't like it and had to search for an alternative.

At last, just over a week later, I went down and knocked on her door, ready to hand it over.

'It's gorgeous!' she said, when I showed her. She'd settled on a colour scheme of sea greens, blues and purples, to go with her purple dress. I'd embroidered the whole thing with a design of seaweed and tiny fish, using pearl beads for eyes. 'Wait,' she said, stepping towards the wardrobe. 'You've got to see the whole thing together.' She picked out her beautiful purple taffeta dress and within a moment was in the bathroom, changing.

'No news I suppose?' she shouted through the door.

I knew she meant about Darrick of course. She'd had the full story of the lunch, wringing out every detail from me, and was keen to get another instalment. I was going to have to disappoint her. 'None, and at this stage I'm quite sure there never will be. It's been over a week since I saw him. He obviously isn't going to call, so you'd better stop asking me. It's only rubbing it in.'

'Sorry.' I could hear the sound of hair being brushed and then sprayed. The smell of Elnett crept under the door. 'But I can't believe it. That lunch sounded quite romantic. And the lengths he went to, to catch up with you … All that hanging around outside hotels and everything. It just doesn't make sense.'

Unless what Radley had said was true, of course, and he had just been using me. I'd waited anxiously after my article in The Enquirer had come out, in case there was some snide gossip piece of the sort Radley had suggested. I'd even Googled my name, just to check I didn't appear in any text other than my own article, but so far none of that sort of fallout had come about.

'Maybe I just didn't live up to expectations,' I said, feeling sorry for myself. 'I should never have let him see me in broad daylight.'

'Nonsense!' she said, appearing at last, her hair piled

high on her head in an Audrey Hepburn-style chignon. The dress was wonderful: knee-length, close-fitting and curvy. She looked fantastic.

'What do you think?' she said.

'One of the loveliest dresses I've ever seen.'

'Not the dress you idiot! What do you think of your bag, as part of the outfit?'

And I had to admit, boasting apart, that it did look good. Its intricate design offset the classic simplicity of the dress perfectly, and the pearls added just the right touch of glamour to the mix.

Sally walked over to the full-length mirror on the wardrobe door. 'Heavenly,' she said. She was totally unself-conscious. It made me feel slightly wistful. 'Now,' she went on, turning back to me again, 'I checked out the going rate for handmade bags. Would a hundred and fifty be okay?'

I sat there with my mouth opening and closing for around thirty seconds before I managed to say anything. 'It's far too much Sally.'

'I wouldn't think so,' she said in a matter of fact way. 'To be honest, it should be a bit more really. If you think about the materials, and how many hours you've slaved over it and so on. The ones I saw in a gallery on The King's Road were two twenty, but I must admit I'm a bit short this month, so if one fifty's really okay?'

'I'll feel guilty for the rest of the year if I let you give me that much.'

'It's either that or I'll take the money back again and you can keep the bag.'

I scowled at her. 'Oh for heaven's sake, all right then.'

'Good.' She wrote out a cheque. 'And there's no need to make such a fuss about it. You don't seem to have any idea how much money people regularly spend on total crap. If you did you'd be quite cross I'm not giving you more.'

It was another week before Darrick finally got in touch again. I'd completely given up on him, though I'd been unable to banish him from my thoughts altogether. However, when he called he behaved as though there'd been no odd gap at all.

'Your friend Jez Ellis is in a film that's just opened at The Everyman on Baker Street,' he said.

'Yes, I know. I was going to go and see it.'

'Come and see it with me then. Can you do tomorrow night?'

I paused for what I hoped struck him as a worryingly long time and then said: 'I'm washing my hair.'

He laughed. 'Oh go on,' he said. 'You'll enjoy it. I feel our relationship so far hasn't conformed to the proper protocol and I want to take you out, in the evening. Seeing a film's a good, respectable way to start again. It would set things on the right course. So, how about it?'

I sighed heavily. 'I hadn't actually expected to hear from you again.'

'Sorry,' he said, whilst sounding distinctly light-hearted. 'Things have been a bit hectic.'

I had a feeling I would never find out what "things" he was talking about. 'Oh, okay then,' I said. 'What time's the show?'

We met outside the cinema at six-thirty so we could have a drink first.

'And afterwards I'll take you for dinner,' Darrick said. He put a finger lightly to my lips when I opened my mouth. 'No arguments. If I don't, the next time I call you'll only accuse me of being neglectful.'

We drank dry martinis because there was a cocktail bar and, as Darrick said, it seemed a waste not to. As we sank into comfortable seats next to one of a number of low, round tables, I asked him what he'd been up to.

'This and that,' he said, raising his glass to me. 'The trouble with travelling so much is that when I do get back to the UK there's always a lot to sort out.'

'To do with your home, and things like that?'

'That kind of thing,' he agreed, smiling.

I felt sure he was irking me on purpose by not letting me have any details. 'So you obviously report on a lot of people and events overseas,' I said, thinking I must Google some of his pieces now that we were back in touch so I could sound more clued up.

'I tend to work on longer-term investigative projects,' he said, 'rather than events.'

'In the arts world?'

'That's right.'

'I see.' I picked the green olive off the cocktail stick that was balanced precariously on my glass and ate it.

'So how did you get on when you went to meet Radley?' Darrick asked.

I'd had the feeling he would shift the conversation to me as soon as I paused long enough to let him. All the alarm bells Radley had set off began to chime again. Was this him pumping me for more information, just as she had said?

'Any sniff of future work?' he asked.

I smiled thinly, and hoped I looked suitably distant. 'There was at first, but I'm afraid we had a bit of a falling out.'

He looked surprised. 'What about?'

'You. She saw us coming out of The Old Faithful together and seemed to feel I'd been a bit disloyal, fraternising with someone who had lied to worm his way into her confidence.'

'How narrow-minded.'

I raised an eyebrow. 'She was also none too pleased when she found out why you were really at the gallery.'

'I hope you told her I was stalking someone unconnected with Seb's place when I sneaked in.'

'I don't think she bought your story. She was fairly certain you'd tracked me down with the sole purpose of squeezing me for information so you could smear the gallery. She says the art world is full of jealous types who'll do *anything* to take a cheap shot at someone as successful as Seb is. Even down to pursuing people like me.'

'What a charming woman she must be.' He took a sip of his drink. 'I might have considered squeezing you occasionally, but information wasn't my end goal.'

Which I knew was pretty good soft soap, though it was rather appealing nonetheless. 'She pointed out that I hadn't asked you about the photograph,' I went on relentlessly.

He frowned. 'What photograph?'

I looked him straight in the eye. 'The one you took of me at the gallery, when I was standing out on the landing.'

'I don't understand.' He did look genuinely mystified.

'That makes three of us. They use CCTV at the gallery and peer at all their guests. Radley saw you take out your mobile – before I knew you were standing behind me – and hold it up to take my photo.' I could feel myself flushing now. It did sound absolutely ridiculous. And the fact that I had believed Radley must make me sound self-obsessed: as though I thought it was totally natural that strange men in galleries might want to take my picture.

'Obviously, it seemed crazy to me,' I said hastily, 'but she insists that's what she saw. So if you could just explain it, then at least I can tell her what you were up to if she does ever call me back in. At the moment she clearly thinks I'm crazy for agreeing to see you.'

'I can't explain it,' said Darrick with absolute finality. He sat back in his seat. 'And the reason for that, is because it didn't happen.'

'I did say to her, right from the start, that she must have been mistaken. I mean, maybe you were reading a text or something.'

He took a deep breath. 'I never even took my mobile out of my pocket, Anna,' he said.

Chapter Eleven

We were prevented from arguing the toss any further as it was time for the film to start. Sitting there with the smell of popcorn in my nostrils and Pearl and Dean blaring in my ears, the whole thing seemed surreal. It was ironic that I was there, next to him at last, his left leg within a hair's breadth of my right, and once again a gulf had opened up between us, so that I didn't know whether I was allowed to want him to brush against me or not.

'Damn,' I said, under my breath.

'What?'

'I'm really confused.'

'You're not the only one.' And he moved then, turning towards me for a second. And at that moment his leg did touch mine, and I found that my brain was going to go ahead and want whatever it felt like, whether it was officially allowed to or not.

The film was one of those coming-of-age movies, filling me with nostalgia for a time when anything had seemed possible and nothing appeared to matter very much. It always struck me as odd that those two feelings should come together. When anything seemed possible, it would be better if you were driven with a desire to get on with what you wanted to achieve.

Come to think of it, maybe the rest of my gang had been. Jez hadn't played the lead in the film – he was one of the friends of the main protagonist – but his part was crucial to the plot and he'd played it superbly. He'd had one or two of these key supporting roles in the last few years and I was willing to bet he'd land a title role within the next twelve months.

'He was good, don't you think?' Darrick said as we got up from our seats.

'He was, wasn't he?' I felt pleased that he thought so.

We went to eat at a place called The Midnight Hour Mediterranean Bistro.

'Even the name's a mouthful,' Darrick said, 'which must be a good sign.'

It was the kind of setting I liked: full of twinkling candles, sparkling glassware and crisp, white tablecloths. The walls were covered with mahogany panels and made me feel warm and cocooned. From somewhere down below us, perhaps a basement bar, I could hear someone playing a saxophone.

'They don't do macaroni cheese,' Darrick said, handing me a menu, 'so you'd better get thinking.'

I searched for the least pretentious thing listed, determined not to rise to the bait, but The Midnight Hour wasn't big on low-key stuff and anyway, that wasn't what I felt like. I went for some glorious-sounding concoction on pasta, featuring artichoke, chorizo and chilli with a whole load of Parmesan chucked on top. Darrick ordered mussels and chips and before long the waitress brought us a bottle of white wine, glistening with condensation.

Darrick poured me a glassful. His well-toned arm was brown next to his white shirtsleeve. 'So all of that business with Radley Summers explains the frosty reception you gave me on the phone yesterday.'

'Oh no,' I said. 'That was just because you hadn't called me for two weeks.'

He laughed. 'Have you decided to forgive me now?'

'I'm still thinking about it.'

'I'll watch my step then.'

The place was thronging and we'd been lucky to get a table. All around us laughter rang out, and chatting voices merged, but I felt we were quite separate from the crowds. They'd given us a table in a little alcove, which was a haven, removed from the main hubbub.

'Look,' Darrick said, 'that Radley woman's completely wrong but, if it makes you feel happier, we won't talk about anything to do with Seb Rice. I want to know about you though. What did you study?'

'English lit. Predictably. Then I did a photography course afterwards and got taken on as a junior reporter at the London Gazette.'

'Starting out on the Gazette's not bad.'

'I got to do all the boring stuff. Council decisions – that kind of thing. But I was straight out of university.'

'Were you pleased to stay on in London?'

I nodded. 'I've always liked it here. I enjoy the bustle; I find it reassuring to be surrounded by people. And it helped that several of my friends stayed on too.'

'Did you move in with Terry at that stage?'

'No. He'd already decamped to Hertfordshire to start his first restaurant; the rent was cheaper, so it was a safer bet than starting up here. I left the Gazette after a while.' I hesitated. 'I wasn't sure I was in the right job, which is an almost constant state of affairs with me.' I made a face. 'I decided to try being a press officer for a company in Barnet, and it was only then that I moved to Terry's.'

'I see.' He poured us some more wine. 'So what about when you were still in London then?'

'I went in with a girl who'd had a room across the corridor at my college. It wasn't all that fun actually. She was one of Seb's ...' I paused.

'What?'

I couldn't believe I was talking about him again. But we'd all been so close, back in the day. It was hard to explain about my life without referring to his. 'I was moving on to a topic we'd agreed to avoid.'

'And are you about to tell me something you think I'll make use of?'

I sighed. 'No. I suppose not.'

He folded his arms. 'In that case I don't want to know anyway.'

'Pig.'

He laughed.

'All I was going to say,' I went on, 'was that she was part of Seb's little group of hangers-on.'

Darrick felt inside his jeans pocket and pulled out a small notebook and pencil. 'Hangers-on ...' he said as he scribbled on the top page.

'If you're going to carry on taking the piss out of me I'm going home right now.'

He put it away again. 'Don't be like that. A man's got to have some fun. You were saying ...'

I thought back to what I'd been about to explain, and rapidly edited it for Darrick's ears. 'He had hangers-on. I expect you know the sort, I think they're around in every college in the country. They're the ones that find out who's the best prospect if they want to cadge cigarettes, or booze, and then stick themselves like glue to whoever it is. In our case it was Seb.'

'Sounds like a generous guy.'

Darrick's tone caught my attention, but his face was in

shadow – his fringe down over one eye – and I couldn't judge his expression.

'There was a similar bloke who lived in my hall at university as a matter of fact,' he went on. 'He always had crowds of people in his room. Mind you, it turned out he was offering more than just booze and fags. Drugs were on the menu too, and he was dealing ...'

He was sounding like a journalist again now. Seb had certainly taken drugs, but I wasn't going to tell Darrick that.

'You're barking up the wrong tree,' I said, leaning back in my chair. 'There was a dealer on our corridor, but it wasn't Seb. It was this really weird guy with eyes like saucers. He had every drug going – both to sell and for personal use, I imagine – and there definitely wouldn't have been room enough for both of them to set up stalls in such close proximity. Even if he'd been tempted, Seb would have had enough business sense to know that.'

'I'm sure you're right.' Darrick sat back in his seat too and held up his hands, a smile playing round his lips again. 'You must have had some wild parties, with a dealer just across the corridor.'

I shook my head. 'Not me. I was far too much of a coward to try any of the hard stuff.'

'But I'm guessing Seb was up for anything that was going? It sounds as though he enjoyed living on the edge.'

I certainly wasn't going to answer that one, although he'd obviously already got a good impression of what Seb would or wouldn't do. 'You do seem very curious about him, you know,' I said instead.

'Of course I am.' He reached over and stroked my arm. 'Through our conversations I got the impression that you were fond of him at one time, and that makes me want to know every detail of your past relationship. There's nothing sinister in that, it's just the bloke in me.'

'He was very popular,' I said, hoping to wind Darrick up some more. 'I think people sensed he'd go places even then. There was something about him, a kind of crackle which turned the tension up a notch whenever he appeared.'

Darrick stifled a yawn.

I smiled sweetly. 'He even had the university staff eating out of his hand.'

He raised an eyebrow. 'What did he actually study? I can't imagine it was art. If he was an artist I presume he'd want to be out there producing work himself, not selling other people's.'

'No, you're right,' I said. 'Business has always been his strong suit really. That's where he channels his creativity. He actually read history of art.' I laughed quietly. 'He always said he chose it because he knew there'd be plenty of girls on the course.'

'Hmm.' Darrick didn't seem to find this all that amusing. 'He wouldn't really have done it for that sort of reason though, would he? He's far too canny.'

'True,' I said. 'No, in fact his parents made their pile out of art and antiques, and I think he always thought he'd follow in their footsteps.'

'As indeed he has, with spectacular success.'

I nodded.

'So what about these academic types that loved him so much?' Darrick went on. 'Were they male or female?'

'Male, actually,' I said, musing on the fact as I took another swig of my Chardonnay. 'I don't remember any of the female members of staff ever visiting his room.'

'It's what I would expect,' said Darrick.

'Meaning?'

'By the time women are old enough to be university lecturers they're probably fairly good at reading people.' He went on before I could respond. 'But he was obviously a hit with the old men of the department.' He speared another chip.

'How do you know they were old?'

'Well, weren't they?'

'Actually most of them were, fairly,' I admitted.

'And they probably wanted to feel young again; to be in with a happening crowd, show they were still game enough to smoke the odd joint, that kind of thing.'

'You make a lot of assumptions.' It rang true, in fact, but I didn't want to confirm what he'd said. Or give him the satisfaction of thinking he'd got them all down to a tee, for that matter. 'There was one slightly younger guy: an overachiever like Seb, who'd been made a professor in his early forties. He was actually an art collector.' In the back of my mind I tried to remember his name. Something double-barrelled, but it eluded me.

'An art collector?' Darrick's voice brought me back to the present. 'He must have been limited in what he could afford. Academics don't usually bring home a lot of cash.'

I thought back to what Seb had told me. 'I think he had family money. But anyway, I reckon meeting him inspired Seb. It showed him his end market and just how much it craved what he might be able to provide one day. People who mind about art mind big time, it seems, whether it's passion, or just because owning important works boosts their status.'

After the waitress had cleared our plates and we'd settled our bill Darrick leant forward, one elbow on the table. 'Don't believe anything that Radley woman says about me,' he said, his intense blue eyes locking onto mine. 'She's definitely the one who's muckraking.' And he moved in even closer, until I was aching for him to kiss me. 'Come on,' he said, standing up suddenly. 'Let's go outside.'

He put an arm round my waist as we left the building, thanking the staff as we went, and this time it was a firm move, without any sign that he was suddenly going to whisk it away again. I felt that same need I'd had when we'd walked along the Thames: that feeling of wanting more, a hollow ache inside me. He drew me closer to him.

'Do you always go out for walks after you've eaten?' I asked, hoping to keep my thoughts hidden.

We took a right down a deserted side street – possibly it was a dark alley – and he turned to look at me, the glow of a street light throwing shadows across his face, emphasising his high cheekbones.

'I was wondering if you might like to walk back to my place. I like physical activity in general,' – he gave me a look – 'but it's always particularly good if there's a proper purpose to it.' Reaching inside the flap of my coat, he put a hand on my waist and moved in so that he was standing up against me, with me leaning back against the wall we were passing. His body was warm, but the contact sent shivers running down me. 'I didn't take that photograph, Anna,' he said. And then he started to kiss me with an urgency that matched the feeling well below the pit of my stomach.

Chapter Twelve

I wanted to go with him, back to his place. I really, really wanted to. I think if he hadn't mentioned the photograph again I might even have gone for it, but that little discrepancy still nagged at the back of my mind, making me wonder.

It was just one extra thing that stacked up against him, along with how little I really knew about his life; how much he liked us to talk about me, rather than about him; and the way that he looked at me when I mentioned Seb.

In the end, I made the usual excuses, and pointed out, quite reasonably, that I hardly knew him and that he seemed to want to keep it that way, for all he'd told me about himself.

He just smiled and said he didn't want to lose his mystery, but he did promise to call, which left me feeling better than I would have done. I kicked myself all the way home, but deep down I had the feeling I'd done the right thing. My jumbled emotions didn't lend themselves to sleep though, and it was well past two o'clock before I managed to drop off.

The next day I peeled myself off my bed rather late, having to combat a strong feeling of inertia. When I arrived in the communal kitchen I found both Sally and Alicia in unusually peaceful silence. I soon saw why. It was the day my article was due out in Epic and they were holding a copy each, both so absorbed that they hadn't noticed me come in.

I'd been careful not to mention the piece when I'd

talked to Darrick the night before; I didn't feel it was his sort of publication.

It looked as though I'd got Alicia and Sally's attention though, and that was what it was all about. I was feeling reasonably pleased until I realised that Alicia had actually got her copy open at the horoscope page. She slapped the magazine shut when she realised I'd rumbled her.

'I read your article first,' she said, sniffing, 'and then I thought I might as well see what else they manage to fill their pages with.'

'And what do your stars predict for you this month?' I asked sweetly.

'Oh,' said Sally, 'is that what you were looking at? I must just check mine next. Great article by the way, Anna.'

'Shouldn't you be at work?' Alicia asked her.

'Later shift today. By two this afternoon I shall be rubbing the hard bits off the feet of the rich and famous, but for now, it's relaxation all the way.' She stretched luxuriously and turned to me. 'Intriguing about Zachariah Shakespeare's lack of underpants.'

'Honestly!' Alicia said, with a loud tut. She got up and left the room.

'It's no use her pretending not to be interested,' Sally said. 'She'd already read your article by the time I came in. She was guzzling up stuff on Pippa Middleton and Samantha Cameron before she started on the horoscopes.'

'The Samantha Cameron piece was quite serious,' a sharp voice said from the hall. 'She'd been visiting a shelter for the homeless.'

'Oops!' said Sally in a stage whisper. She flicked her own magazine to the horoscope page. 'What're you?'

'Virgo.'

'Hmm. Sounds like you're in for a difficult time,' she said, frowning. 'It says a conflict of interest is going to make things tricky at work.'

'Except I don't actually go to work.'

'You mustn't be cynical. You need to look at things more broadly.' She scanned the page again. 'It doesn't seem to mention anything that might relate to your date last night, which is weird because I'd say it was a pretty significant event.'

'Gosh yes,' I said. 'That really is inexplicable, isn't it?'

'Sarky! How was it anyway? Did you have a nice time?'

'I'm not sure nice is quite the way I'd put it,' I said, poking my head into the hall to check that Alicia wasn't still listening.

'Sounds like there's more to tell,' she said, so I closed the door and filled her in.

She sighed. 'I do like a man of mystery. I can't believe you didn't go home with him. You could have found out so much more that way.'

I think she was frustrated I couldn't give her any extra salacious details. 'I thought you said I should be careful.'

Sally waved away my comment with a perfectly manicured hand. 'Up to a point, Anna, up to a point.'

Epic was mailing me a copy of the latest issue for my records, so I didn't have to dash out and buy one. Unfortunately, this meant I had no excuse to mooch about and fritter away my time, but Sally seemed to have spotted I was in that kind of state when it's hard to settle to anything.

By the time she came and put her head round my door I'd already picked up a file of copywriting jobs that needed doing three times, on each occasion slinging it back down again with a sigh. Desk tidying had been next on my list of distractions.

'Fancy coming shopping?'

'I'm supposed to be writing about a computer chip manufacturer.'

'I should think that settles it then,' she said. 'Come along.'

So I went. I trailed about after her as she bought little bits of jewellery, a scarf and a new pair of shoes. Then we passed the shop she'd told me about, where the handmade bags were over two hundred pounds.

'You ought to get yours in there,' she said, nodding at the window, where the bags were displayed on silk-covered pedestals. 'They're definitely good enough.'

I shook my head. 'It's only a hobby, Sally.' I was about to say I wouldn't have time to turn it into more than that, but then it occurred to me that that wasn't really true.

'You like it though, don't you? Next time I come this way I'm going to bring the one you made for me and see if they'd be interested.'

I was about to tell her not to when my mobile rang and Sally continued to browse as I fished it out of my pocket.

Glancing at the screen triggered an adrenaline rush. Seb Rice.

Chapter Thirteen

I gave myself a moment to calm down before I answered. 'Seb! I haven't spoken to you in ages.'

'I know darling, and it's entirely my fault. I wanted to congratulate you on the piece in Epic.'

'It's horribly frivolous, as well you know,' I said, twisting on one heel as I stood there, feeling awkward.

'It's pushing the gallery further into the mainstream. That kind of thing's great for creating hype. Okay, so Epic readers probably won't come along and buy Zachariah's paintings, but they'll make a buzz that means every art collector looking for something poppy will be queuing up to get them. Even the teenagers in high school will be talking about his work now.'

'Well I'm pleased you're pleased,' I said.

'I am. Look, can we meet? I'd love to buy you lunch.'

After the ongoing lack of contact this was unexpected, but I needed to take it all in my stride, I knew. 'Sure, lunch would be good.'

'What are you up to now?'

'Oh,' I said, glancing at Sally, 'I'm not sure I can do today.'

Sally made shooing "go ahead" motions with her hands.

'Or maybe I can,' I said to Seb. I never could manage a three-way conversation of this sort with any style.

'I love a woman who knows her own mind.'

As Sally walked off towards Farquharson's I made my way to the restaurant Seb had suggested. It looked horribly exclusive from the outside, and there were no prices on the menu, but then Seb had said he'd like to buy *me* lunch. I reckoned if this was a reward for my hard work – a perk, effectively – then maybe it was okay to let him.

He wasn't there when I arrived, but a deferential waiter took my coat and knew all about the booking. He drew a seat out for me to sit down, and I got the timing all wrong, so that he knocked the back of my knees when he tucked the chair in again for me. I was thankful when he scuttled out of sight, no doubt to laugh at my lack of savoir faire in the kitchens.

Our table was by the window, so I could look out onto the street and see all the shoppers teeming past. The Christmas rush was already well underway, with November almost over.

Then, through the crowd of other people, I glimpsed Seb. It was odd. His photo appeared in the press every other week but it was actually a long time since I'd seen him in the flesh. His height meant I managed to pick him out quite quickly, and it gave me time to watch him as he walked the last few metres towards the restaurant. He was dressed in a dove-grey suit with a white shirt, open at the neck, and had a grey overcoat slung over one arm.

The feelings I'd had for him in the old days didn't come back when I saw him. They always had up until now, during those intermittent times when we'd been in more regular contact. It was a relief to find that on this occasion I felt a rush of fondness, but nothing more.

He was still handsome, there was no doubt about that, but I found myself comparing him with Darrick. Seb was lean and elegant but there was a coolness and reserve that went with his physical beauty. He lacked Darrick's humour, as well as his rough edges, his strength and some kind of inner fire. At that moment he caught me looking in his direction and smiled, waving a hand.

As he came through the door I stood up to say hello and he bent to give me a hug. He smelled of cologne that I guessed was too expensive for me to recognise. The hug was the acid test. All was well so far.

'It's so good to see you,' he said, pulling back for a moment to give me the once over. 'You look well.' He tweaked a lock of my hair. 'I'm glad you decided to grow it long again; makes you look like a Botticelli. It's such a glorious colour. So.' He moved to sit down. 'How are you enjoying being back in London then?'

'It's great. I mean it was lovely sharing with Terry, but I'd begun to feel like a bit of a gooseberry after Steve moved in. It wasn't fair on them. And you know what it's like: you either love London or you loathe it, but if you love it you're never really quite happy when you're living anywhere else.'

'Well it's great from our point of view, at the gallery,' he said. 'The work you did for The Enquirer was excellent.'

The waiter hovered nearby and handed Seb a menu.

'I have a friend who works there,' Seb went on, without looking up, 'and he said how much they'd enjoyed dealing with you. I think they found you unusually reliable.'

'I'm glad about that!'

We chose our food. It was several grades on in ostentatiousness from the menu at The Midnight Hour and I wasn't quite sure what I'd ordered. I hoped it would be all right.

'And a bottle of the Chateauneuf-du-Pape please,' Seb said.

'The '95 sir, or the 2002?' the waiter asked.

'The '95,' Seb said, without pausing.

It was a far cry from house red. I'd only just left behind calculating which wine to buy based on cost per unit of alcohol.

'So what have you been up to, other than the work you've been doing for us?' he asked.

'Other profiles, some copywriting, you know, the usual mix.'

'And in your free time? Been enjoying the London nightlife?'

I wondered if he was probing, having spoken to Radley. 'Not on a very regular basis,' I said, 'but I did see Jez's new film last night.'

He sat back in his seat and I thought how fit he still looked, in spite of all the cocktail parties and vol-au-vents. 'I must make time to go and see that. It's great that he's doing so well.'

In the old days he would have found missing something of Jez's unthinkable. 'I heard he tried to catch up with you when he was last in London,' I couldn't help saying. 'I think you were busy though.'

He sighed. 'I haven't been all that good to the old gang, have I? Not really a loyal member.'

I felt guilty. 'It was very kind of you to put the Shakespeare work my way,' I said. 'I know you think about us all.'

'Providing work contacts isn't quite the same thing as being a good friend though, is it?'

I looked down at the table. It was only at that point I realised how much he had hurt my feelings by keeping away for so long. The past was the past, but we had been through some fairly intense times together: shared experiences that we could have tackled jointly. But I was being unfair. He was the one who'd had to deal with the trauma.

'I know you find it hard to be with us,' I said.

He put a hand out to touch mine. 'In the immediate aftermath it was mainly you that got me through it. I didn't treat you fairly then, Anna.'

'Under the circumstances …'

'The circumstances don't excuse the way I behaved.' He leant forward and the waiter, who had been about to hand over our wine, stepped back. 'I wanted to say I'm sorry.'

'You don't have to apologise for anything.'

'Yes I do. I acted like an idiot all those years ago and there's a whole list of things I regret doing ever since. It all came to a head when I had a talk with Radley a couple of days ago. She was filling me in on your last meeting. I would have asked about it sooner, only things have been frantic. She was pissed off because you'd been out to lunch with that man who said he was Max Conran.'

I looked up. 'I know,' I said. 'She left me in no doubt whatsoever about how cross she was.' I couldn't keep the edge out of my voice.

He gave me a rueful look. 'What cut me to the quick was that she said she'd had a go at you for disloyalty. She'd wanted to know why you hadn't thought to give me a call, once you found out more about our mystery guest.'

'That's right,' I said, remembering.

'And you told her, quite rightly, that we were barely in touch with each other any more. Why should you think of calling me?'

'I should have thought of it really,' I said, though I wasn't entirely sure I meant it.

'I can quite see why you didn't. It made me realise I need to put the past behind me. I don't want to lose you too, Anna.'

There was a momentary pause. 'Do you think we should let the waiter give us our wine?' I whispered. The tension broke: he laughed suddenly and sat back in his chair.

Things got a bit more relaxed when our food turned up. I still couldn't tell what mine was, but it tasted pretty good.

'So how has life been with you?' I asked.

'Good,' he said. 'Everything's been going brilliantly at the gallery. But the man you attracted at the private view is a bit of a worry. Radley tells me he's a journalist who'd done something to offend one of my friends. Is that right?'

'So I gather.'

'Did he ever explain what he was up to when he took your photo that evening? I know Radley was sounding off, but I think she was genuinely concerned for you.'

'He denies ever having taken his mobile out of his pocket,' I said.

Seb frowned. 'That's worrying. You know, I still don't like the sound of him. And what was his real name again?' He paused. 'Radley said something like Derek?'

'Darrick,' I said. 'Darrick Farron.'

'And that's another reason I needed to see you.'

'What do you mean?'

'He said he'd come in under a false name so I wouldn't throw him out?'

'That's what it amounted to.'

'Thing is, when I think through all the dust-ups I've had in the past, I can't imagine what incident he's referring to.' He held up a hand to stop what I was going to say. 'And what's more to the point, I've quite definitely never had a run-in with anyone called Darrick Farron.'

Chapter Fourteen

A frown traced its way across Seb's face. 'Darrick's not a name I'd forget. He explicitly said he was a journalist?'

'Yes,' I said. I felt as though he was treating me like a child, but then I pulled up short and thought again.

What had he actually said? I was pretty sure he'd mentioned reporting on things and ongoing investigations, and said he was an art specialist. Had I just assumed the rest? I'd certainly thought that had been what he'd meant. And Darrick must have known that.

When I looked up I realised Seb was registering my uncertainty.

'So you have seen him again?' he asked. 'I presumed you must have, if you'd asked about the photograph.'

I felt it was none of his business, which made me pause for long enough to confirm his suspicions.

'I'm not having a go at you,' he said, running his finger round the rim of his wine glass. He looked up at me. 'I know you're a grown-up, and Radley's already had her two pence worth, which was wrong of her. But in spite of the way I've been recently, I do care about you; I just want you to look out for yourself, that's all. There still seems to be a chunk of Darrick Farron's story that doesn't fit.'

The waiter brought the pudding I'd ordered and I sat there, pie-eyed with Chateauneuf-du-Pape, coming to the grim realisation that I was actually too full to eat the meticulously presented helping of champagne cheesecake with its raspberry and elderflower garnish. Wine at lunchtime was also awful, I concluded. It made me feel all sleepy and stupid and was the one seemingly constant theme of London life that I could do without.

Talking about Darrick had given me indigestion anyway. It seemed I was always getting upset or disturbed by him, either in an animalistic way by the sheer nearness of his physical presence, or else at a distance, as I found out yet another discomforting thing about him.

The silence between us was broken by the sound of a text coming in on Seb's phone. He reached into his jacket pocket, drew his mobile out slowly and smiled as he read the message.

'Radley,' he said. 'She knows me too well.'

'Is she wondering where you are when there's work to be done?'

'Not quite.' He put the mobile away and smiled at me, looking, I thought, slightly guilty. 'I don't want you to think I didn't mean it when I said I wanted us to be friends again,' he said. 'I mean proper, outside work, friends.'

'I sense a "but" coming …'

'But, well, I did have a business proposition to put to you as well.'

I raised my eyes to heaven. 'I might have known it would take something like that to draw you out here.'

'Not true and unfair.'

'But to come to the point …'

'To come to the point, I was so pleased with the work you did on Zachariah that I wondered if we could persuade you to do a bit more for us.'

'Radley mentioned something …'

'Oh, she was just talking about the odd freelance bits and pieces,' he said. 'I was thinking of something rather more permanent.'

I looked at him, wondering what was coming next, and if it really would be much less complicated if I never had to hear it.

'I've been on the lookout for a director of communications for a while now.'

'But surely you've already got someone dealing with all your marketing and PR.'

He nodded. 'Sure, all the usual types of things: placing ads, organising the events and all of that but, up until now, Radley's been doing the lion's share of the more strategic stuff. She's overworked and also, don't tell her I said so, but it's not really her field.'

He grinned. I didn't.

'And how would she feel about having someone else brought in to take over those jobs?' My legs felt slightly wobbly at the mere thought of her reaction.

'I've decided to promote her to director of exhibitions, so that ought to shut her up.'

'Seb!' Now I couldn't help laughing. 'You are awful.'

'But would you consider working for me, that's the point, awful though I am?'

I could feel myself being silent for a long time.

'You don't really want that pudding, do you?' he said, and I shook my head, wincing at the thought of how much it probably cost. Not that Seb seemed bothered.

'Maybe I could just have a coffee to knit myself together again.'

He signalled to the waiter. 'Could my friend just have an espresso instead?' he asked, and the waiter quietly took my plate away.

Seb looked at me and raised an eyebrow. 'You don't seem very keen on my offer.'

'It's just a bit of a shock, that's all.'

'I was hoping to achieve "nice surprise" rather than "shock".' He divided the last of the wine between us and sat back in his chair.

I managed to summon up a smile. 'It's a lovely surprise of course. It's just that I've been trying to make a go of it as a freelancer and, to be honest, I'm still not sure it's going to work, but if I bottle out now and become employed again, I suppose I'll never know.'

He was quiet for a moment. 'Well, I don't want to dash your dreams,' he said, without any hint of rancour. 'Look, I tell you what. How about I offer you the directorship with two safeguards thrown in?'

'What have you got in mind?'

'Well, first, it can be a short-term contract. You could try it out for, four months say, and then we can each agree to renew if we think it's working.'

That already sounded quite a lot less threatening, even though I knew it was only psychological. 'And what was your other suggestion?'

'That if you get wind of a good interview opportunity, you can take unpaid leave to follow it up and work on it as a freelance. So long as it doesn't interfere unduly with gallery business then I'm sure we can be fairly flexible.'

'You're being very indulgent, Seb.'

He held my hand again, and just for a second, it felt like it had years ago, and without the emotional pressure that there had been then too. 'The question is, is it working?'

I was worried that it might be. 'Can I think about it?' I said. 'Just for a day or two?'

He gave my hand a momentary squeeze. 'Of course you can,' he said. 'Just give me a call. If you go for it though, I'd love it if you could start straight away. We've got a whole load of stuff coming up, so time's rather of the essence.'

Neither Alicia nor Sally were there when I got home. Sally would still be on foot duty of course, and Alicia had gone off to some very posh afternoon tea function where she'd been specifically asked to provide cucumber sandwiches and a Victoria sponge. ('It's hardly a challenge,' she had said, with a heavy sigh, 'but at least I can show them how it's meant to be done.')

I knew Alicia was supposed to be going out for dinner afterwards with an old friend, and Sally was in the habit of indulging in after work drinks with her mates. The result was, I had the strong urge to tell someone about what had happened, but there was no one to tell it to.

The job offer and the fresh news on Darrick fought for space in my head. Eventually, I tried Terry. It was too unfair really; he was always the one I turned to at tricky moments, even though I was supposed to be letting him get on with his own life.

Luckily for him, his phone was switched to voicemail. I thought for a moment but decided against leaving a message. Knowing him he'd call back as soon as he could, even if it was a bad moment, and that wasn't what I wanted. Seb had said I could have a day or two's grace, and the weekend was coming up. I'd sit it out, mull it over and come to a decision.

So with that shelved, the matter of Darrick came to the fore. It was time to find out just what was really going on. Of course, I could call him; I did have his number. However, I certainly didn't want to talk to him about the job offer at the gallery. Whenever he talked about Seb his tone of dislike was unmistakable, however hard I fought to ignore it.

And in any case, if I did call him he'd probably just lie to me again. Instead, I got out my laptop. It was time to find out for myself.

Darrick certainly wasn't a journalist. That much was quite clear from my search.

A friend of mine once said that if you didn't show up on Google you were no one. And by that definition, that's exactly who Darrick was. I didn't get a single hit.

Chapter Fifteen

Things went to the opposite extreme the following morning. Instead of having no one to go to for advice, I was suddenly presented with two people who were as keen as anything to put forward their opinions. Sally seemed to spot I'd got something on my mind the moment I went into the kitchen.

'You look a bit rough,' she said, putting down her coffee mug. 'No offence. Bad night?'

I nodded. I'd spent the whole time tossing and turning in my bed, trying to relax enough to drop off.

'Things on your mind?'

I nodded again.

'You're not very chatty this morning. You might feel better if you told me all about it.'

'Possibly.'

'I'd feel better anyway. I'm curious now. Besides,' she looked at her watch, 'it's that party tonight. I swapped my shift today so that I'd have time to get ready, but I don't actually need all day. I can give you several hours of my undivided attention.' She smiled.

'Mmm,' I said. 'Very kind.'

And it was at that moment that Alicia put her head round the door. She must have been lying in wait. 'Trouble?'

Yes, I thought, it's just arrived. 'Not exactly. I'm in an unexpected situation and I'm not sure how to resolve it, that's all.' Why had I said that? Alicia would never leave me alone now. She considered unresolved situations very unsatisfactory. She would see it as her duty to get me sorted out and wouldn't let up until I'd told her everything.

I scraped back my chair and stood up. 'D'you know, I think some fresh air might be good? Clear my head. Maybe I'll just walk up to the Heath or something.'

'But what about breakfast?' said Alicia, seizing on practicalities. 'You won't be able to think clearly on an empty stomach.' To be fair, food was her specialist subject.

'Oh don't worry about that. I'll just stop by at Café Rouge or somewhere and grab a coffee.'

Alicia looked at me severely.

'And a croissant,' I added.

'Oh, good idea,' said Sally. 'I haven't been to Café Rouge for ages and it will set me up for the day. I'm right with you about a decent breakfast, Alicia.'

'Oh well if you're both going,' Alicia said, 'then I'll join you.'

Although I had wanted to tell someone all about it, this wasn't what I'd had in mind. Sally was one thing, but Sally plus Alicia was quite another. The fine drizzle in the air didn't enhance my mood; it was a bit like walking through a cloud. I stomped crossly along Flask Walk, a few paces ahead of my so-called house "mates". Alicia strode after me and Sally trotted along behind. Fat chance of having a quiet think now.

'Breakfast first then?' Sally said.

'Why don't you two go for breakfast,' I said ungraciously, 'and I'll have mine later. I need to have a think.'

Sally giggled and herded me under the awnings of Café Rouge. 'Remember the empty stomach thing. Anyway, I can guarantee you'll feel better once you've got it all off your chest.'

Inside it was warm, and of course dry, which did make me feel – grudgingly – that coming straight in instead of going onto the Heath had its advantages. And the smell of warm bread was making my stomach rumble. The cafe was quite crowded, but we managed to find a table in a corner and I sat there, feeling I was probably steaming slightly.

'I'm tempted by this basket thing where you get a bit of almost everything,' Sally said.

Alicia gave her a repressive look. I knew she regarded choosing food based purely on quantity as very low indeed.

'That does sound good,' I said, snapping out of my crossness for a moment when presented with the chance of annoying her. 'Slight shame about the lack of marmalade, obviously, but maybe having a cappuccino alongside would make up for that.' I saw Alicia's frown deepen. She ordered a warm French baguette with a small pot of posh jam and a black filter coffee.

'So what's going on?' Sally said, whilst we waited for our order.

I looked at them. I wasn't going to say anything about Darrick, but I knew I'd have to give them something. They wouldn't leave me alone all day otherwise. 'I've been offered a job,' I said.

They both looked at me and then at each other.

'That's normally a good thing, isn't it?' Sally said.

'Not when you're building up a very promising career as a freelance journalist it isn't,' said Alicia, keen to show that she had seen the point. I was a bit surprised by her reaction though. I'd never got the impression she thought my career was remotely promising.

'Oh ...' said Sally. 'I see. I hadn't thought of that.' She

paused for a moment. 'Though I suppose you could still carry on writing in your spare time, couldn't you?'

'Yes,' I said. 'I'd been wondering if that was the way forward.'

Alicia shook her head. 'If you want to make a success of the freelancing, you have to show some commitment, Anna. You can't just give the matter your fleeting attention when some opportunity comes your way.' She leant back to let the waiter put down her coffee. 'Thank you.' She turned back to me. 'Although I have to say that's exactly the approach you seem to have taken so far.'

I knew she was right really. I should have been pushing more, networking, knocking on people's doors. 'I don't find it that easy, thrusting myself forward and bullying people into taking my pieces or letting me interview them,' I said, feeling small.

'Well of course not,' said Alicia. 'It's not easy, that's why. So what are you going to do about it? Just give in?'

As a matter of fact, I realised that was part of the appeal of Seb's job offer. I could just give in. I'd be able to write brochures, and interview his artists and so on, without having to go out and sell myself at all. Alicia wouldn't like that though.

'Actually,' I said, thinking of how to put the best spin on his offer, 'it's possible that if I took this job, I'd increase my contacts.'

'Well that sounds brilliant,' said Sally.

I smiled gratefully at her, without knowing quite what I was up to. I wasn't actually convinced taking the job was the best move. And I would be throwing away my pursuit of journalism at the sharp end. I might get cushy security, but I probably wouldn't end up feeling as proud of myself as I would if I decided to go it alone.

Alicia clearly needed more convincing too. 'Where is this job, anyway?' she said, as the waiter set down our food.

'Um, at Seb's gallery,' I said.

'What!' The word was like a pistol shot.

Sally looked up expectantly. 'Is that bad?'

Alicia folded her arms and gave me a meaningful look.

'Alicia doesn't really approve of Seb,' I said.

'But don't you do all his catering?' Sally asked, taking a bit of pain au chocolat from her basket.

'That's business,' said Alicia. 'I'm sure you don't like all the people whose feet you de-scale, do you?'

Sally laughed.

'Alicia got the gallery work through Seb's ex-wife, Mel,' I said. 'And since they've remained friends she came in for all the gory details about his shortcomings when they broke up.'

'What she told me wasn't just to do with their married life,' Alicia said. 'They were business partners for years too, don't forget. And he had a ruthless reputation even before that. There was all that hoo-ha at university with his tutor.'

I cut in. 'That was absolute rubbish.'

'Sure?' She put down the bit of baguette she'd been about to eat. 'Anyway, that's beside the point. Let me warn you now, Anna, that it's the gallery and business all the way with him. He may be an old friend, but his work interests will always come first.'

'Well it would be work I'm joining him for, not anything else,' I said as soon as her mouth was full again, 'so that should be a good thing. Besides, I thought you'd approve of his single-minded approach.'

I paused to take another sip of my cappuccino. 'And

although I'm sure you're right about his dedication, Alicia, I have managed to negotiate a couple of concessions out of him that will apply if I do take the job.' Okay, so I hadn't really had to negotiate, but it sounded better that way. 'If a good freelance opportunity comes up I can take unpaid leave to pursue it.' I didn't mention the little caveat about this being okay, so long as it didn't interfere too much with gallery work.

'Hmm,' Alicia said, her eyes boring into mine. 'It'll be interesting to see that work in practice. And not that many great freelance opportunities will come up, if you're not even going to be out looking for them. So what was the second concession then?'

'That I can start on a temporary contract and see how I go. If it doesn't suit me I can drop the whole thing after four months.'

'Oh great,' said Alicia, breaking another bit of baguette off violently, so that crumbs sprayed over the table. 'And meaning that if he doesn't need you at that point he can also let you go without any compensation.'

'To be fair,' said Sally, 'it would be usual to have a no-strings probationary period anyway, so Anna wouldn't be worse off at the gallery than anywhere else.'

'It's very odd that he suddenly wants you there, I must say,' Alicia went on relentlessly.

'Something cropped up recently that made him realise he didn't want to cut off all his old friends,' I said.

'Well it's certainly about time he came to his senses on that score, but it doesn't mean he has to employ you all.' She sipped her coffee. 'Why now, I wonder? You can bet it won't be for sentimental reasons.'

'Why was he going to cut off all his old friends in the first place?' Sally asked.

'Not now, Sally!' Alicia said sharply.

Sally stuck her tongue out at her as she turned back to me again.

'Long story,' I said. 'I'll tell you later.'

'Good.'

Turning back to Alicia, I said, 'Okay, so he doesn't want me to go and work with him for sentimental reasons – well that's good, isn't it? Sentimental reasons would be a dreadful basis on which to appoint me. The alternative is that he really does need someone, and because I've been doing the Shakespeare stuff I sprang to mind. I'm available and convenient and I've got roughly the experience he needs. That's not so awful is it?' I could see she wasn't going to give any ground. 'And there would be lots of advantages,' I went on. 'I'd have a regular income, something good to go on my CV, lots of contacts in the arts world ...'

Alicia cut across me. 'I'm surprised he wouldn't want someone with a degree in art or art history, under the circumstances.'

It occurred to me at that point that I might be able to afford to move out of her house if I took the job.

She looked at me and shook her head as though I was the most witless person in a classroom full of dense people. 'Never mix business and friendship, Anna,' she said. 'I would have thought what Mel went through would have convinced you of that.'

Chapter Sixteen

By the time we left Café Rouge the fine rain had turned heavy so I decided to give the walk on the Heath a miss. It wouldn't have helped by that stage anyway. I was so cross with Alicia that I almost wanted to ring Seb and accept the job straight away, just to spite her.

I thought Sally might follow me back to my room, to sympathise, but in fact she headed down to the basement. Alicia said she needed to get on with some accounts, so I went upstairs on my own, ready to gnash my teeth in solitude, but it was only twenty minutes before there was a knock at my door.

'Thought I'd better wait until she'd got ensconced with her paperwork,' Sally said, coming in. 'If I'd come up straight away she'd probably have followed me.'

I laughed. 'Thanks for trying to pick holes in her arguments.'

'Hey, that's no problem. It's instinctive really, isn't it?' She walked in and sank down into an easy chair. 'I'm mystified though.'

'Why?'

'Well, you seem pretty keen on the idea of the job, so why all the agonising? And why did you let Alicia stick her beak in?'

'Did I let her? I thought she just sort of foisted her opinions on me.'

Sally smiled. 'Seriously though, why not just go for it if it fits the bill? You're not really bothered about what Alicia thinks, are you?'

I sighed. 'Not unless she's right.'

'Oh, I see. So you think there's something in what she's been saying?'

'I have got some of the same worries.'

'Did this Seb guy really treat his wife badly?'

I shrugged. 'I don't know, to be honest. She certainly does seem quite bitter from what Alicia says, but as far as I know he's made all the right provisions financially. In fact, I got the impression he'd done more than he needed to. And I actually thought the split had been her decision too.'

'Hmm. Sounds odd,' said Sally. 'And what was all that about the upset with his tutor?'

His tutor had been that same professor I'd mentioned to Darrick. Perhaps he might have regretted hanging out with the students by the time the rumours hit …

I focused back on Sally's questioning face. 'Oh just old tittle-tattle.' I'd begun to wish I'd never told Alicia about it. 'When Seb got a first at university, the whisper went round that he'd blackmailed him.'

'Really?' said Sally, sitting forward in her chair. 'Wow, you do provide good gossip, you know.'

'Delighted to oblige,' I said wryly. 'The story was that he'd sold the tutor drugs, and that he was therefore able to exert some pressure to improve his chances of getting top marks, but it was rubbish really.'

'You think?'

'Definitely. It's true Seb missed a lot of lectures, and he was always late with handing in his essays, but he didn't need blackmail to get him through. He was just one of those people who was clever enough to get by without working hard.'

'Sounds like quite a bloke. So who started the rumours then?'

I shrugged. 'He did put some people's backs up. I think he made them jealous, to be honest. He was in with everyone, had lots of girlfriends, mainlined on wild parties and drugs … And you know how annoying it is when someone does well without even trying.'

Sally nodded.

'But, speaking of annoying people, Alicia's still quite right. I won't really be able to pursue my freelance career if I've got some high-powered job at Seb's place.'

'Would it be high-powered then?'

'Well, it's got a posh title.'

She raised an eyebrow.

'Communications director,' I supplied.

'Wow! That sounds good.'

'Sounds a bit scary.'

'So it's scary and it affects your freelance plans,' said Sally, itemising my reservations on her fingers. 'Any other downsides?'

'It's true that working with friends can put pressure on your relationship.'

She counted off a third finger. 'There's something else, isn't there?'

There was. For me it was sitting there larger than all of the other items put together: Darrick wouldn't like it. Whether it really was down to jealousy, or whether there was another reason, I was quite sure he would hate the idea. After my Google search, I knew I shouldn't care. Talk about not owing him anything. But it wasn't about owing him. It was the way he made me feel. I pushed the thought aside. It was crazy.

'No,' I said. 'That's probably about it really.'

'So what's he like, Seb Rice?'

I walked over to my bookshelf and took down an old

photo album. 'He's very driven,' I said. 'Passionate about his work, and well,' I paused, 'passionate about everything else too.' Sally gave me a look and I rolled my eyes. 'In a focused way; *not* in the way you're thinking.' I turned to the album, flicking through the pages of photos from my sixth form to get onto the university ones. 'Here he is.'

'Dishy,' she said, looking up at me. 'Did you fancy him when you first got to uni? I bet you did!'

'If I did, I wasn't alone. He was sought after.'

'I can imagine. So what about all that you and Alicia were saying about him cutting off his old friends?'

I turned more pages of the album, until I found one of Seb and Julia.

'Wow,' Sally said. 'Who's she? She's gorgeous.'

'The first girl Seb was really serious about, in the time I knew him,' I said, and explained what had happened to her.

Sally put her hands up to her mouth. 'God how awful. The poor, poor man. He must have felt so guilty as well. I mean, if he'd been planning to go up and see her the weekend it happened, and then he'd called it off because of work.'

'I think after that he decided never to get that close to anyone again. I suspect the Mel thing was a distraction, but that his feelings for her were never as intense. Maybe that's what made her leave him in the end. She knew he'd never love her as much as he'd loved Julia. I get the impression he keeps all relationships at surface level now. There's always a reserve in his manner, at least on the rare occasions I see him.' In spite of his moves to make things up to me, that was how his approach at the restaurant had seemed too, I realised. There was something clinical about it, the scene carefully acted out, all planned, with no loss of control.

'But you and Alicia were talking about his university friends especially?'

I nodded.

'That seems a bit weird.'

'Alicia thinks so,' I said. 'It's one of the reasons she doesn't like him. She's very hard-nosed about personal tragedy. She doesn't believe he avoids us because of what happened when we were all together. She reckons we started to bore him.'

'On the one hand that sounds a bit harsh but ...'

'But you think his reaction's extreme, if it is just due to the fact that we bring back memories?'

'After so many years, it does seem a bit surprising. Not that I'm grudging him any feelings he wants to have, given what happened.'

I got up. 'Is it too soon for more coffee?'

She shook her head and I went to fill the kettle from my basin, edging it sideways to jam it under the mixer tap. Whilst I waited for it to boil I wondered how to answer Sally. She had a reasonable enough point.

'I think it was to do with what happened just after Julia died,' I said, bringing over a mug of coffee for each of us. 'You see, Seb had no role to play. Julia had no immediate family; almost no family at all in fact. She'd really been existing up there in Cumbria in total isolation, apart from when he was with her. So when she killed herself, there was no one for Seb to go and talk to up there, no one he could support, or be supported by.

'The old guy who was the executor of her parents' will reappeared, and sorted out paperwork and dealt with the police. And of course Seb had to give evidence and everything too. Julia had some aunt up in Scotland, and I think she might have made contact with Seb to commiserate, but other than that he was suddenly totally cut off.'

'So what did he do with himself?'

'He went between us, the university gang, one after another. He got totally manic: couldn't stay in one place for more than a day or two at a time.' I could feel tears welling up in my eyes. 'It was awful. He was searching for solace, but there was none to find.'

Sally came and put an arm round my shoulder.

'So now, we're all a big part of those very worst memories,' I finished.

I couldn't tell her the whole truth – I'd never told anyone – but memories came flooding back to me now, with horrible clarity. Seb arriving, doped up on whatever he'd taken and crying, holding me tight and looking for that way out that he had so wanted. And I had tried to give it to him. It didn't seem wrong at the time. Our affair – if you could even call it that – had only lasted for a few days. He had remained largely drunk and incoherent, as though he'd shut down and wasn't allowing the real world in any more.

And then suddenly he seemed to come to again, and I could see the torment in his eyes when he looked at me. I was disgusted with myself.

Was Seb really going to put that behind him at last? And if so, my mind followed Alicia's train of thought, why now? One thing was certain, if I was going to go and work with him, it wasn't just him who would have to deal with old memories. I really didn't know if I could do it.

Chapter Seventeen

I stayed up late that night. Darrick sent me a text in the early evening, saying he'd been called away, but that he wanted to see me. He said he'd ring on Sunday. His sudden appearance in note form on my phone shattered any shreds of composure that might have been quietly gathering themselves together. How could I make him tell me the truth when he called? A nagging feeling in the pit of my stomach told me I shouldn't even give him the chance to try. If I couldn't Google him successfully, maybe I still didn't have his correct name, let alone accuracy on lesser matters, like his job.

Then at eight, Seb emailed. 'Not hassling you,' the message read, 'but I realised I hadn't even mentioned salary. Does £60K sound OK? Hope to speak to you soon, S xxx'

Sixty bloody thousand. He had to be joking. I wasn't the sort of person who got paid that kind of money.

Thoughts overlaid one another in confusing patterns. With that sort of salary I could definitely move out and I wouldn't have to worry about chasing work. What's more, the job ought to be interesting and it would be fun to belong somewhere.

But then the negative thoughts flooded back in. On top of the objections I'd itemised to Sally, I had a nasty feeling the rest of the gallery staff would feel nepotism was at the root of my appointment.

On Sunday morning I called reinforcements.

'You're not at the restaurant or anything?' I said.

'Naaah,' said Terry. 'Other people do the opening up these days, you know that.'

'Oh good.'

'Actually I was just having breakfast in bed.'

'Oh God! I'm sorry.'

'You are so easy to wind up, Anna Morris,' he said, laughing. 'Just tell me what's on your mind.'

And so I did. Of course, he gave his advice without knowing the full extent of what had happened between me and Seb, but it still seemed to make sense.

'I need hardly say that you must ignore Alicia,' he said. 'But when all's said and done, if you do take the job, you can always do what Seb said, and jack it in again after four months if you hate it.'

'That's true,' I said.

'The main thing is to keep up with your journalism in the meantime,' he went on. 'Just for those four months, really reach out for anything that's going, even if you have to work all night. Keep up the pressure on that score. That way, if you do decide the gallery's not for you, you can take up where you left off. And at least you'll have twenty grand under your belt. That'll buy you the time to look for more writing work.'

Suddenly, it seemed like a no-brainer.

Seb sounded genuinely pleased and a little relieved when I rang him.

'We've just got so much on,' he said. 'Is there any chance you could come in tomorrow?'

'I suppose …'

'Great. Look, one of the first things is to get you bedded in properly.' He paused for a moment. 'We're a fairly tight-knit bunch so it's best if I introduce you to the main people you'll be working with straight away. Then they can see how likeable you are.' I felt my nerves jangle again. 'I'll arrange a group lunch. But, if you come in at eleven, I can show you round first. Does that sound okay?'

It sounded awful.

'Great. I'll look forward to it.' I'd already slipped back into employee mode, and lied with ease.

'By the way,' he went on, 'I Googled your friend Darrick.'

'Ah yes,' I said. 'So did I, as a matter of fact.'

'Oh, well then, you know as much as me, which is pretty well nothing. I'm going to have a dig around though, Anna. I'll let you know what I find.'

It was five hours later when Darrick finally rang.

'I'm sorry it's so late,' he said. 'I only just got back.' He sounded tired and immediately his tone conjured up the image of him the night we'd first met: that sleep-deprived, faintly rough look that suited him so well. 'I thought I could ring and tell you a bedtime story.'

'Will it be about a mystery man who keeps appearing and disappearing again?'

There was a pause. 'Is that the type of story you like?'

'I'm not sure,' I said. 'I think I could cope with one that had slightly fewer twists and turns.'

'I've got a nasty feeling I can't do that sort,' he said and I realised he meant me to take him seriously. 'What have you been up to all weekend, anyway?'

In the ordinary way it should have been me asking him the questions. Like what he really did for a living, and why he didn't show up on the internet. But the job for Seb and his likely reaction filled my mind again now. I wanted to tell him, and get it over with. Nothing seemed like the right way, so I plunged in, feeling I could provide twists and turns too. 'Oh just the usual,' I said. 'Several rows with Alicia, and a £60K job offer.'

'Fairly eventful then,' he said quietly. 'And the job offer?'

'Seb. He contacted me out of the blue. I know you thought he might put more work my way, but I wasn't expecting it to be in-house. He wants a communications director.'

'Swanky.'

'Not really me.' Here was my chance to play it down. 'I get to try it for four months before I sign up to a permanent contract, so that makes me feel less claustrophobic. And the salary means I'll be able to build up a bit of a buffer to support me whilst I look for more freelance work.'

'If you decide not to stay on.' His lightness of tone didn't disguise what he thought.

'Yes, if.'

'I thought you wanted your independence.'

'I have to be practical.' I cursed myself as soon as I'd said it. Darrick wouldn't respect me for taking the easy option.

'You don't feel odd about going to work for someone who's effectively been cold shouldering you for years?'

'Not if he pays me enough, no,' I said, hoping to get a laugh out of him, but it fell flat.

'I was going to ask you to have lunch with me tomorrow.'

Suddenly I was angry. 'What, and now you're not as a punishment? Just because I've taken a highly paid and responsible job that's going to get me lots of new contacts?'

He sighed, but didn't raise his voice. 'I just wonder why

you've agreed to it. It doesn't seem to fit with what you wanted at all. I thought you were braver than that.'

'I feel quite brave taking the job actually.' He didn't know how brave.

'The offer of lunch is still open, if you want to come.'

I was fuming. Probably it was because I knew he was right about the job, coupled with the fact that he'd been anything but honest with me. What gave him the right to wade in with opinions on how I should run my life?

'I can't make it,' I said. 'I've got a working lunch.'

'Right.'

But a moment later I realised my approach wouldn't get me the answers I wanted. 'How about meeting up in the evening instead?' I said. 'That will give you the chance to explain why your name doesn't show up in a Google search.'

'I can't,' he said. 'I've got to go away again. If you don't trust me you'll just have to put up with it.'

And he hung up.

Chapter Eighteen

I hadn't seen Sally since the party, and was wondering if she'd fulfilled her plan to ensnare one of the rich young men she'd thought she'd find there. When she came in to breakfast on Monday I was convinced she'd been successful. There was a spring in her step and the corners of her smile almost reached her ears.

'What was he called?'

'Hey! What do you mean? Is it that obvious?'

'Yup.'

'Oh all right then. Jeremy Drinkwater. He didn't though. He drank lots of champagne, and so did I. We spent all day yesterday in bed, except for one brief romantic walk in Regent's Park.'

'You must be very hungry then,' I said. I was feeling a bit sour.

'He ordered food in.' She looked me up and down. 'So you decided to take the job then.'

I was wearing director-of-communications clothes; even I had to admit it. 'Yes, but I'm still not sure I'm doing the right thing, and I'm dreading today.'

'Never mind. Eat your rolls and you'll feel better.'

I'd given myself three, for extra strength, with a dessertspoonful of marmalade in each.

'You do know you could give Paddington Bear a run for his money, don't you?' Sally said. 'I can't quite work out how you can consume food at the rate you do and remain so tiny.'

'Nervous energy,' I said. 'And I'm bursting with it today, hence the extended rations.'

'Well, you can always leave the job if you hate it, remember. Anyway.' She reached into her pocket. 'I hope you'll still have some free time left over.' She handed me a scrap of paper which had a couple of names and phone numbers written on it, as well as a red wine stain on one corner.

'What's this?'

'A couple of people who'd like to commission your bags,' she said airily, pouring herself more coffee. 'I told them the cost was two fifty. I thought that would be better really.'

When I'd finished spluttering over my orange juice and checking that Sally wasn't just winding me up, I went back upstairs to get my work bag ready. I really was going to have to put in a lot of hours, just as Terry had said, and hope that one of the horses I was backing turned out to be a winner.

But my workload worries were swiftly replaced by musings about Darrick. He had absolutely no right to make me feel guilty about the way I earned my living; I didn't even have the luxury of passing judgement on his job, given that I still didn't quite know what it was. I picked up my things and headed towards the door.

But though I stamped down the stairs, feeling angry, I still wanted to talk to him again, and what's more, I hated the idea that he might be thinking otherwise.

I started the tour of my new workplace on the fourth floor of the gallery, where most of the staff were based. The offices all had glass panel walls and venetian blinds, just like Seb's did. I could see Radley's shadow behind hers, and even that hint of her presence made me slightly uneasy. I had an office to share with someone called Sinem, who had been helping Radley with press releases and the like, and an intern called Elsie. Neither of them were in evidence, but Seb said they'd both be at the lunch. I couldn't help noticing that he rolled his eyes when he mentioned Elsie's name. I decided not to ask.

Down on the third floor, a handful of visitors were wandering around the Shakespeare exhibition.

'How's it going?' I asked Seb.

'Really well. They've been selling like hotcakes.'

'What kind of people buy them?' I tried to keep the incredulity out of my voice.

'A really wide range actually,' Seb said, walking slowly along the length of the room. 'So far we've had a rock star, a businessman from Dubai and an American record producer, amongst others.'

'Any interest from Lawrence Conran?' I asked.

He gave me a look. 'Given that he didn't even bother turning up to the private view and sent an imposter in his place ...'

'I'll take that as a no then. Is he persona non grata?'

Seb shook his head. 'He's never going to be that. He's far too valuable to us. In fact, he did mention he might pop in, in a day or two, and I shall be very polite to him, as always.'

'But he can't be all that interested in the Shakespeare stuff, if he's left it this late?'

Seb shook his head, causing his blond fringe to flick over his eyes. 'Doesn't rate it,' he said. 'But he'll take a look at what's downstairs. I'm expecting a couple of new portraits by Bailey Forrester. He'll be the first to see those.'

On the second floor I knew Seb had a wide range of artists exhibiting. They tended to be people who would sell for less than the celebrities with individual exhibitions on floor three, and so represented bigger potential winnings for those investing to sell again.

'Is Lawrence good at picking out stuff that will go up in value?' I asked.

'He's a genius at it. In fact I think it's self-fulfilling now, because of his reputation. The moment he starts buying someone, everyone else thinks he must be onto something and before you know it they're all jumping on the bandwagon. Within a couple of months he's created enough of a market to sell the paintings back to the people who only got interested because of the stir he originally caused.'

'Did you ever think of going into business that way?'

He shook his head. 'I prefer it like this, just taking commission on the paintings that get sold here. In some ways it feels more certain. But I still have the same challenge of picking out the up and coming stars.'

We walked down another set of stairs.

'After a year or two,' he went on, looking at me over his shoulder, 'the hope is that the people I've backed produce the sort of work that changes hands for a fortune at auction. So long as that keeps on happening, I still have the trust of my buyers.'

'Is that always what it's about then?' I said. 'For the buyers, I mean? They're mostly looking to sell on after a bit?'

'Oh no,' Seb said, 'not necessarily. But if the paintings rocket in value it reassures them they haven't been taken for fools.' He gave me a look. 'Now that really is what it's about half the time: the ego boost a buyer gets when they know they made the right decision, and everyone else can see they did too.'

We worked our way down through the rest of the

exhibition halls to the ground floor, where there were prints and books for sale for mere mortals like me who didn't want to bankrupt themselves.

'Time for lunch,' said Seb. 'I told the others we'd meet them there.'

The venue was a half-timbered pub called The Flag. We went up stairs that creaked and complained in protest, to an attic room with a sloping floor and a fire burning. The air smelled of wood smoke and rich beef casserole. Our table was just next to the hearth.

We were the first ones there, but the peace wasn't destined to last. I looked up and saw Radley come in, a posh-looking carrier bag on her arm: sky-blue paper with ribbon handles.

'Out on the spend?' Seb asked.

'Birthday present,' she said, drawing out a chair and sitting down in one quick movement. Her mouth was set and she didn't say anything else.

Seb took our drinks order and went off to the bar immediately; I had the feeling he was after an excuse to leave us alone.

'Look, Anna,' Radley said, right on cue, 'I was out of order when you came in last. I should never have had a go at you like that – it just came as a bit of a shock to see you together with our imposter, that's all.'

'I should have called you or Seb about him, Radley,' I said. 'I'm afraid because he didn't seem to be a threat, it just didn't cross my mind.'

'It's unfortunate that we have to be so careful.' I could tell she still hadn't forgiven me. 'Our reputation's the thing that makes our whole operation work,' she went on. 'If there was ever a problem we could lose everything.'

I nodded. 'I can see that now.' I reckoned I'd better let her get it out of her system.

Seb returned with the drinks, followed by a woman with grey hair, clipped into an unforgiving cut, carrying a lime juice.

'This is Monica Smith,' Seb said with a half smile. 'She heads up our accounts team, so be nice to her. She'll be the one passing on the good or bad news about how much money you can spend on your publications.'

I was ready to match Seb's jovial tone, but as she looked me up and down, one eyebrow raised, I could see it would have been a mistake. She was wearing a wrap-around cardigan of the sort dancers put on to keep warm when they're not exercising, and she had ballet pumps on her feet too. Both sat rather oddly with her nylon, crease-in trousers. She looked as though she might have adopted one style thirty years earlier and only added the other more recently.

'I understand from Mr Rice that we can expect a lot from you,' she said. *And woe betide you if you fail to deliver*, she might just as well have added.

Out of the corner of my eye I could see a small smirk on Radley's face.

Before I had to cope with Monica's appraising look any longer, two women I assumed must be Sinem and Elsie joined us.

Sinem had long, dark hair and sparkly, mischievous eyes. She was a similar height to me, meaning I wouldn't get a crick in my neck when we spoke, which was a bonus.

'It's a great surprise to meet you, Anna,' she said. 'Seb only told me you were coming – or,' she looked at Seb with a grin, 'might be coming – last Thursday.'

I gave Seb a look.

'But it's good news,' she went on. 'We certainly need the extra help. When Seb told us some of his grand ideas for the coming months, I was feeling slightly faint until I heard we'd be getting an extra body on board.'

Elsie, however, looked less impressed. She was picking at a loose bit of table mat and looking at me as though I'd got a slug on my nose.

What struck me most about the lunch was the manner in which Radley behaved. The others, at least, carried on in much the same way as promised by their initial behaviour. Elsie was sullen and quiet, Sinem the exact opposite and Monica just watchful.

But with Radley it was as though she was gradually thawing. Seb kept bringing her into the conversation and each time she contributed she seemed a little friendlier. At first it was as though she was just going through the motions ('Well that's something Anna would know about, with her newspaper experience,' said in a stiffly polite tone) but gradually it began to feel more natural ('I'd want to discuss that with Anna later. What do you say, Anna? Maybe we could do that tomorrow over a coffee?').

When she made this last suggestion, I caught Seb give her an approving look, and a small private smile, which I was quite sure I wasn't meant to have noticed.

Chapter Nineteen

I spent the afternoon looking at databases and profiles of Seb's past buyers. At one point Elsie left the room, which was a relief. I didn't feel as though I could ask any questions in front of her; her silence was oppressive.

'Is there something wrong, as far as Elsie's concerned?' I asked Sinem.

She snorted and ran her hand through her hair, her bangles jangling down towards her elbow. 'That's a constant state of affairs,' she said. 'In particular, she resents you coming because she thinks you'll be getting a director's salary in return for writing a few press releases.' She sat back in her chair. 'In her opinion, Seb should have offered her a permanent post instead.'

'Would that have worked? In your opinion?'

Sinem let out a bark of a laugh. 'Are you kidding? I'd go insane if she stayed. No,' she said, looking at me, 'in my opinion Seb should have promoted me and got a new assistant in.'

I looked at her for just one moment with my mouth open before she said: 'Oh I'm only kidding! This is my first job actually, so I'm not quite ready for director level posts yet. But if you get a chance to put in a good word for me with Seb I'd be grateful. I don't think the "assistant" title is quite commensurate with what I do.'

I stopped hyperventilating and said, 'And what's the deal with Monica? She seemed very reserved at lunch.'

Sinem shrugged. 'Partly just the way she is, I think. I sometimes feel there's a bit of a generational thing going on between her and Seb. She's the only member of staff who calls him Mr Rice.' She laughed. 'And I'm not quite sure she approves of all of his methods.'

I wondered what these might be, but I didn't want to interrupt her flow. I had a feeling there might be more to come.

'But the other thing is, I think she feels a huge sense of ownership over the gallery.'

'Why's that?'

'I reckon it's because she used to work for Sir Anthony Peake.'

'The chair of the board, who owns this building?'

Sinem nodded. 'Apparently, when Seb and Mel first rented this place they had no one to do the admin side of things for them, so Sir Anthony "lent" them Monica.

'She's been here ever since. I think she sees herself as his representative on earth.' She giggled. 'She's got it quite clear in her own mind that she ought to be in charge of the gallery's direction, who's hired and fired and so on. The word on the street is that there's another complication with Monica too. It's before my time here, but I understand she was very fond of Seb's ex, Mel. Of Seb, not so much. I guess that colours her view of gallery matters.'

Mel's supporters seemed to be everywhere. For a moment I imagined Monica and Alicia teaming up to fight her corner. The idea was quite frightening.

'Anyway,' Sinem went on, 'she doesn't really have much say in how things are run; it's Seb who's ultimately in charge of the purse strings, Monica just nit-picks over the details. All the same he likes to keep her on side. We suspect she reports back to Sir Anthony, and there's no doubt we need to be on good terms with him. He could probably squeeze a higher rent out of us if he chose.'

* * *

Just before I was due to leave, Seb popped in.

'Have you got five minutes, before you head off?'

I followed him and, once we'd reached his office, he closed the door in that careful, deliberate way that tells you a person's about to tackle something delicate.

'How's it been today?' he asked.

'Fine,' I said, knowing this was just small talk.

'Good.' He motioned for me to take a seat. His venetian blinds were half open and, as I sank into a chair, I turned my head and saw Radley watching us. She looked away quickly.

'Look, Anna,' Seb said, 'I've just had a call come in that's put the final jigsaw piece into the puzzle.'

I raised my eyebrows.

'I know exactly who Darrick Farron is now,' he said, letting out a sigh. 'In many ways it's good news. I mean, he's not an undercover reporter and it does look as though he's given you his correct name this time.'

I had a trembling feeling in my stomach as I waited to hear what he had to say. 'What is the truth then?' I asked.

'It turns out he's involved in undercover art investigations.'

'He works for the police? Or customs or something?'

'Nothing quite as traditional as that,' Seb said. 'He's a freelance. A gallery might hire him, or a rich art buyer trying to track down a particular work, or in some cases a government.'

I felt relief wash over me and took a deep breath. 'I'm glad. I thought you were going to say he was a mass murderer at the very least.'

Seb's mouth tightened. 'Just because he's an investigator doesn't mean he operates inside the law. He might be working on a legit job – going after an artwork that's been stolen, or someone who's avoided paying vast sums in tax – but there's plenty to suggest he's not picky about the work he takes on. And he's known for using some brutal methods to achieve his ends. What he does, he does very quietly and privately. He covers his tracks. It's no wonder we didn't find him on the internet.' He leant across the desk, much as he had done at the table in the restaurant, and took my hand for a moment. 'You like him, don't you?' he said.

I tried to look him in the eye, but didn't manage it.

'I know you do, Anna, and I'm sorry, but I'm worried for you. I don't want you to get hurt.' He picked a piece of paper from his in tray. 'This is a printout of the email I got this afternoon,' he said, 'detailing all the people who've hired this guy. Some of them are the sort who'd stop at nothing, and he'll be abiding by exactly the same principles as they do, believe me.'

I looked away for a moment and caught Radley watching us again. Once more she averted her gaze as soon as it met mine.

I couldn't work out what to say to Seb. He made me feel cross and trapped, and in spite of what he claimed to know about Darrick, every part of me resisted his message.

'You're thinking you can stay involved with him without getting embroiled, aren't you?' said Seb. He didn't sound cross, only sad and sympathetic. 'The trouble is, that kind of work tends to follow you around. You don't just do it nine to five. When you're with him, the next person you meet might be one who'd rather he was dead. Is that how you want to live?'

When I didn't say anything he went on, 'I'm guessing he hasn't been around much?'

I shook my head.

'The people who pay him will always come first, Anna. I don't want you to have to go through all that; you're too precious to me. The heartache might be bad now, if you break it off, but it'll be worse if you get more deeply involved and have to finish it later.' He sat back in his chair again. 'There's one more thing too,' he said. 'It's a hundred times less important but I've got to mention it.'

'Go on.'

'Well, it's an issue for the gallery too.'

I looked up at him.

'In one way, as I was saying, I was quite relieved when I found out who he was. I mean, we deal with the artists themselves, face to face. There's no question of fraud, or stolen works or anything that he'd be interested in.'

I waited for him to spit it out.

'But it does mean he was after one of my guests. Now, I can't be responsible for what they get up to. It may be that some of them have dabbled in something criminal at one stage or another, and if so I'd naturally take a very dim view of that. But at the same time, your involvement really would cause complications.'

'How do you mean?'

'Can you imagine how it would look if he caught up with one of my guests now, and you were still seeing him? I can visualise the headlines: "Gallery's communications director tips off hired gun".'

I sat up straight. 'Bad for business, you're saying?'

He responded to the coldness in my voice: 'Don't think I wouldn't want criminal dealings unmasked, Anna,' he said. 'Don't think that for a moment. But if my clientele think they're going to be under scrutiny whenever they come to me, and that I'm aligning myself with the sort of gangland art collectors Farron works for, I think they might be put off. And, in all honesty, I can't say I'd blame them.'

I took the stairs down, rather than the lift, my footsteps echoing on the concrete treads. Seb hadn't spelled it out, but then he hadn't needed to. If I wanted to stay at the gallery, it was time to give up on Darrick Farron. Always supposing I got the chance. I had a feeling he'd given up on me already.

Chapter Twenty

By the time I got home I'd been having hypothetical arguments about what to do if Darrick called for well over an hour and, given that they were leading nowhere, I really wanted to close my mind to the whole thing. I wished it was that easy to push the thoughts away, but they kept sneaking in again each time I tried to focus on anything else.

I'd dismissed all the hints about Darrick being tantamount to some kind of gangster almost immediately. The more I thought about it, the more I reckoned Seb was probably exaggerating to convince me I had to dump him, and save any possible threat to his business. This made me furious that he should back me into a corner with his ultimatum.

Then again, if Darrick didn't call anyway, which in all likelihood he wouldn't, there was no choice to make. But I still didn't like the feeling of being coerced.

Having said that (the argument in my head had continued, as we rattled between tube stops), could I really blame Seb? I could see what he meant. It might be that clients guilty of very minor misdemeanours would still run scared if the gallery became associated with someone like Darrick.

The one thing that made me feel slightly better was that he hadn't exactly lied to me a second time around, though he'd certainly been economical with the truth. Then again who, in that sort of job, would want to go into details with a virtual stranger?

And so the arguments began all over again as I reached

Hampstead and walked out into the evening air, my shoulders hunched against the cold.

Back at Alicia's, I could tell that Sally's day hadn't gone smoothly either. She stomped up the stairs from the basement when she heard me come in and I could smell that she'd been on the bottle.

'Jeremy Drinkwater is a bloody bastard!' she said, leaning against the hall wall.

'Oh dear,' I said, moving towards her. I was keen to get her back downstairs again before Alicia joined us.

'Bloody bastard!' said Sally at a more extreme volume.

I was too late. Alicia appeared in the hall, her eyes popping. She looked very dolled up: lots of go-get-'em make-up and some impressive leather boots, along with an impeccable mini-skirt-and-jacket suit.

'What do you think you're doing, Sally?' she said. 'Quieten down at once! I've got a dinner guest!'

On the plus side, Sally received this admonishment with gales of laughter, which echoed through the hall and stairwell as Alicia stalked back into her dining room again. I wondered who the mysterious visitor might be. It was actually very rare for her to entertain when it wasn't for work.

'She's such a big bossy boots,' Sally said loudly.

'Come on,' I said, shoving her so hard I almost sent her careering down the stairs. 'Back to your place so you can tell me all about it.'

'Have a drink,' Sally said, once we'd closed the door. I could see she'd made serious inroads into a bottle of gin.

I poured myself a tiny measure (my stomach felt empty and I knew it would go to my head), topped it up generously with tonic, and sat down.

Sally sloshed some more into her tumbler – without tonic – and did the same.

'So what happened?' I asked, taking a sip.

'Spent the whole day dealing with some particularly horrible feet, then finally went off duty, only to get a message from that little shit on my mobile.'

'And?'

'And it seems he forgot, on Saturday night, that he actually has a long-term girlfriend called Gloria.' She tutted. 'I mean, Gloria! Can you believe it? Anyway, amazingly, he managed to carry on forgetting, even once he'd sobered up, right until I left on Sunday evening. Then it seems she got back at lunchtime today, and it jogged his memory, so it's all off.'

'I'm sorry,' I said.

Sally looked at me, her eyes squinting slightly, and patted my hand. 'It's all right,' she said comfortingly. 'It isn't really your fault.'

'What about Greg?' I asked. 'I mean, I thought you two had a good thing going together, and he sounded really nice from what you said. You showed me his photograph that time, remember? He's very good-looking.'

'Lovely boy,' Sally said. 'Dear sweet boy, but just a boy, Anna. Just a boy ...'

She let her sentence trail off. At that moment there was a knock at the door.

It was Alicia. She glanced at Sally for a second and then jerked her eyes away, letting out a noise which expressed deep disgust. She turned to me. 'I thought you must be down here, Anna. There's someone I want you to meet. Come on up to my dining room.'

Sally looked at me pitifully. 'Don't leave me, Anna,' she said. 'I really need to talk to someone.'

'Don't be an idiot, Sally,' Alicia said. 'You're in no fit state to communicate with anyone at the moment. You ought to be sleeping it off.'

I turned to Sally. 'Don't worry,' I said. 'I'll come straight back down as soon as I've been to say hello.'

'Promise?'

I nodded, and got up to go with Alicia. Loyalty to Sally would certainly bring me back to her again, but if my cousin was about to unveil a new love interest, I couldn't bring myself to miss it.

Chapter Twenty-One

We went upstairs – I was still in my coat – and Alicia ushered me through to her dining room, where she and her companion looked to be between courses.

'This,' said Alicia, 'is Lester Frayn.' She took in my blank expression in a fraction of a second and rolled her eyes as she explained, 'He's a top theatrical agent, based in New York. He discovered people like Faye Banks and David Wentworth-Tait.'

Okay, them I had heard of.

'He was very interested to hear that you're a friend of Jez Ellis,' Alicia went on.

'Don't worry,' the man called Lester said, 'I know he already has an excellent agent of his own. I was just keen to ask you to pass on my compliments to him. I guess you could say I'm a big fan of his. He's got a great career coming up.'

He had a very pleasant American accent, and one of the most disarmingly friendly smiles I'd seen in a long while. Alicia, who had been looking slightly anxious, seemed to calm down a bit. I heard her let out a breath that sounded as though it had been under starter's orders for some time. She pulled back a chair for me. 'Sit down and join us for a moment, Anna,' she said. 'Glass of champagne?'

I was conscious of the empty stomach and the gin, but it seemed rude to refuse, so I slipped off my coat and made myself comfortable. As she poured, it struck me as odd that they wanted me to come in and gatecrash their party.

I think Lester might have sensed this. He turned towards me and said, 'We've just had the most wonderful appetiser. Alicia sure is a number one cook. We were going to wait a moment before our next course, so we can appreciate it properly.'

Which still didn't quite explain my presence.

'I wanted to get you up here for another reason, Anna,' Alicia said suddenly. 'I knew you'd be furious with me if I didn't introduce you to Lester, since he'd be the perfect person for you to interview next. I explained to him how you were building up your freelance career.'

This was actually really kind of her. I was sure Lester would make an interesting interviewee. I would need to do lots of swotting up, since his work wasn't really my field, but it sounded like a great opportunity. Lester was busy making self-deprecating remarks and explaining how the publicity would help him too.

'It was Alicia's suggestion,' he said. 'You mustn't be bounced into it, Anna, if it doesn't suit.'

'I think it would be great,' I said, 'if you really don't mind. I'd be delighted.'

Lester beamed. 'I think it'd be a blast.' This made me rather anxious. I hoped I could make the interview as fun as he seemed to think it might be, without having to resort to questions about Mary Poppins again.

'You'll have to make it snappy, though, when it comes to arranging something,' Alicia said, casting a sharp glance at me. 'Lester flies back to the States the day after tomorrow, and he's already booked in at a big event tomorrow evening.'

I looked at her and I could see the challenge in her eyes. Scheming cow! She was doing this deliberately. She knew how hard it would be for me to get time off during the day. I'd claimed that Seb was going to be flexible, and now she was putting him – and me – to the test.

'Say,' Lester said, picking up on my dismay with remarkable sensitivity. 'Looks like that might be inconvenient for you, Anna. We can always do something by email perhaps.'

'But face-to-face is so much more authentic, isn't it, Anna?' Alicia said. 'And you wouldn't want to miss an opportunity like this. Surely you'd be able to slip into town for an hour or so? Lester's staying at the Savoy. Why don't you aim for three o'clock?'

Lester was looking rather pink. 'Just you give me a call tomorrow if you can't make it after all, Anna,' he said. 'I'll be back at the hotel getting ready by that time anyway, so if you have to cancel you've no cause to worry about it. Is that understood?'

I finished my wine and left them to their main course. As I walked back down to the basement, I hoped Alicia would get indigestion.

I had expected that Sally might be out cold by the time I went back to her, but amazingly she was still in a sitting position and actually looked relatively cheerful.

'It's all right,' she said to me, getting up unsteadily. 'I've decided now, he was just a bastard.'

'Yes, so you said. Look, Sally, I've got to eat something. I'm so hungry. It would do you good too.'

I ended up calling for a delivery pizza because she wanted to come with me to the shared kitchen, and I dreaded her letting off more expletives in Lester's hearing, however much I wanted to pay Alicia back.

Over the food, Sally wanted to know about my day. I told her about meeting the gallery crowd, and what Seb had said about Darrick. I didn't really expect her to take it in, in her condition, but the pizza seemed to be helping sober her up, at least enough to engage on the subject. Meanwhile I had begun to join in the drinking, having opened a bottle of red, so we met somewhere in the middle on the sobriety scale.

'See, what it comes down to, is this,' Sally said. 'How bad are the people that Darrick works for?'

I watched as pepperoni and mozzarella slid precariously towards the edge of the droopy slice of pizza she was holding.

'If they're goodies,' she said, 'then he's a goody.'

'But if they're baddies,' I added, taking another large swig of red wine, 'then he's dodgy.'

Sally pointed a finger at me and the pepperoni fell on to her lap. 'Exactly.'

'The trouble is,' I said, 'how can I tell?'

'Good point,' Sally said. 'What you need to do ...' She put her pizza down on her bedside table. '... is to ask him.'

'Do you think he'd tell the truth?'

Sally frowned. 'Yes,' she said eventually, with no further explanation.

I felt too sleepy to ask her why she was so convinced. 'Do you think you should have a plate?' I asked. 'For your pizza, I mean?'

Sally peered at the abandoned slice. 'It's all right,' she said. 'Because it's on the table, you see. What you need to do,' she said again, 'is to see him, so you can find out the truth.'

'The trouble is, Seb doesn't want me to,' I said. 'To him it's a case of don't see Darrick if I want to keep my job.'

Sally refilled my glass, spilling red wine onto the floor. She rubbed at it with a stockinged foot and was silent for a while, pondering the problem. At last she looked up brightly and said, 'S'all right. What you need to do, is to not tell him.'

Upstairs the matter seemed simple. Sally was right: I had to find out more. And anyway, Seb wasn't in charge of my life. I noticed that the walls of my room moved slightly as I sat down on my bed to compose a text to Darrick.

Later, as I lay there in the dark, my mind swam with various thoughts of the day. I imagined Darrick huddled in conversation with moustachioed gangsters and thought it was very funny.

At some point between waking and sleeping Radley popped into my head. I wondered again about why she'd seemed to enjoy telling me off so much, that day in her office. It was as though she'd got some extra reason to dislike me.

And then I thought of Seb, smiling at her when she was civil to me in the pub.

My first thought on waking was the fact that my head hurt. This was swiftly followed by a vague feeling that I'd considered texting Darrick the night before. I looked at my phone and found that it had been more than just a thought.

I'd written: 'Want 2 c u. Need 2 ask about gangsters. Hope u r a goodie. A xxx.'

Oh God. And he hadn't texted back. No surprises there.

Chapter Twenty-Two

At the gallery, I wondered what to do about Lester. The fact was, Alicia was right: a face-to-face interview would be much better. I'd be able to put across the way he looked and his surroundings. The Savoy would add a bit of glamour and emphasise his jet-set lifestyle. Besides, he'd sounded quite keen on the idea and he seemed like a really nice man. I liked the thought of being able to get to know him better. And it would certainly be a great interview to add to my portfolio.

On the other hand, I knew it would take me much longer than an hour by the time I'd travelled over there and back, and it was only my second day ...

I glanced at my watch. It was already half-past ten and the later I left bringing it up, the worse it would get. If I was going to go through with bunking off, I needed to address the issue now.

Elsie sat nearby, huffing and puffing over some website updates. Sinem was zinging through some flyers for an exhibition happening in March. She really might start to feel she should have been promoted in my stead if I swanned off for the afternoon. I spent ten more minutes agonising, the hands on the wall clock seeming to move at double speed.

At that point I went and knocked on Seb's door. I think I must have looked so anxious by the time I opened my mouth that he thought there was something terribly wrong. When I explained what I wanted, he seemed relieved.

'It's no problem,' he said. 'No problem at all. If you've

got anything desperate that needs doing, maybe you could finish it off afterwards?'

'Of course.' I should never have doubted he'd be supportive. I wondered why I had worried.

'Do take stuff home if it's more convenient than coming back here.'

'I know it sounds silly, Seb, but I think it might be best if I'm seen to be at the gallery.'

He raised his eyebrows.

'Sinem's very capable. If I want her loyalty, I need to make sure she knows I'm committed and actually adding something to the team, not just freeloading. And there's Elsie to consider too ...'

Seb laughed. 'Don't take any notice of what she thinks,' he said. 'With the best will in the world, that really would be a waste of time. I bow to your judgement on Sinem though. She's a good worker and I'm glad you're keen to keep her happy. Of course, you could just tell her you're going off to a meeting.'

I gave him a look.

'Up to you,' he said, shrugging. He got up and rubbed my arm in a friendly way. 'I'm pleased to see you're considering these things. Shows you're thinking long term.'

I felt a twist of anxiety in my stomach.

'I did hope I hadn't put you off yesterday with my worries over Darrick Farron,' he added.

I thought of the text and hoped I wasn't blushing.

After leaving his office I went along to the ladies' and when I came back out again I could see Seb was in Radley's office. I really needed to head in the opposite direction, but I paused for a moment. I had a nasty feeling he was telling her about my afternoon appointment.

Radley was standing up, one hand on her hip leaning towards Seb. She didn't look pleased. His stance was just as aggressive; I hoped he was backing me up.

The interview with Lester went well. I'd barely had the chance to do any background reading – just some web browsing on my phone at breakfast that morning – but he made me feel totally at ease and was kindness itself when it came to filling in my vast areas of ignorance.

I wondered how he'd got to be where he was with such a controlled ego. He insisted on us having tea and scones together too, and in the end I thought, what the hell.

'When will you be back in England again?' I asked, putting down my plate. His cheeks went slightly rosy.

'As a matter of fact, I may come over on a flying visit as early as January,' he said. 'Alicia and I have been having a little talk about that.'

It seemed an unlikely pairing but maybe he was kind and patient enough to see beyond her sharpness. And, of course, given his successful career, she wouldn't feel the need to boss him around so much or interfere with how he ran his life. If they did make a go of it I hoped he would alter Alicia's pH a little. Something less acidic would be much more acceptable.

I was back at the gallery just before everyone else was due to leave.

'Seb said you were going to burn the midnight oil,' Sinem said, 'so I've left you some notes here on what I've done so far and a couple of calls that came through. Did he explain that you have to go out down the side staircase if you leave after seven? The rest is all alarmed at that point and you'll see the security guards knocking around.'

'Thanks, Sinem,' I said. 'I presume Elsie's already left?'

She nodded, pulling a face. 'She went early as a matter of fact.'

'Oh dear. Some kind of problem?'

'Radley overheard her moaning about you going off this afternoon,' Sinem said. 'Well, you know how she can be. She let Elsie have it – told her how it was in your contract, and how it was good for the gallery if you were happy and stayed on. She said if Elsie was rude to you about it, her internship would be over on the spot. And then she basically let her know how far from indispensable she was.'

'Oh dear.'

Sinem shrugged. 'It was her own fault really. We were told you'd made that arrangement with Seb, and that it was all above board, before you even came in on the first day.' She picked up her coat, ready to leave.

'It wasn't great timing, having to duck out of work so soon after I'd started.'

'It was always going to irritate people,' Sinem said cheerfully, over her shoulder. 'But that's life for you.'

At least Radley had backed me up though; Seb must have used all his powers of persuasion to get her on side.

Seb popped his head around my office door at 6.50 p.m. 'Don't stay just to make a point, will you?' he said. 'Do whatever you really have to and then get off home. Not every day will be like today. It'll all get easier.'

'Thanks, Seb. You've been so supportive. I feel bad that I've given you the run around already.'

'It's no problem.' He paused for a moment, a smile flickering on his lips.

'What is it?'

'To be honest, I'm about to give you the run around back; just so you can stop feeling shifty about this afternoon of course.'

'Very thoughtful of you,' I said, wondering what was coming.

'You won't have heard of Henry Feldenstein?'

'Actually Sinem mentioned him when we were talking about your really high spenders.'

Seb nodded approvingly. 'He happens to be flying into Glasgow on Friday afternoon for a meeting on Saturday. I was wondering if I could persuade you to go up there and have dinner with him?'

After Lester, I felt it was the least I could do, though the idea filled me with dread. 'Sure. What do you want us to talk about?'

Seb handed me some notes. 'He's interested in the Marcus Oriel exhibition and he's worth a fortune to us if we handle him correctly.'

Which didn't do anything to settle my nerves. 'I'll do my best. Maybe you could brief me some more over the next couple of days, once I've had the chance to read this lot?' I held up the papers.

'Of course. Don't worry though. He'll be putty in your hands. He was delighted when I told him it would be you joining him for dinner rather than me. I tend to rub him up the wrong way. And I must admit, I did mention you were a redhead.'

Seb's asking me about Friday was clearly a formality then; it was all already signed and sealed. On top of that, I wasn't wild about the implications of his final sentence. 'Bloody hell, Seb!' I said. And I would have made more of it, except we were both momentarily distracted by the sound of a text coming in on my phone.

'I'll leave you to see to that,' he said, moving swiftly towards the door. He waved a hand as he left the room.

The text was from Darrick. It read: 'If I'm a man of mystery u r female equivalent. Meet u 2morrow? 8pm yr place? Text me yr address. D.'

Suddenly I was aware that my office door had opened again.

'Sorry,' Seb said. 'I forgot to say I'm out all morning tomorrow, but I should be back by two p.m. if you need anything. In fact,' he went on, 'let's meet anyway – say three-thirty? – It'll give me the chance to tell you all about Henry Feldenstein's weak spots.'

I didn't get back to Alicia's until gone 9.30. I sent Elsie an email from my work account just before I left. That should show her.

Once home, I went straight to the kitchen, planning to make pasta and pesto before I went up. It seemed the fastest possible way of installing food into myself, so I could go and get some sleep. I'd been feeling rather rough all day after the session with Sally.

Alicia pottered in as though she'd just happened to be passing. 'So I hear the interview with Lester went ahead,' she said. 'He called and said what a nice time he'd had.'

I longed to tell her what I thought of her low tactics, deliberately forcing me to test Seb's promise of flexibility so soon after I'd started work. However, I needed to be adult about this. Instead of fuming at her, I could just gloat over how kind Seb had been. I was still tempted not to compliment Lester, because that would be congratulating her on her conquest, but in the end, I couldn't resist it.

'He's such a nice man, Alicia,' I said.

She flushed. 'He is, isn't he? I met him a few years

back at an awards dinner where I was catering. We've kept in touch ever since, and had the odd drink. I never really thought it would come to anything more.' She was being totally un-Alicia like. 'Then this time around, same awards, he suddenly suggested dinner. He took me out, and so I invited him back here to reciprocate, and the next thing I knew we were making plans to see each other again.'

'I'm so glad,' I said. 'Really, Alicia.' And I was too, in spite of it all.

Though I felt a little less warm and slushy when she said, 'So how did Sebastian react when you told him you needed the afternoon off?' with great relish in her voice.

'He was wonderful,' I said.

She gave me a look.

'No, really. It was no problem at all. I think when I first went in he thought I was going to discuss some problem I had with the work, or ...' I thought of Darrick. '... some other kind of hitch. But as soon as he knew what I wanted he relaxed completely and just told me to go and get on with it.'

Alicia let out a long breath. 'I'm quite surprised, I must confess.' At least she was honest enough to admit it.

'I gather even Seb's exhibitions director, Radley, who can be tricky, backed me up. They genuinely want me to be happy working there I think.'

'Very modern of them,' said Alicia, looking disappointed. 'What is he up to? That's what I wonder.'

'What do you mean?'

'Well, Sebastian gets you in, pays you a very decent salary, and gives you the most amazing terms, seeming quite happy for you to duck out of your work almost as soon as you get there.'

'It's just good management practice,' I said, picking up the saucepan, ready to drain my pasta. 'It encourages staff loyalty.' The moment the words were out of my mouth I thought of the date I'd arranged with Darrick.

'Well it's going a hell of a lot further than any employer I've ever come across,' Alicia said. 'You know what Sebastian's like, Anna. He's a very driven man; no way does he do things by accident. It's still my bet that he's after something more than just your work skills if he's treating you this well.'

Chapter Twenty-Three

The following morning I felt as though someone was playing a series of erratic tunes on a stringed instrument in the pit of my stomach. I knew the strange quivery sensation was down to my approaching date with Darrick. I was really nervous about seeing him again. It wasn't because I was anxious about what he might say regarding his job. The reasons behind my inner flutterings were rather more basic than that.

I needed to focus on work. After being out for half of the day before it was important to put my all in now, and not to get distracted.

'Fat chance,' said Sally, when I voiced this intention to her over breakfast. 'Bet you don't go for five minutes between now and this evening without thinking about him.'

I had a nasty feeling she was right. 'I've got lots to do though,' I said.

'What kind of stuff?'

'Seb's got a couple of people coming in from public galleries and he's really keen for them to take some of Shakespeare's paintings. I've got to put together a package to convince them.'

'What will you put in it?'

'Reviews that say how innovative Shakespeare's work is, and what a huge, world-class star he's destined to be, that kind of thing.'

Sally smiled. 'I think it's really great that Seb wants to get them into public galleries – you know, so that ordinary people will be able to see them whenever they want.'

'Hmm.' I thought of the paintings. 'Well, I suppose ...'

'You're meant to stick up for him you know.' She went to make herself another slice of toast.

'It's not just that I'm uncertain about the public benefit,' I said. 'I also think you're being a bit idealistic about Seb's motives.'

'Really?'

I nodded. 'He's keen to get the paintings into public galleries because if people see that that sort of institution wants to collect Shakespeare's work it'll boost his selling power elsewhere.' I took a swig of my coffee. 'If Seb can tell a potential buyer that a chunk of Shakespeare's work has been saved for the benefit of the nation, it'll raise his status and make him even more desirable. So then he'll sell better to private buyers.'

'Really?' Sally looked shocked.

I nodded. 'And the more private buyers are interested, the more galleries will want to collect him, and so on, forming a virtuous circle. If you see it as virtuous.'

She brought her toast over to the table. 'I'm beginning to think your Seb's a bit of an operator.'

I laughed. 'He's got a business to run. I suppose you can't really blame him. And by the way,' I said, putting down my coffee for a moment, 'he's not *my* Seb.'

'But he is being very decent to you, from what Alicia's been telling me.'

'The old gossip! But it's true, he is. Then again, he's scuppered the first part of my weekend in return.' I told her all about the trip to Glasgow to meet Henry Feldenstein.

'Hmm,' Sally said. 'It does sound as though he's planning to get his pound of flesh then.'

'So long as Feldenstein's not expecting any kind of

flesh,' I said. 'I rather get the impression Seb wants me to use my feminine wiles to convince him to buy Marcus Oriel's work.'

'Wear brown tweed and look forbidding,' said Sally. 'It's the only defence left to you.'

At work I began to piece together what the art critics had said about Shakespeare. Elsie was trawling through a series of Google alerts to find every positive piece that had made its way on to the web. At 10.30 a.m., she emailed another link through and I clicked to see the article.

The headline was *Zachariah Shakespeare: a very, very silly man*.

'Um, Elsie,' I said, 'you know when I mentioned that I was specifically looking for *positive* reviews of Shakespeare's work?'

She looked up and rolled her eyes. 'Uh-huh?'

'Well, by that, I meant articles which say nice things about him, okay? The ones that imply he's a money-grabbing fool are of less use to me.' It was the third such article she'd sent through in the last forty minutes and I had a feeling she was doing it on purpose.

'What about if the article calls him something like a "Shock Jock"? That's what this one here says.'

My head was aching slightly. 'To be fair, that could appeal to some people. Better bung it through.'

Elsie let out a huffy noise. 'You see. It's not simple, is it?'

I kept looking at my watch in spite of my resolve to knuckle down. I hoped Sinem hadn't noticed. She was deep in a batch of letters to buyers who might be interested in our February exhibition.

All my clock-watching made the morning seem

interminable. At last it was midday and I felt it wouldn't look too odd if I went out to get some lunch. I walked for a few streets first, to try to settle my nerves, and eventually found a place called Beatrice's Bites. The baguettes in the window looked tasty enough, although the name of the shop made me think of mosquitoes.

The day was unusually mild, and I sat on a bench in a square, munching through mozzarella and tomato, and watching the world go by. A couple of pigeons pecked around near my feet, edging closer and looking hopeful. Glancing through a cafe window, I could see a man in a red cravat talking to a woman with a very pronounced chin.

It was a while before I was conscious that I'd carried on staring at them, but without seeing what was in front of me. I was back to thinking about the evening again. I roused myself, and shook my head to clear my thoughts and focus on reality.

It was at that moment that I realised I was now gazing gormlessly at Radley. What's more she was looking right back at me. She'd been in the same cafe as the guy with the cravat, and was now emerging from the door, followed by a man. He was mature, with thick iron-grey hair, and attractive in that kind of way that successful men often are, before you pull yourself back and remember to think straight. There was a paisley silk scarf round his neck and he had the air of a man who wants for nothing.

Radley gave me an odd, quick little nod in acknowledgement, which he spotted. He glanced in my direction, and frowned for a moment, a faint look of recognition in his eyes, then turned back to Radley. As they walked swiftly past she was saying something to him, possibly telling him my name, because his look flicked back in my direction and, just for a moment, I caught his eye.

It was another five minutes before I made my own way back to work. I wracked my brains as I walked, trying to think who the man with Radley could have been. As I crossed the square to the gallery entrance, I suddenly wondered if I'd got it; he looked like the guy who'd been visiting Seb, the day I'd come in to talk to Radley, and she'd torn me off a strip about hanging out with Darrick. I remembered noticing him the foyer, because he'd been so well dressed then, too.

Back at the office, the meeting with Seb drew near and I began to feel uneasy. My evening out with Darrick was high in my mind and my guilt levels were soaring.

He smiled when he saw me outside his door and got up to usher me in. 'How's it going?'

'I'll have the package for the public gallery reps ready by five-thirty,' I said.

'Great. And is it shaping up okay?'

I nodded. 'It's pretty convincing.'

'Wonderful.'

He spent some time telling me how to handle Henry Feldenstein, which included lots of psychological tactics, but beyond this nothing much more than a bright smile and a ready line in flattery, which was a relief. When we seemed to have come to the end of what he needed to tell me, I started to gather my things together, but he held up a hand.

'There's just one more thing I needed to talk to you about, on another subject.' He paused. 'One of our buyers from the private view was in touch this morning.'

'Oh yes?' I said, wondering what was coming. Seb's

expression told me they hadn't called to arrange the purchase of a painting. I hovered by the door.

'Funnily enough, this guy had recognised Darrick Farron.'

'Oh?'

'Yes.' He paused for a moment. 'Of course he didn't realise he'd come in under a false name and he wanted to know what connection we had with him, and why he was here.' He walked over to me. 'It does back up what I was saying the other day, doesn't it?'

I didn't reply.

'What I mean is,' he went on, 'I was right to worry that any link between us and him could harm the gallery. You do see, don't you, Anna?'

I nodded and he rubbed my arm in that characteristic way of his.

'Thanks. I knew you'd understand really.'

As I walked from his room I became aware that two people had been watching us. I caught Radley's eye for a moment but, as usual, she looked away quickly. Monica Smith, on the other hand, continued to stare at me from where she was standing by the printer, without any signs of discomfiture. Her cool, appraising glance gave nothing away, and I walked back to my own office wondering what was on her mind.

I was on my way down the stairs, ready to leave for the day, when Radley caught up with me. 'You recognised my lunch companion I expect,' she said.

I was surprised by her question, and took a moment to answer. She took my silence as assent.

'Professor Maxwell-Evans came in to see Seb recently,' she said.

Maxwell-Evans. Good grief, that name was a blast

from the past. And now I knew, it made sense that he'd recognised me, albeit not well enough to remember why. He'd clearly had to ask Radley to jog his memory. The professor was Seb's old tutor: the guy who'd collected art and indulged in the odd illicit substance. He'd changed, but that wasn't surprising given the intervening years. I certainly hadn't put two and two together when I'd seen him going in to Seb's office that day. But why did Radley seem so shifty?

'He left some papers behind, so I was just returning them to him.'

'Right,' I said, mystified. 'Good idea.' And I clattered my way down the rest of the stairs and out of the door.

Chapter Twenty-Four

'So what are you going to wear then?' Sally was darting around my room, skipping from foot to foot as though it was her date, not mine. Her exuberance was partly explained by the arrival of a new man on her scene: someone called Jasper, who'd been regularly dropping his mother off at Farquharson's and had spotted Sally's lingering glances. She was going out with him on Friday night.

'I don't know yet,' I said in answer to her question about clothes. I secretly wished she'd go away. 'I haven't had a quiet moment to think.'

She started rifling through my wardrobe, failing to take the hint. 'Ooh, what about this?' she said, pulling out a short, black party dress with a plunging neckline.

'For the pub?'

'Is that where you're going?'

'Well, he didn't say, but I presume we're not going clubbing at eight in the evening.'

'The thing is, if he mixes with gangsters he'll probably be used to women in dramatic dresses with guns tucked in their stocking tops.'

'You know,' I said, walking over and taking the dress from her, 'you are so not helping.' I returned it to its hanger and thrust it to the rear of the wardrobe.

'Oh I get it,' Sally said. 'You want something more moderate – I mean, just in case you don't get the chance to change your clothes before you go into work tomorrow morning ...'

'I'm going to treat that remark with the contempt

that it deserves,' I said, but Sally just gave me a naughty, knowing smile.

'You must remember,' I went on doggedly, 'that this is an information gathering exercise.' I gave her a look. 'I shall be displaying the utmost caution.'

She raised an eyebrow that said, 'yeah right', as clearly as if she'd uttered the words, and I felt the excitement bubble up in my stomach again.

In the end I decided on a black top with a ruffled neckline – reasonably low, but not excessive – a funky mini skirt with huge, unnatural orange daisies embroidered onto a green background, and my long brown boots.

'You will take care of yourself, won't you?' Sally said, suddenly sounding anxious. I think she felt slightly responsible for me. After all, it had been her suggestion to see Darrick again specifically to find out if there was anything dodgy about him or not.

'Of course.'

'And text me if you're not planning on coming back home tonight?'

'Sal-ly!'

She raised an eyebrow. 'Oh come on!' she said. 'Don't tell me the thought hasn't entered your head. Just text me, that's all. Then I'll know you're staying out of choice and haven't been bundled into the back of a black limo with mirrored windows.'

I steered her towards the door. 'All right. I'll text you! Now, could I please have some privacy, so I can get changed?'

Despite getting all tetchy and wanting space to myself, so I could be ready on time, I actually found I had twenty minutes to spare when I'd finished. I hovered on the stairs, wondering whether I should go down and wait in the hall, or if Sally and Alicia would laugh at me for behaving like a teenager.

At last there was a ring on the bell. They both appeared, as though they too had been listening out, but I got there ahead of them, hastily shouting my farewells and pulling the door closed behind me.

Glancing over my shoulder, I could see Sally peering out of the hall window, the curtain hitched to one side. Her nose wasn't actually pressed to the glass, but I'd say the tip of it was touching.

'Is that your cousin checking me out?' Darrick said.

'Oh no, that's not Alicia,' I said. 'I think you'll find she's staring out of the dining room window.'

He looked round. 'Oh yes, I see her.'

'The face at the hall window is Sally,' I said, 'my fellow lodger.'

'Do they always keep such a close eye on you?'

'Only when there's something exciting going on. You've achieved folk hero status thanks to what Seb said he'd found out about you.'

Darrick raised his eyebrows. 'You'll have to tell me all about that.'

'That's just what I was intending.' I wanted to choose my moment though. Blurting it all out in the street didn't seem like a good idea.

I had thought that Darrick coming to pick me up might mean he was in the car. Perhaps he had some special outing planned or something. In fact, it became apparent that he was on foot.

'So what's with the home visit?' I asked.

He raised an eyebrow. 'It seemed friendlier than demanding you meet me in a pub you'd probably never been to before, in a neighbourhood you might not know.'

'But I met you in The Old Faithful.'

He shook his head. 'A whole different ball game. That was lunchtime. Besides,' he gave me a half smile, 'I wanted to find out where you live.'

'That's not fair,' I said lightly. 'I don't know where you live yet.'

He put an arm round me, pulling me in close for a moment, his fingers edging round the top of my skirt. 'If you remember, you were invited, only you came up with some transparent excuse.'

I blushed as I recalled the scene in the backstreet near The Midnight Hour. 'I enjoyed that evening,' I said.

'And so did I.'

We walked to the tube station and caught a southbound train.

'Where exactly are we going?' I asked, as the tube rattled through the tunnels.

'An old haunt of mine,' Darrick said. 'You'll see.'

I didn't have long to wait. He made us get out at Chalk Farm.

The night was bitter, the sort where the air's cold enough to make you catch your breath, and it was slightly damp and misty. 'Is it warm, this place you're taking me to?' I asked.

He nodded. 'Don't worry, we're nearly there now.'

We walked towards Primrose Hill, and he led me down a tree-lined street, where we kicked our way through piles of leaves. Ahead of us, just to the left, was a white apartment block, built back off the road. It was a crisp series of flats with large windows and curving balconies. The gardens at the front were spacious enough to accommodate the odd cedar tree, as well as several smaller varieties besides.

'Here's the old haunt I was mentioning,' Darrick said.

'It looks modern, not old,' I said, giving him a sharp look from under the lamppost where I had paused. 'And it's not quite the restaurant or pub I was expecting.'

But as I finished my sentence he put an arm round my shoulders and began steering me up the drive. 'I thought you wanted to see my place,' he said. 'And besides, if we're going to talk about gangsters it's only really safe to do it somewhere where we won't be overheard.'

I pulled away but he took my arm and propelled me forwards again. 'Anyway,' he said, 'I've got steak, chips, mushrooms and onions all ready to cook. And a really good bottle of red.'

'Oh well, that's different then.'

'I knew you'd see sense.'

Darrick's flat was quite something. It was on two levels and the inside was painted white. Downstairs there was an extensive living area stretching from a kitchen at one end, through a dining section to a wide seating area beyond, with a balcony. There were a couple of doors off the hallway that I guessed led to a cloakroom and maybe a broom cupboard or something like that. Upstairs ... well I didn't know anything about upstairs, except that there was one. Leading up to it was a substantial moulded spiral staircase, also in white, arcing majestically towards the ceiling.

'It's an amazing place,' I said, as Darrick took my coat. 'I'm guessing working for gangsters pays all right then.'

'Is that what Seb told you?'

'It's what he implied. He didn't actually say gangsters. I think he used words like ruthless and muttered things about operating outside the law.'

Darrick hung up our coats – I'd been right about the cupboard – and walked towards the kitchen range. 'Tell me exactly what's happened since I saw you last then,' he said, opening a bottle of wine and reaching down glasses from a high shelf to the left of the dining table.

So I went through everything, starting with Seb's job offer and going through to what he'd said about the sort of people Darrick worked for, and the effect he'd be likely to have on potential buyers at the gallery.

Darrick was getting the steak out of the fridge; he'd prepared everything so it was ready to go. He looked thoughtful as he heated the oil for the chips.

I took a sip of my wine. 'Can I do anything?'

He shook his head. 'Everything's under control.' He turned to look at me and smiled as he flipped the steaks over.

He didn't seem to be about to volunteer anything, so I plunged in. 'So what is the truth about your work? I presume you knew I'd assumed you were a journalist.' It was only as I said it that I realised how angry I was.

He gave me a look and a half smile that told me he'd been well aware I'd been deceived. 'Did you really? Sorry about that.'

I took a deep breath. 'So what is it that you do do, exactly?' I asked.

'I assumed Seb had filled in all the details.'

'He said you tracked down stolen works of art, that kind of thing.'

'And he portrayed that as being pretty much unacceptable in his world?'

'He said you used brutal methods to achieve your goals.' I sighed. 'In any case, you've got to be fair, Darrick. You can see his point of view. He doesn't want some rich buyer who left the proceeds from a mediocre watercolour off his tax return to be frightened away by you. I'm quite sure he supports everything you do in principle.'

Darrick turned off the heat and lifted out the chips, dishing our portions onto large, white plates. 'Do you know how hollow that sounds?' he said. It was his turn to fight to control his temper. His blue eyes were blazing, though he kept his voice level. As he put the plates on the table he said, 'You have to live according to what you believe, Anna. If you operate by Seb's rules you're giving in just to make a fast buck.'

'We all have to earn our keep,' I said, making a show of sweeping my eyes over the palatial surroundings.

'I'm not ashamed that what I do pays well. It's a tough job and it can be dangerous. I get called off to God knows where at a moment's notice and half the time I'm not allowed to tell anyone what I'm working on. It doesn't seem unreasonable to take a decent wage.' He took a large slug of wine.

'And what about the people you work for?'

'I'd never do a job for someone I didn't respect, and I'm quite at ease with the methods I use.'

We sat in silence for a moment. My food steamed in front of me. Suddenly Darrick laughed. 'For God's sake, Anna, we seem to be making a habit of this. Eat!'

So we ate and drank and talked about Primrose Hill and Hampstead and films and music, just as any other couple might.

I couldn't leave the subject of Darrick's work altogether though. I felt there was more to discuss. Finally, when we'd finished and were sitting over glasses of brandy, I asked, 'Why weren't you more explicit about your job? It did feel as though you were deliberately misleading me.'

'The reason's going to be a lot more prosaic than you imagine,' he said. 'It's quite simply that my work isn't that much of an asset when it comes to relationships.'

'Oh!' I said. That put a slightly different complexion on things. 'What, you mean because you get called away at short notice and things like that?'

He nodded.

'So there wasn't anything underhand about it after all?'

Darrick looked at me across the table. 'It was about as underhand as you can get, as moves go. I was hoping that if you got to know me first, before you found out about my career-related shortcomings, I might have a chance of conning you into seeing more of me.'

After we'd finished our drinks Darrick stood up, and I automatically followed him across the room. He turned to face me, looking straight into my eyes. I found myself oblivious to everything else around us, losing myself in his gaze.

'So Seb forbade you from seeing me whilst you're working for him?'

'That's what it amounts to.'

'What are you doing here then?' he said.

'I think it's possible that physical instincts have led to a lapse in judgment.'

'That's very much what I was hoping,' he said, leaning forward.

Every fibre in my body seemed to strain towards him, waiting for him to touch me. Then in a moment he was pulling me to him, kissing me hard on the mouth, slipping a hand under my top. A sparking, shivering sensation crackled down through my body. What followed was intense, ungentle and exhilarating.

It was quite a while later that I realised I hadn't texted Sally to alert her to my loose behaviour. Darrick shifted slightly in his sleep as I sneaked out of bed to go to the bathroom where I could see what I was doing without waking him up.

When I got back in again he was stirring. 'Okay?'

I nodded and explained that, given the gangster connections, Sally had insisted I let her know I was okay if I decided to stay out.

He laughed and lay behind me, stroking me softly. 'So have you thought any more about Seb's ultimatum?' he said into the darkness.

In fact, I realised now I'd been seeing it as something that could be ignored – at least for a while. But perhaps it couldn't. Perhaps Darrick wouldn't carry on seeing me if I was effectively treating him as a secret that could be kept at my convenience.

I imagined what Alicia would say. Okay, so she hadn't approved of me working for Seb in the first place, but what would her reaction be if she knew I was considering giving up a £60K job for the sake of someone I'd only just met, who might not last five minutes in a relationship? I smiled to myself for a moment.

'You're taking a long time to answer,' Darrick said, touching me more firmly and persuasively.

'I'm not sure I should be making decisions about my future career based on carnal desire,' I said.

'Seems like quite a good reason to me,' he replied.

'Would you still see me if I stayed at Seb's?'

'Would you carry on working for a man who controls who you go out with for the sake of his petty criminal friends?'

'No,' I said eventually. The slowness of my answer was down to the distracting stroking, and where it was leading, rather than indecision. 'I don't think I would.' The idea of giving it all up for him was suddenly daring and exciting. Throwing caution to the wind ran hand in hand with the passion I was feeling.

He rolled me towards him and began kissing me again with all the urgency of earlier in the evening. 'When will you leave the gallery?'

'As soon as I can,' I said, when I was able to say anything. 'But I can't just walk out tomorrow.' I drew in a sharp breath as he touched me again. 'I'd be leaving them in the lurch. I'll have to finish off a couple of things and then I'll go.'

'Good,' he said. 'I need you with me.' And if we said anything more, I didn't take in what it was.

Much later I woke again. Darrick wasn't in bed, but I could hear him next door. There was a faint sound of the tapping of keys on his computer.

I suddenly wondered if an urgent message had come in from one of his employers. I had to be realistic about what he had said: he got called off at a moment's notice to do some hazardous job or another. What would it really be like, being involved with someone like him if our relationship lasted?

I rolled over and lay on my back. It was too late now, I thought. Whatever it was like I had to be with him, for as long as he wanted to be with me. This simple thought and the absolute conviction I felt left me oddly calm. The upheaval of leaving the gallery seemed unimportant. What was happening now was meant to be.

I slept for a couple of hours. When I woke I glanced at the clock to see it was only 5 a.m. Darrick was back in bed again, deeply asleep by my side. I lay there for half an hour. I was having the kind of adrenaline rush that must get people addicted to riding in fast cars. My pulse raced at the thought of the night we'd spent together, and the decisions I'd made. I knew I needed to get on calmly with my day-to-day life until I'd sorted things out with Seb, but part of my brain was running away on a whole new track, already released from the confines I'd so recently placed myself in.

I felt fidgety, as though all the energy coursing through my veins would burst out at any minute. I didn't want to sleep; I wanted to hold the feeling to me and relish every minute of it. As quietly and gently as I could, I slipped out from under the duvet, grabbed a jumper of Darrick's from a chair, and tiptoed downstairs.

In the kitchen I made coffee, standing there cocooned in the warm wool that smelled of him. Then I carried my steaming drink over to the living area, which was covered, wall to ceiling, with shelves containing books and CDs. The reading matter was interesting: everything from George Orwell to John Grisham. There were lots of travel guides thrown in, along with rows of art books that occupied the bottom two shelves, I presumed because of their size and weight. I began work on scanning the CD collection. He owned several of the same albums as me; there was certainly a music overlap, which was always an encouraging sign.

I moved along to the next bookcase. Ah, photo albums. I spent a moment or two wondering if it was too intrusive to look at them, but the temptation was strong. Outwardly, they didn't seem to be his style. Their covers were pink and purple in swirls, with a bow on the spine. Yuck. I giggled, still with that feeling of excitement bubbling up inside my stomach. Probably an old girlfriend had bought them for him. If I looked inside I would see some leggy blonde – probably twice my height – looking back at me.

That would serve me right for snooping. I reckoned I was grown-up enough to cope, but all the same, why ruin the mood?

Instead I drew out the book next to the albums: Brewer's Dictionary of Phrase and Fable, thinking I'd take it over and curl up with it on the sofa until Darrick got up. The books were tightly packed, so I had to tug to shift it. When it finally moved, the volume to its left and the photo album to its right came out too, and several loose snapshots fell onto the floor.

Just like a bloke. Some ex might have given him the albums, but he hadn't spent any time laying out the pictures inside. The pages themselves were pristine and untouched. There weren't even that many loose photos, but I guessed that those there were dated back some years. Darrick looked much younger in the first picture I found of him. Probably all the recent ones would be in digital format on his laptop.

Now I was desperate to get the pictures tidied away again before Darrick came down and thought I'd been digging my way through his personal stuff. It seemed unfair that I'd pulled back from the brink and not snooped, only to be put in a position where I looked guilty. I hastened to replace everything and return the album to the shelf.

It was as I was stacking the pictures up that I saw one of the photos featured a face I knew. I felt the hairs prickle on the back of my neck.

The picture had been taken at a wedding. A woman in a bridal dress stood to one side, laughing with one of the guests, and several other suited men and women had been caught side-on in mid flow. But all these people blurred away as I stared at the one face I recognised.

It was Seb's old girlfriend, Julia.

Chapter Twenty-Five

It's funny how your brain comes up with any number of explanations for something that's unexpected, providing several ridiculous ones to explain away an anomaly you'd rather not accept.

My brain simply told me it was a coincidence; that Darrick wouldn't even have realised this was Julia. After all, she was only one of a group and, in any case, it was clear from her black dress and white apron that she was a member of the serving staff. She must have been there to earn a bit of extra cash.

Darrick would have known the people who were getting married, but not the ones serving the champagne. It was quite obvious. That was the way my brain explained the picture. No matter that Julia was looking at the camera and smiling, as though there was some connection between her and the photographer. It was a coincidence; a startling one, but a coincidence nonetheless.

But then I turned the photograph over. Written on the back was "Julia at Margot and Matthew's wedding, August 2000".

I wasn't familiar with Darrick's handwriting, so I compared the script on the back of the photo with samples I found around the room. There was a half-filled notebook on a sideboard, and a pad by the telephone base station; all the scraps of writing matched the inscription. And now my brain was forced to look at a new explanation.

Darrick had known Julia; that was the plain truth.

It was as though I'd been punched. I'd heard other people claim to feel like that after a shock, but I'd always assumed it was a throwaway remark. Now I understood: it was like being winded. I couldn't breathe for a moment.

Even in that state, I knew there was information I had to assimilate and also that I was keeping it at bay. The photograph carried a message I didn't want to read and so, for the time being, I rejected it rather than analysing what it might be.

It took a moment – maybe several – before I realised that Darrick must be awake. I heard a door closing up above, and then the sound of a tap running.

Mechanically, I slid the photograph under the others and slipped them all back between the pages of the album.

He hadn't told me, my mind kept saying, as I pushed the album and the books back on to the shelf. He hadn't told me he'd known Julia. More than that, he'd actively misled me. He'd asked about her, got me to describe what she'd looked like.

I managed to dress whilst he was in the bathroom, retrieving my crumpled clothes from the bedroom floor.

'I'd forgotten I was meant to be in early for a meeting,' I said, when he came back to the bedroom, his hair damp from the shower. I knew I wouldn't be able to keep up my facade if we had to sit down to breakfast together.

On my way out Darrick pressed a bag of things to eat into my hand, his fathomless blue eyes meeting mine.

'Are you all right?' he said.

'A bit hung-over, that's all.'

He was still looking at me closely. 'I've got to be away for a few days,' he said. 'I'm not sure how easy it'll be to keep in touch, but if I can't reach you before, I'll call again as soon as I'm home.'

I nodded, backing out of the door, hardly hearing him. I only knew I had to get some space between us so I could think.

Chapter Twenty-Six

I would have done anything not to have had to go into work. I just wanted somewhere I could be alone and piece together what was going on.

On the tube I strained my memory to think of all the times Darrick and I had talked about Julia. He'd been so deceitful, that was what I couldn't get over. I knew there were things he'd never be able to tell me about his work and that that part of his life might remain totally separate from anything we had going together. But with Julia it was different. I was already involved. I'd met her; she'd been the lover of one of my best friends. And all the time Darrick had known her too; well enough to take her photo at that wedding, just a few weeks before she'd died.

What was he after? That was the question. The only conclusion I could draw was that he wanted some kind of information from me. I remembered him asking whether Seb ever talked about Julia now.

It was becoming horribly clear that this was why he'd taken an interest in me. That first evening at the private view he'd quickly found out that I'd known Seb for a long time, and ever since then he'd been after me. It wasn't for my own sake, but because of Julia.

I wondered if they could have been lovers. If they had, and it had been going on when that photograph had been taken, then it would have been whilst she was officially with Seb. She hadn't seemed the type, but then who knew what might happen in the heat of the moment? I could testify to Darrick's sex appeal, I thought bitterly. And if she had been dealing with that type of emotional maelstrom, on top of everything else, might it have contributed to her suicide?

I reached Waterloo and decided to walk from there. I didn't take in my surroundings at all, but went on autopilot. The image that kept coming back to me was that of Julia in the photo, laughing, looking happy, very beautiful and very alive.

In the office I found Sinem had bought us all advent calendars. I hadn't remembered the date, my mind had been so full of other things. I struggled my way through the jollity and chocolate eating. And then Seb wanted me to join him to talk to the public gallery representatives. As we walked them round Shakespeare's paintings I felt terribly conscious of my secret knowledge; it seemed to hang in the air between us. Once or twice Seb looked at me as though he sensed there was something wrong.

After the visitors left we had a quick update with Radley.

'I think they'll each take something,' Seb said. 'The pack Anna put together was very convincing. There were some influential names in there saying all the right things.'

'Which paintings were they looking at?' Radley asked.

'The two cheapest ones,' said Seb, laughing. 'Budgets are very tight, but one of them already has some finance secured from a local business sponsor. My guess is they'll be back in touch to confirm before the day's out. I told them one of our most regular buyers was coming in shortly and so it wouldn't be wise to hang around.'

Radley made a face. 'Meaning Lawrence Conran, I take it, who isn't due for days and wouldn't touch any of Shakespeare's paintings with a bargepole anyway?'

'Quite. I didn't highlight Conran's views on the matter.'

'Well,' said Radley, 'Monica will want to know as soon

as any sale's confirmed, so she can plot it all on one of her spreadsheets.'

I began to get my files together, ready to go back to my office, but Radley still sat at Seb's desk, making notes.

'Are you all right, Anna?' he asked, and although I was looking at him, I could feel Radley's eyes on me as I answered.

'Fine. Sorry – bit of a headache, that's all.'

He frowned for a moment, looking into my eyes as though there might be more to see, but he let it go. 'Don't stick it out if you're not well. After all, you've got a long journey ahead of you tomorrow.'

Just as I turned my head away I saw Radley raise her eyes to heaven. 'I'll be fine,' I said. 'I might take an early lunch break though, and get some air.'

However much Radley was sticking up for me officially, I had a feeling she felt Seb was being kinder and more lenient than was necessary. I was sure her management style would have been much tougher than his. Perhaps it made sense, given that she had to deal with a whole load of staff, whereas he only worked with a few people directly.

I went to get my coat and walked out of the building, cutting through towards the river where I stood and watched the water go by, grey and choppy in the dull morning light.

I wasn't sure what to do about Seb. Should I tell him about the photo of Julia at Darrick's flat? I wasn't convinced it was worth the upset.

It could cause him to think, as I had, that Julia might have been unfaithful to him. It would alert him once again to Darrick's interest in me and the gallery, but he was on his guard as far as that went anyway. Keeping the information to myself would hopefully just protect him from any hurt that might result.

It seemed odd that, in the early hours of that morning, I'd made up my mind I really couldn't work for Seb any more. Now I was at a loss. The same should apply, whatever else was happening, but suddenly I just felt sorry for all that he had been through. Walking out didn't seem like such a reasonable option after all.

And what was I going to do if Darrick called? Our relationship certainly wasn't proceeding on the basis I'd thought it had been. In fact, it probably had no basis at all. Except what had happened the previous night had felt passionate and real.

I walked further from the gallery and then took out my phone. 'Terry?' He'd answered straight away. 'Can we talk or are you making a soufflé?'

He laughed. 'What's on your mind? Or no, don't tell me, you're just calling to see how I am.'

'I'm sorry.' I felt awful. 'I am calling to share something with you.'

'Thought as much. What's happened? Seb hasn't pissed you off already has he?'

'No. He's been fine. I wish it was something that simple.' I went on to tell him pretty much everything that had happened. It was the first time I'd even mentioned Darrick and I found it slightly awkward admitting we'd already spent the night together.

'I had no idea you'd been holding out on me,' he said. 'I thought you'd have shared the news if you'd got a new beau on the horizon. Just saying.'

'I'm sorry. I would have explained about him normally, but it's been kind of complicated.'

'That's one way of putting it. And it doesn't sound as though it's getting any less so.'

'You can say that again,' I said. 'And that's why I need your advice. I can't really see any reason to tell Seb. I mean, I don't know what the photo's all about, but bringing it up will only open old wounds.'

I heard Terry sigh. 'You do pick them, don't you?' There was a pause. 'Are you sure you aren't just putting off telling Seb because it will mean admitting to seeing a man you'd promised to give up?'

'I never promised him anything of the sort. He just assumed that's what I'd do. And anyway, I've already thought about that and yes, I am sure.

'I didn't like him telling me who I could or couldn't see though, even if it was relevant to the success of the gallery. I'd be quite prepared to come clean and resign over that, if necessary. But is there any point in telling him, that's what I'm asking, given that it's all such old history?'

'It might be old history, Anna,' Terry said, 'but whatever significance it has – which is more than either of us knows – it's affecting the here and now, isn't it? It sounds as though Julia has been one of Darrick's chief topics of conversation since you met. Whatever he's up to, I'd say it was current.'

Chapter Twenty-Seven

I went and bought a sandwich, even though I wasn't hungry, and then went back to the gallery, not feeling any better. I could see the truth in what Terry said, but I hadn't promised him I'd tell Seb.

As I walked up the stairs to the administration floor I was still wondering what to do. The place was fairly deserted. If I was going to have it out with him this might not be such a bad time. I'd taken my lunch early, but now the bulk of the staff had gone off to get theirs. If Seb was in his office ... But as I reached his corridor I could see that he wasn't. I hung around for a moment in case he came back; it was quite usual for him to skip his lunch break.

A second later, Monica Smith came past, in a V-necked jumper and slacks, her mouth sour. 'If you're looking for Mr Rice you can give up for at least another hour,' she said. 'I saw him go off with Radley just after twelve-thirty.' She made sure she had my attention and then added, 'They tend to take quite some time, when they go off together.'

The tone she used and the way she emphasised her words made me pause. Was she saying what I thought she was saying? I looked at her but she made no other comment. Perhaps I'd imagined the nuance I'd thought she had applied.

Later on I was about to ask Elsie to go and collect some budgets I'd been promised from Monica's office when I changed my mind and decided to go myself.

I saw her glance up as I approached her glass cubicle

and then instantly duck her head down again and busy herself with her calculator.

I took no notice and went on in. 'I came for the budgets for the next two exhibitions,' I said.

'I've signed this one off, but I'm afraid I've had to make considerable alterations to this second one.' She didn't sound afraid, she sounded pleased. 'I felt you were being rather extravagant.'

'Really? Perhaps you could explain.'

She seemed to relish this idea giving her, as it did, the opportunity to rub my nose in my failings some more. From my point of view, I was just intrigued by what she'd said earlier. I wondered what sort of malicious gossip she'd been peddling and whether I could goad her into spreading any of it in front of me. I would be delighted to go and tell on her.

'Here,' Monica said, pointing to an area she'd marked in highlighter pen. 'The people we usually use could do that for you at half the price.'

'Oh, that's interesting. Elsie said they *were* your preferred suppliers.'

She let out a snort. 'Elsie! Well, no more need be said. It's best to ask Radley about something like that.'

'I will in future.'

'I'd certainly say she's the one to stay friends with at the moment.' Monica gave me a meaningful look.

I tried not to rise to the bait, but was overpowered by temptation. 'How do you mean?'

'I've noticed she's seen a lot of Sir Anthony lately,' Monica said. 'And he's been telling me how helpful she's been. Apparently she takes rather more care over what he wants than Mr Rice ever has.'

'She's clearly got time on her hands.'

Monica leant forward. 'All I can say is, Mr Rice had better watch out if he's going to rock the boat with Radley. The power base may be shifting.'

I wasn't going to give her the satisfaction of probing any further, so I made to get up from my seat.

'You're getting on all right with her, are you?' she said, stopping me in my tracks. There was a speculative look in her eyes.

I sat back down again. 'With Radley? Yes, she's been very kind, very helpful.'

She raised an eyebrow. 'I wondered how it would be when you got here.'

'Why?'

'Mr Rice has his favourites and he's given to changing his mind about who is ...' She paused for emphasis. '... flavour of the month. When that happens it can make for a bad atmosphere.' She still wasn't being explicit, but her tone meant there was no mistaking her meaning.

'I'm sure if Radley's "flavour of the month", as you put it, she's got nothing to fear from me,' I said tartly. 'Seb and I are old friends, but we're more like family; cousins, say.'

'In my position you get to hear a lot of things, and that's not quite the impression I got.'

'You listen to all the tittle-tattle that's going, do you?' I stood and picked up the budgets. I wondered who on earth she'd been talking to.

'I tend to know what's true and what's not,' she said. 'After all, I've known Mr Rice for a long time, so I know what he's like. The stories about him often involve women, so I usually find new ones of the same sort quite credible.'

'He was loyal to Mel for years,' I said. 'It's only natural if he has relationships now he's free.'

'Loyal? To Melanie?' Her tone was incredulous. 'That relationship started to go wrong before they'd even signed the lease on the gallery. You can take it from me.'

Chapter Twenty-Eight

Later that afternoon, when I saw that Seb was alone, I went to knock on his door. I was planning to tell him about the photo. I'd decided Terry had a point: whatever it was that was going on, he had a right to know.

'Everything okay?' he said.

I nodded. 'I just needed to talk to you.'

He pulled out a chair for me. 'And I wanted to talk to you too, as a matter of fact. I just had a call from David – you remember? The second of the two gallery buyers? Well he's confirmed they're going ahead with a purchase and what's more, you know you highlighted *Corpse* as being highly acclaimed?'

I nodded.

'Well they've decided to go for that, rather than *Blame*. I didn't think they'd stretch to it, but apparently once he'd called one of their sponsors and conveyed the relative impact, they decided to opt for the work with the wow factor.'

I wondered what line of business the sponsor was in. Undertaking perhaps?

Seb put his arm round my shoulders and gave me a squeeze. 'It's all down to you,' he said. 'I knew the work you'd done would pay off, and I think you're also someone people trust. You were great. You'll have no trouble with Henry Feldenstein tomorrow.'

Suddenly he slipped his arm from round my shoulders to round my waist and drew me in a little, looking at me in a way that reminded me of the old days – not in that rush of emotion just after Julia had died, but before that, when life was less complicated.

Now I found I had an entirely different conversation in mind from the one I'd been planning. 'Seb?'

'Yes?' he said. He was smiling at me, looking so young suddenly.

'I spoke to Monica Smith today ...' I had to say it. '... and she hinted very heavily that you're having an affair with Radley.'

He looked absolutely horrified and stared at me for a moment before saying, 'Oh my God!' and quickly withdrawing his hand. 'I'm sorry, Anna. And you thought I was flirting with you too?'

'I didn't think you meant anything by it, but I didn't want to give Monica ammunition for any further mischief she might make.'

He turned his head, glancing behind him.

'I haven't actually seen her peering in at us, but she's just the sort to be hiding behind one of the office rubber plants, so I'm glad you don't have any.'

Seb laughed, but then his expression was sober again. 'Seriously though, Monica Smith is a menace.'

'It's certainly not fair of her to comment. You're your own man and it's no one's business who you see, least of all hers.'

'You're right of course, but all the same, the Radley thing's nonsense.' His eyes were wide. 'I had no idea Monica was under that impression. I don't mean there's anything ridiculous about it,' he added. 'Radley's great, but neither of us is the other one's type. You know how it is. Either you are or you're not.'

He looked at me and sighed. 'I'm sorry if I seemed to be making up to you, Anna. I suppose when we're together now it takes me back to university days, when everything was simple, before I ever knew Julia and things changed.'

He looked into my eyes. 'I didn't see what was under my nose then, or appreciate what we could have had. But I know time's moved on now. I suppose we've both been through too much for us to turn back the clock.'

He got up and walked over to the window where the lights of London were sparkling before us. When he turned back towards me again he said, 'You don't look much older now than you did then. I think that's why I keep thinking I can put all that's happened behind us and shut it away in a box.' He looked at his watch. 'It's late, isn't it? I expect you want to get off home. Take it easy on your way up north.'

I nodded. Suddenly I felt exhausted.

It was a relief to get back to Hampstead, but there were downsides. Sally met me, demanding a blow-by-blow account of what had gone on during my evening with Darrick, which didn't help. I'd been so looking forward to telling her. As I'd texted her the night before, I'd imagined us analysing the date together and how much fun it would be. As it was, I just didn't want to talk about it.

Under normal circumstances I would have found it hard to sneak off to my room without providing a proper explanation, but timing was on my side; Sally had more updates on her date with Jasper. He was taking her to the opera, and whilst she filled me in I managed to edge my way stairwards.

'I hate opera,' she said standing there in the hall, her eyes sparkling, 'but I shall live for what comes afterwards.' Before she let me go, she added, 'I still want to know *all* the details of your date you know. Bung all your stuff upstairs and then come and tell me over a glass or two of Chardonnay.'

But, before I'd made it to the first-floor landing, Alicia appeared. 'You don't look too good,' she said. 'Do you want to pop in for a drink?'

'I'm not sure,' I said. 'I'm not feeling too great.'

'Bad day at work? Or did the date go awry?'

I thought for a moment. The whole thing had been an emotional rollercoaster from start to finish, but there was a limit to what I wanted to share with Alicia. 'Neither was as straightforward as I'd anticipated,' I settled for saying.

In the end I went to have a glass of wine in her sitting room. After all the hours I'd spent at work, wanting to be alone, I now found I was actually putting off the time when I would have to go upstairs and face my thoughts. And, for once, it was better ensconcing myself with Alicia than with Sally; she was more likely to badger me with questions about work than about Darrick. After all, she was dying to prove my decision to take up the post had been flawed.

'So what's up at the gallery?' she asked.

I shrugged. 'Just the usual politics really, I suppose. There's a rather poisonous woman there called Monica Smith.'

'Now that name rings a bell.' Alicia rubbed her brow as though it might make the memory materialise, like a genie.

'She used to work for the gallery owner apparently, Sir Anthony Peake.'

'Oh yes!' Alicia said. 'I do remember. Mel said she was hard to deal with. On the one hand she always seemed to be on her side, when she and Sebastian disagreed, but on the other she said you could never relax with her. She was always stirring up trouble. I got the impression that half the time there wouldn't have been a side to take if Monica Smith hadn't been meddling in the first place.'

'That sounds like her all right,' I said. 'She basically implied Seb was having an affair with Radley.'

'Hmm.' Alicia took a sip of her wine. 'That's certainly what Mel thinks.'

'Really?'

Alicia nodded. 'I was on the phone to her today as a matter of fact. We're going out for a meal together at the weekend. So what about Sebastian then? Did he deny the affair, or didn't you ask him?'

'He denied it. He seemed totally knocked sideways by the idea as a matter of fact.'

'Mel did say he could have had a second career as an actor.'

'If you'd seen him, Alicia, I think you'd have been convinced too. He was just matter of fact about the whole thing. Said he thought Radley was great, but she wasn't his type, any more than he was hers.'

'Hmm.' She got up and walked over to the fireplace. 'And did Sebastian make any move towards you today by any chance?'

'Oh no,' I said. 'I must admit I thought for a second he was going to, but the moment I told him the rumour I'd heard about him and Radley he pulled right back. He realised I'd thought he was going to get fresh and apologised.'

Alicia gave me a knowing glance over her shoulder as she put another log on the fire.

'It was nothing. He was always quite affectionate when we were at university. Demonstrative. He's like that with everyone.'

'Even Monica Smith?'

'Oh play fair! Okay, he's not like that with her, but with most people.'

'Especially you and Radley.' She smiled. 'Another glass of wine?'

I didn't stay for a second drink with Alicia. We were clearly going to come to blows if we maintained a presence in the same room for longer than five minutes or so. Instead I went up to the attic bathroom for a shower and stood there with the water running down my face, thinking. I remembered Darrick's touch, his mouth on mine, how certain I had been about belonging in his arms.

As I was drying myself, my mobile went. It was his number. When he'd said he was going away I had thought that might give me some space to work out what to do. Now clearly he was making the effort to get in touch, for whatever reason.

I paused, undecided. Should I pick up and confront him? And if I did, what would he tell me? Had he really only seduced me because I had access to some kind of information he needed? And how did it all involve Seb? My feelings for Darrick aside, I didn't know whether I should be trying to find out more, or stepping back and cutting myself off.

Maybe the only way forward was to talk to him. Then again, that was the approach I'd taken so far, and each time it had consistently led me deeper into whatever he'd been doing, without really providing me with the truth.

At last I made a grab for the phone, ready to press the green button, but it went dead. My indecision had made the choice for me.

Chapter Twenty-Nine

I was feeling churned up about Darrick and wound up about the journey the following day too. It made me queasy and so I wasn't in any hurry to go to the kitchen and make supper. I knew I'd have to get down there soon though, and I couldn't hold out on Sally forever either. She'd probably come up and bang on my door if I didn't go and feed her gossip before the hour was out. Still, I delayed my visit, faffing around with overnight stuff for Glasgow.

I was busy deciding what to wear for my dinner with Feldenstein when Darrick's text came in. It read: 'Didn't get much sleep when you were with me. Will get even less without you. (Sleep that is. Won't get any of the other.) Back Thurs eve. D xxx'.

It took me straight back to how I'd felt when we'd lain next to each other: that longing and a connection stronger than anything I'd ever known. Was it possible to feel like that and yet to be mistaken?

Suddenly I did want to go down to talk to Sally. Of course, I wasn't going to show her his message, but now I had to decide whether to reply or not. The need to share the gist of last night and get a second opinion had gone from being daunting to being essential.

I poured out the whole story of our date to her almost as fast as she poured out the wine. She made appreciative noises in all the right places, whilst I ploughed on, knowing the bombshell I had in store.

'Bloody hell,' was all she said when I got to the bit about the photograph. It was the first time I'd known her stuck for words.

'That just about sums it up,' I said.

At last Sally added, 'Just what is he playing at?'

'I wish I knew.' I took another slice of the pizza we'd ordered. It was becoming a habit, but at least we were both enjoying it in a relatively sober and decorous way this time. My hunger hadn't really come back, but I was aware of my journey the following day. It would be good to line my stomach, and not have a hangover.

'And what will you say to him when he gets back in touch?'

'He's already been trying,' I said, and explained about the call and the text.

'So the text was friendly?' Sally reached over to turn on her fan heater.

'It was intimate. He used just the same tone he did when we were last together.'

'So what are you going to do?'

I shrugged my shoulders. 'The thing is, Sally, the more I think about it, the more I'm inclined to take the same approach as before.'

She looked across at me. 'How d'you mean?'

'See him again, face him with it and ask for an honest answer.'

She opened her mouth to say something, but I got in there first. 'The fact is, when I found the photo, my initial reaction was that he must be using me.'

'Which does seem like a reasonable conclusion,' Sally said.

I nodded. I could hear the heat in her voice. 'I know. After all, I don't understand what he's up to, but if it's got nothing to do with me personally, then why not just tell me all about it in the first place?'

'Exactly.' She gave me a meaningful look.

'But now, I feel as though perhaps his interest in me is more genuine than I thought. I mean, he still seems keen and I can't see what else he hopes to gain from me … other than the things a man normally gains from a woman in a relationship.'

Sally sighed and I went on, 'Okay, so maybe he and Julia were lovers. Maybe he happened to be in London and because he knew about Seb he thought he'd find out more about him, out of some sort of morbid curiosity. Does that have to mean that he and I can't make a go of it?'

Sally got up, walked over to a corner cupboard and fetched a second bottle of wine. Once she'd topped us both up she sat down and I could tell instantly that she was about to take on the role of big sister, even though she was so much younger than I was. 'I'm sorry, Anna,' she said, 'but it seems to me that you've already given him a lot of second chances.'

I stared down into my glass and wished I hadn't come looking for encouragement.

'From the moment you met him he's been spinning you a line, one way or another,' Sally said. 'You've gradually found out bits and pieces of the truth, but only because you've dug and pushed.

'Do you really think he would even have told you his name wasn't Max if you hadn't made it clear you'd found him out?'

It was unpleasant to think back to our first meeting at The Old Faithful and realise that perhaps she was right.

'It's true that you could keep forgiving him and going back for more, but who's to say what you'd find out next, and what else he'd be prepared to keep from you if you carried on seeing him.' There was a seriousness and sympathy in her eyes that I hadn't seen before.

I tried to help her out, even though I was squirming inside. 'It's nice of you to be honest.'

She smiled. 'It's horrible doing it. The thing is, Anna, I've seen it happen before. No one I know has ever been out with anyone quite like Darrick, I have to say, but the forgiving, going back and getting hurt again cycle is very familiar. It's happened to me more than once.' She finished off her wine. 'Maybe you need to sleep on it and see how you feel in the morning. The trip to Glasgow sounds like a slog, but at least it'll give you the chance to get away, and a bit of distance might help you see things in perspective. You'll get some time to take stock.'

I went back upstairs feeling utterly deflated and gave in to the tears that had been threatening to arrive in Sally's room. In the end, I did as she'd suggested, and though I glanced at Darrick's text twice more before switching out my light, I didn't send a reply.

The next morning I woke at 5.30 a.m. and mulled over my plans for the day. I'd been meaning to take the train up to Glasgow, my mission being to do the Feldenstein job in one quick hit and then get home again.

Lying there in bed, I had plenty of time to consider what Sally had said. Maybe she was right about getting some distance from the situation I was in. And Darrick was away anyway, it wasn't as though there was any chance of him turning up.

I wondered about using my car instead, and then taking off somewhere on Saturday. I could stop overnight at a nice, faceless motel on my way home and make a weekend of it. It would be good to get some peace and quiet and I wouldn't have to face however many hours of small talk in a crowded carriage. I let the idea play around in my head between periods of dozing and by 6.30 a.m. I was up, and looking at a road map.

I went downstairs for an early breakfast and planned my day. If I set off quickly I could stop for a decent break over lunch and still manage to fetch up at my hotel with plenty of time to preen myself before my dinner date.

The drive was good. I set the radio to a music station and focused my mind on the journey, pushing out other thoughts. Suburbs slipped by in a blur and the idea of submitting a nice big diesel bill to Monica played pleasingly in the back of mind.

At the restaurant I had a surprise. Henry Feldenstein had been called away at the last minute and instead, I got his business adviser, one Morgan Rose. He was intense, and not a bit flirty. He had a jutting cleft chin, wore a dark suit and black-framed designer glasses and sat up very straight, listening to every word I said. No assertion I made went unquestioned. I had a feeling he'd see straight through the flattery that Seb had recommended for his boss, so I modified my behaviour accordingly. My conscious scheming increased my distaste for what I was doing. It was all so calculated. Still, I'd made my pact with Seb, and he'd helped me out with Lester. I just had to swallow my sensibilities and get on with it.

Eventually Rose cut across me and said, 'How much does Rice want to let Feldenstein see Oriel's work in advance of any other buyers?'

Seb had said this would happen and I had all the right answers to give him. There was no way he was going to exclude the possibility of a bidding war, so Feldenstein was out of luck. My job was to keep him sweet, yet desperate, by telling him the private view would be very exclusive. I was anxious that having to do this through

Rose might weaken the strategy, but there wasn't much I could do about that.

My worries about an endless evening, possibly winding up in some dodgy club, were dispelled. He was clearly one of those people who measured every minute of their time, never wasting a second on unnecessary fripperies. By 10.30 p.m. I was back at my hotel, soaking in a hot bath and rinsing away my manipulative performance, which I felt was clinging to me like dirt.

Even as I looked at the road map the next morning I was aware that my imagined intention of giving myself space was under threat. I wondered if, subconsciously, the idea had been at the back of my mind ever since I'd lain in bed that morning. If you looked at the route from Glasgow to London, veering off to stay overnight in the Lakes seemed like a very reasonable plan.

Though the Dales would make just as much sense, an inner voice argued. But I already knew I was going to ignore it.

Chapter Thirty

There was no earthly use in going to Cumbria. Julia had been dead for fourteen years and Seb's parents no longer lived there; there would be nothing to see, nothing to find out. But the desire to go built up as I sat over my hotel breakfast. The more partial information I had on Darrick, the more I wanted to know. It was like having an itch: the more I scratched the more I felt the need to.

And if I was going to go somewhere, it might as well be the Lakes: beautiful destination of my childhood holidays, and a place where I wouldn't need to get my bearings. After all, I only had one night. I booked myself into the Penrith Travelodge, keeping to my plan to stay somewhere faceless at least. Once I'd been back to my old haunts I could shut myself away for the night.

I drove straight to the hamlet where Seb and Julia had once lived; I couldn't help myself. It was the first time I'd been back since Julia's funeral and suddenly it seemed important to make the trip, a way of laying the past to rest. The urge made me realise how strong my sense of guilt was for sleeping with Seb so soon after she'd died. I suppose it was the knowledge that I'd wanted him, all that time they were together, that made me feel so bad. Crazy really, in the grand scheme of things, but now was the time to face up to it, and let it go.

It was raining lightly as I parked opposite Julia's old house. I got out and stood in the tall, damp grass, looking at the building. The smell of mud mingled with that of the wood smoke which wove its way from one of the chimneys. The house had changed. Someone had added a conservatory to its west side and there was an ugly brick-built garage near the entrance gates. But the atmosphere was the same; the grey stone was forbidding in the overcast weather. I felt the echoes of fourteen years earlier. I could still see Julia as she had been when I'd first met her: leaning against Seb, his arms around her, her silvery hair spilling over his jumper.

A man with a terrier came up the road. 'You lost, love?' he said, dragging me back to the present.

I shook my head. 'Just visiting an old haunt.' I paused a moment. 'I remember there was a village shop round here somewhere, but I can't recall how to find it.'

The man rubbed his chin. 'Could be Henley's? Just a mile up the road and then turn left and you'll see it.'

The shop had an old-fashioned bell and its sound took me back to my last visit. The effect was unexpected, giving me an odd pulling sensation inside. Memories tugged at my emotions as the smell of sweets and newsprint filled my nostrils. Even the woman behind the counter looked familiar, with her beaky nose and bright bird-like eyes. She wore a blue checked overall and had a bit of a hunch, as though she'd spent too many years stooping over her till.

I bought a newspaper, a Coke and a sandwich. 'You won't remember me,' I said, as I handed over my fiver, 'but I used to come and stay near here. I remember this shop.' I stood there thinking, letting the past come back to me. 'We used to buy you out of fudge when we were feeling hungry.'

The woman smiled. 'Family holidays was it? We get a lot of little ones in here, spending their pocket money on the local sweets. We still do the fudge, if you're interested.'

She waved a small, bony hand at some shelves near the

window and I went over and picked up a packet, feeling the familiar cellophane crackle under my grasp.

'Actually, it was when I was a bit older than that.' We'd bought the fudge as a morning-after-the-night-before treatment. Kill or cure. 'I used to come up to see Seb Rice and his girlfriend Julia, when she was living up at the big house.'

Her eyes widened. 'Oh, well I knew Sebastian and his mum and dad of course,' she said. 'That's how it is if you run the only shop in the village.'

'It must be nice, being at the heart of the community.'

She nodded, the corners of her mouth jumping up again, covering her face with laughter lines. 'You get to know everyone, so if you're interested in people it's the ideal job. I've been working here for thirty-eight years too, so I've seen all the changes. Villagers coming and going, babies born, growing up and getting married ...' Then her expression changed. 'And that poor child, Julia. I knew her too of course, though she wasn't around for as long as the Rices. It was her parents' house before she inherited, but they travelled so much I barely caught sight of them. It was mostly tenanted until Julia turned up.' She sighed. 'Terrible tragedy, wasn't it?'

'Awful,' I agreed. 'I couldn't believe it when I heard.'

She nodded. 'And young Sebastian seemed so smitten with her.' She leant forward on the counter, pushing grey hair out of eyes that glistened slightly. 'She was just coming out of the woods. She'd had such bad luck, poor pet, and there he was, ready to take care of her. I remember I was quite struck by the romance of it at the time – it seemed like the happy ending she deserved. And then ...' She tapped her fingers down on the counter. '... all of it gone overnight.' She took the extra money for the fudge and sighed. 'How is Sebastian now? Do you still see him at all?'

I nodded. 'He's all right, though I don't think he'll ever quite get over what happened.'

She shook her head. 'How could he, when all's said and done? We can't go through life untouched by our experiences. But he's coping?'

I explained about the success of the gallery, and how kind he'd been, giving me my job.

'Well, I'm glad to hear that,' she said. There was an odd look in her eye. 'I worried for him after she died. Even more than I might have done for a different person, I mean. He'd been looking after her of course, but, in many ways, my husband Harry and I thought she was the making of him.'

I looked at her but she waved away what she'd said with a quick flick of her hand.

'There, it doesn't matter now, in any case. And of course, Sebastian had lots of other nice friends to see him through.' She nodded in my direction, smiling, and then her eyes were far away again. 'I do remember there were a couple of larky lads he brought up here once.' She paused, rubbing the small of her back as though it hurt her. 'They certainly livened the place up. Mind, they did wake me up in the middle of the night one time. Seemed to think they could buy my sweets at two in the morning. But I didn't get up, and they bought me the most enormous bunch of flowers to apologise the next day, which was a nice touch.'

I smiled myself then. 'I'll bet that was Terry and Jez. They were always like that: extremely well meaning, but with a tendency to get overexcited.'

She nodded, beaming. 'That fits all right. And then there was one man who used to come and pick Julia up to go sailing on Derwentwater. He told me she was having lessons, but she didn't have a car, so he would drive over and get her. Always turned up in a Range Rover all covered in mud. They used to park across the road and come in for sandwiches. Of course, he must have been local though, so you may never have known him.'

I shook my head. Then it suddenly came to me that she might remember Julia's other visitors too. Knowing would hurt, but I made myself ask, 'You don't by any chance remember another friend of mine, do you?' and gave her a description of Darrick.

'Sounds like Irish colouring,' she said. 'Dark hair, and very blue eyes?'

I nodded.

She shook her head. 'Sorry love, you've got me there; we get so many visitors. The man who took Julia sailing just happened to stick in my head – because he was semi-regular. And then the two lads I mentioned made an impression because they were so young.'

'And noisy,' I added.

She laughed. 'In fact, I think that's what I meant when I said they were young. They were the same age as Sebastian, I suppose – but they acted young; full of the joys of youth. Some of the others he brought up here were just the opposite. From a different mould, so to speak; older and harder.' She reddened for a moment. 'Stuck up Londoners, Harry and I used to call them, I'm afraid. Proud of themselves they were, plumped up with their position in life. We often wondered which way Sebastian would go – whether he'd stick with the fun-loving, innocent sort, like your two friends, or if he'd be swallowed up by that adult, money-grabbing world.'

Back at the Travelodge I made myself a cup of black coffee to avoid the long-life milk and sat on the sofa, scalding my mouth as I failed to distance myself from Darrick.

True, the woman who ran Henley's had never come across him, but it wasn't reasonable to draw any conclusions from that. She couldn't possibly have seen everyone who visited. In any case, he and Julia could have met elsewhere – and the wedding photo proved that they had – but they couldn't have done this on a very regular basis. After all, Julia didn't drive, so whenever she went further afield she'd be relying on buses or lifts. Rather than putting the lid on any thoughts I had of seeing him again, the lack of information just made me more restless.

And then I wondered which of Seb's friends the shopkeeper had been talking about when she referred to that nasty, tainted adult world. None of my friends fitted the bill, but then Seb had probably already been making more high-powered contacts. I realised that whether I admired him for the fact, or wrote him off as an operator, entirely depended on my mood at the time.

Chapter Thirty-One

Back in London on Sunday evening, I went to get some things ready for supper in the kitchen. I was halfway through chopping an onion when Alicia appeared, as was her habit. I think she looked for any excuse to come and check up on either me or Sally, seeing it as her duty to watch over us and fulfil all necessary nagging duties.

'Eating in?' she asked. I hadn't treated her to the same résumé of my evening out with Darrick as I'd given Sally, so she was still probing for details in her usual unsubtle way. This particular tack was her method of trying to draw me out about any further dinner dates I might have planned.

'That's right,' I said, refusing to be goaded. 'I'm going to have spaghetti bolognaise.' I brushed my streaming eyes with the back of my hand. Bloody onions.

'Want any help?' Alicia appeared unaffected by the vapours.

'It may not end up being cordon bleu,' I said, 'but given that I learnt to cook it when I was ten, I think I can manage, thank you.'

She sniffed. 'It was just a thought.'

'Very kind.'

She peered at the mushrooms I'd bought. I could see her struggling with herself and then managing not to tell me that they weren't really the best sort, and that I hadn't been storing them correctly.

'So what are you up to tonight?' I asked, realising that she wasn't going to go away just because I was ignoring her.

'Tonight's my meet up with Mel,' she said. 'We're going to that Vietnamese place just off Leicester Square I told you about.'

'Lovely,' I said, swiping the mushrooms from under her nose and starting to wipe them with kitchen paper. I wondered if they would talk about Seb and his fictitious affair with Radley. 'So what's Mel up to these days?'

'Just starting up a new venture as a matter of fact,' Alicia said. 'She's opening up a restaurant.'

'Really?' I was interested. 'I thought she was still involved in galleries.'

She sat down at the table. 'Oh she is. She's still got joint ownership of the one in Putney. But this isn't entirely unrelated and it's quite ground-breaking. She's planning to have up-and-coming artists working whilst people eat. They're going to produce things quite quickly so that, if the clients want, they can buy the pictures and take them away there and then.'

'Will people want to buy them?' I was slightly sceptical.

'Well, Mel does quite well in the art world, you know. She's good at spotting talent just as Sebastian is, and the success of his gallery is partly built on what she achieved too.'

'So she'll pick the right artists?'

'I'm quite sure she will.' Alicia looked up and spotted the bottle of red I'd opened. 'Mind if I have some of your wine?'

I felt guilty I hadn't offered first and passed her a glass. It wasn't that I grudged her a share, just that I hadn't wanted to prolong her visit. 'So presumably she'll be after people who are early in their career,' I said, 'if they're willing to stand around sketching all evening?'

Alicia picked up her glass. 'She's aiming to fine tune the

whole thing to perfection,' she said. 'She'll pick people who are just bubbling up and starting to sell. She'll market them as the next big thing to the restaurant goers, so that their sketches will seem like a bargain, to be snapped up by the discerning art collector.

'And because they'll literally be the work of an hour, the artists will be willing to sell the drawings for a reasonable price. It'll be good from their point of view too, because they'll get to keep most of what they charge.' She took a swig of her wine. 'And let's face it, it's so much easier trying to sell people things when they've had a few drinks. After a well-oiled meal, Mel's quite sure her clients will be loose with their cash, and I suspect she's right. Also, she thinks the pictures will sell well to couples, as romantic mementoes of their evening out.'

'It sounds like an interesting idea,' I said, putting down the mushroom I'd been holding. 'So what cut will she get of the artists' profits?'

'Just a small percentage,' Alicia said. 'She'll make most of her money by having a hip new restaurant everyone wants to be seen at. And the artists that feature will be on display at the Putney gallery too.'

'So Mel's hoping to attract the restaurant goers back to her exhibitions to buy something more valuable?'

'That's right,' Alicia said, nodding.

'She must be planning to draw in a rich crowd.'

'Oh they don't have to be super rich; just the sort who'd be willing to spend the odd thousand to make themselves feel superior to their friends.'

'That is the super rich,' I said. 'And may I say I find you horribly cynical?'

'Or out of a love for art, of course,' Alicia said, topping up her glass. 'And in any case, Mel looks set to do very well out of the venture, even if they don't all spend thousands. The food'll be upmarket and she's having a champagne bar that people can visit on the way in. It will all help to create that feel-good atmosphere she's aiming for, to make sure the customers cough up.'

'So when's she launching all this then?'

'I'm not sure exactly,' Alicia said, 'but it must be quite soon because I know she's been interviewing for ...' She paused suddenly, her eyes taking on a knowing look. 'Ah! I see what you're getting at. You're wondering if the press have already got hold of it ...'

'And if not, whether I might be allowed first dibs,' I said. 'Well, the thought had crossed my mind. It would make an interesting feature, and I bet I could sell it to the arts section of The Enquirer.'

Alicia came over to where I was standing and patted me on the shoulder. 'I'm glad you're still thinking like a journalist,' she said. She picked up the mushrooms I'd been about to chop and put them back in their bag.

'What are you doing?'

'Well,' Alicia said as she slid my chopped onion into a Tupperware box, 'as far as I know she hasn't gone public on it yet. And now I think about it I can't imagine why I didn't suggest you should cover it before.'

She put the onions and mushrooms into the fridge. 'They'll keep until tomorrow,' she said, 'in spite of the condition they're in. Time is of the essence, so you'd better come along with me now, to Leicester Square. You might as well tackle Mel about it straight away. For all I know she's working out which journalists to call as we speak.'

I argued with Alicia all the way to the station. 'I can't just gatecrash your dinner,' I said. 'Mel's not expecting me.'

'I could call ahead if you like.'

'That won't help; it's still presenting her with a fait accompli. I'd rather you went and talked to her about it first. Then, if she's happy for me to interview her, I can arrange a time when she's not expecting a quiet evening out with a friend.'

Alicia looked round at me, her expression exasperated. 'Honestly, Anna, you do make the most tremendous fuss about everything. I'm quite sure she won't mind you being there, and she can always say no.'

Everything was consistently black and white as far as Alicia was concerned. She'd never been held back by tact or self-doubt. 'As a matter of fact,' she went on as the tube doors slid shut, 'she'll probably be delighted that you're with me. The only person from the gallery that she sees occasionally these days is Sebastian himself. And he's not going to be honest about what's going on. She'll want all the gossip.'

'Which will put me in a great position,' I said through gritted teeth.

'Fair's fair, Anna. If you scratch her back she'll probably scratch yours.'

We spent most of the journey in silence. I didn't really think Mel would mind me just turning up. If she'd wanted a heart to heart with Alicia (which seemed extraordinary) then she might be mildly annoyed or disappointed, but nothing more than that. No, what got me was simply Alicia's habit of railroading people – and possibly my own failure to stop her in her tracks. It was quite nice to be out and about though. Maybe it would stop me from thinking about Darrick for an hour or two.

From Leicester Square tube we walked along Cranbourn Street and then cut off down a side road to find the restaurant.

'Now,' said Alicia as we went in, 'don't go all shy and apologetic. It'll be good for her to get some publicity and you're just the person to handle it. Don't forget that.'

I had been feeling just about all right until she opened her mouth. The moment she assumed I would naturally be feeling unconfident and generally rubbish, my mood plummeted.

I hadn't seen Mel for a number of years. We'd met every so often in the early days of Seb's gallery, but since then I'd only seen her once, very formally, at a drinks do and then after that she and Seb had separated. I wasn't even sure I'd recognise her now, and the room was rather dark.

Alicia spoke to a waiter who ushered us over to a table in the far corner. 'He's going to lay an extra place for you,' she said to me. 'So you see, it's quite all right.'

'Are we early?' I said, glancing at my watch.

'Just by a few minutes, but Mel's a very good time keeper so I'm sure she'll be along any moment.'

The waiter came over with a large tray and transferred cutlery, napkin and glass to my place with great ceremony.

Just as he was leaving us again Alicia nudged my arm. 'Oh look,' she said. 'There she is.'

I glanced up and there was Mel, over by the doorway. I did recognise her of course. She'd had her hair cut short into a bob, but other than that she looked very much the same: statuesque and sleek.

Alicia waved a hand – unnecessarily, as the waiter was already directing Mel towards us – and she peered over, trying to make out who I was.

Then the strangest thing happened. She was about halfway from the door to our table and suddenly she just stopped. I'd swear it was when she realised it was me. And then it was all a bit embarrassing. I got the impression that she just couldn't think what to do. It was rather like watching a rabbit in headlights.

'What on earth's the matter with her?' Alicia said. She spoke quite loudly, so that anyone on neighbouring tables who hadn't already noticed the situation was alerted to the unfolding scene.

At that moment Mel seemed to snap out of it and gave Alicia a look, so that she got up and went over to have a quiet word – in the middle of the restaurant, with everyone watching. A minute later, Mel disappeared and Alicia came back to the table.

'What on earth's the matter?' I said. 'And where's she gone?'

'She's gone to the powder room.'

'And you're about to tell me I was right, and she doesn't want to talk to me about the new restaurant, aren't you?' I said, fiddling awkwardly with my specially laid fork.

'It's not something I could have foreseen,' Alicia said. 'And it's nothing to do with the interview.'

Thinking about it, I realised this must be true. Alicia hadn't had time to explain my presence in that much detail.

'But I'm afraid it won't work out, us pursuing that this evening,' she said.

I gave her a look. 'So what gives?'

'I don't know, but apparently she needs to see me alone. I said I'd explain before she comes back out again.' She looked across at me. 'Will you be all right getting back to Hampstead?'

I had the insane feeling she was about to check I had enough money on my Oyster card. 'I think I'll manage.' I got up and felt several tables' worth of eyes on my back. I was glad we'd managed to create some passing excitement.

'Oh and, Anna,' Alicia called, in a carrying voice as I made my way towards the door. I turned my head. 'Mel did say to say that she was very sorry to put you out.'

I bought a burger from a stand and held onto it with numb fingers as I walked through the wind, back to the station.

Really weird. That was the only conclusion I could come to. That Mel wanted a private chat with Alicia about something was fair enough. Odd choice of companion but still, there was no accounting for people's tastes. What made it peculiar was that she felt the need to hide in the ladies' loo until I'd left the premises; that and her reaction when she'd realised that it was me sitting there. She'd quite clearly not known how to handle the situation for several seconds. It wasn't often that a circumstance like that occurred.

Whatever she'd said to Alicia, I thought, as I stuffed the burger wrapper into a bin, it wasn't just that she didn't want to spend the evening with a third person. It was that she didn't want to spend the evening with me.

Chapter Thirty-Two

The following week plodded on without any further contact from Darrick. Twice I had composed a message to him, but each time I deleted it without pressing the send button.

It was dank and murky as I walked from the tube station into work on Thursday. He was due back that evening and I wondered if he would text again. Damp hung in the air, chilling me to the core and leaving a queer, metallic taste on my tongue.

I'd only been in the office for half an hour before Seb came in. The suit and shirt he wore were black. He had no tie; instead his top shirt button was undone. Privately I thought he looked great, but didn't like to say so in case it gave him the impression I was making up to him, which would be bad, or buttering him up, which would be worse.

'Morning,' he said, including Sinem and Elsie in his greeting. 'Anna, I could do with a word if you've got a minute.' Behind his back I saw Elsie give an elaborate roll of her eyes.

I walked down the corridor with Seb towards his office. As he closed his door behind us he said, 'Lawrence Conran's coming in today, as you know.'

I nodded.

'He was meant to be here this morning, before opening time, but he's just called to say he can't make it until this afternoon now.

'It shouldn't be busy though,' Seb went on, 'and he doesn't stand on ceremony, so that's all right. Besides, it'll be good for business if people see a serious buyer looking around.' He paused and glanced across at me. 'I'd like you to lead on his visit.' He moved back to perch on the edge of his desk and motioned for me to take a seat.

My immediate thought was that Lawrence Conran knew Darrick. Whatever Sally had said I felt a little leap inside me at the idea of spending time with someone who might know what made him tick. 'Sure,' I said, keeping my tone casual.

'I'm still livid with Lawrence honestly, over that business with Darrick Farron,' Seb said. 'But I can't risk getting into a situation where I'm grilling him about why he helped an imposter. Lawrence buys a lot from us and getting into some kind of argument with him would be too high a price to pay.'

'I understand,' I said. 'You'd like me to talk to him because I'll be able to stay neutral, and you can keep your distance until it's all blown over?'

He nodded. 'Partly that, and also two other reasons. Firstly I think he'll like you and buy more if he deals with you.'

I glanced up at him.

'Honestly,' he said. 'You did a great job with the guys from the public galleries, Anna. Even if Lawrence hadn't betrayed my trust, I'd still be sending you off to deal with him.'

To cover my embarrassment I said, 'And you mentioned there was another reason?'

'Well, it did occur to me that Lawrence might give something away about what was behind Darrick Farron's unorthodox visit. I don't imagine he'll provide you with the whole story or anything. And ...' He put up a hand, seeing the look on my face. '... I'm certainly not asking you to actively probe for information. That said, he's more likely to open up with you. If he does mention anything you think I ought to know, perhaps you could tell me?'

'Of course,' I said. 'But don't forget that Darrick ...,' I paused, realising I should use his surname. '... Farron did say he was at the gallery looking into one of your potential clients. Do you still want more information, even though his work wasn't directly connected with us?'

He nodded. 'Anything that affects my clients affects me too. And anyway ...' He got up, walked across to his window, and looked out across the rooftops. '... he hasn't been renowned for telling the truth so far.' He turned back to face me. 'If anything does crop up that indicates he has an interest in anything else – something that involves us more closely – I'd definitely like to be the first to know.'

I thought of the photograph and of how I'd ignored Terry's advice and still not told Seb about it. As soon as I'd seen Lawrence Conran I would have to weigh up the overall impression I got of Darrick's motives, and then decide what to pass on.

As Lawrence wasn't due until after lunch I'd assumed I'd have a clear morning to get through some of the jobs that had been piling up. Sinem had a variety of press releases for me to sign off, there was a phone call I needed to make to another one of Seb's rich buyers, and a whole load of text to write for a brochure. However, I'd only been back at my computer for ten minutes when the front desk called up.

'Visitor for you,' Debbie, the receptionist, said. 'Could you possibly come down? I'd bring them up but Baz has had to nip out.'

She hung up before I could ask who it was.

'Off out again?' Elsie asked, as I got up from my desk.

It couldn't be Darrick, I reasoned as I got into the lift. Despite the fact that he'd said he wouldn't be back until that evening, and that the gallery was the last place he'd visit, he was still the first person to come to mind when Debbie called. It was so ridiculous: that automatic little flutter of anticipation I couldn't quite suppress.

So if not Darrick, then could it be Alicia, come to inspect my desk? I couldn't think who else would drop in on me. Sally would be at work.

I got out of the lift and walked towards the foyer. Well, it definitely wasn't Darrick. I felt my insides right themselves as I looked ahead to see a middle-aged lady I didn't recognise. There was no one else by the desk.

As I got nearer she must have heard my footsteps and turned round to smile a greeting. 'You must be Anna, yes?' She held out a hand for me to shake.

She was one of the most elegant women I'd ever seen. Her hair was a beautiful slate grey, her eyes huge, and she was standing up very straight.

'My name is Nadine Constantin,' she said, after we'd shaken hands. 'Call me Nadine please. Do you have a moment? We could use your lovely gallery cafe perhaps?' She spoke with a soft French accent. 'I should explain that I am a friend of Zachariah Shakespeare's mother.' She put a finger up to her lips. 'It is not the kind of thing I can say in front of dear Zakkie,' she said. 'He hates to admit he even has a mother. It is far too conventional for him.'

I grinned, enjoying a momentary image of Shakespeare drinking sherry with ladies of a certain age in a respectable drawing room. 'I can imagine that.'

I went up to the cafe counter but the waitress seemed to recognise me and instantly volunteered to bring our coffees over, taking great care to make sure we were comfortable and had everything we needed. It felt very odd and, I suddenly realised with a guilty little shock, rather nice at the same time.

'So,' Nadine said, 'fate has been at work.'

I wondered what on earth was coming next.

'One day I was round having dinner with my old friends Beatrix and Reggie Shakespeare ...' I loved the fact that he had a father called Reggie. '... and in came Zachariah, fresh from being interviewed by the press, which tends to make him bad-tempered.'

'Oh dear,' I said, thinking of my own rather bizarre session with him. 'I'm sorry to hear that.'

'But no,' Nadine said, holding up a hand, 'do not be sorry because on this occasion he was in a very good mood and actually made quite amusing company at dinner.' She took a sip of her drink. 'It is good coffee,' she said, smiling again. 'So, we asked Zakkie about his day, and he said he had been interviewed by someone who was anything but ordinary.' She looked at me over the rim of her cup and raised her eyebrows. 'You my dear, evidently!'

I felt my cheeks go red. 'To be honest, I didn't feel I'd done a very good job at all.'

She put down her cup and waved away my comment with her hand. 'He said you did not stick to the script that his awful PR lady was insisting on. He said you let him talk about Chitty Chitty Bang Bang. He thought that was fun. Partly because it irritated the PR lady, admittedly.'

'Yes, I noticed she wasn't too pleased.'

Nadine laughed. 'Zakkie liked what you spoke about because it was ...' She sought the right word. '... quirky. That was how he put it. He does not want to seem ordinary, that is true, but what is ordinary about an artist, that paints such pictures, talking to the press about films watched by children?'

I hadn't thought of it like that before.

Other people had started to filter into the cafe now it was past opening time. The woman from behind the counter still found a minute to bring us a plate of cakes though.

'How delightful,' Nadine said to her, picking up a chocolate brownie. 'It must certainly have its rewards, working in this place.' She took a bite. 'But I presume you are just here for the short term? With all your other commitments, I mean?'

'I'm fitting my journalism around work for the gallery at the moment,' I said, not wanting to admit the fact that I might be letting my writing slide.

'But it must be hard to fit in all your interests, what with the bags as well,' she said, opening her eyes wide.

I swallowed a mouthful of coffee to provide thinking time. 'The bags?' I wasn't keeping up.

'Ah, I should have explained,' Nadine said. 'That is the coincidence of which I spoke. One day I hear your name at the house of Zakkie Shakespeare, and the next I hear it from my niece, Camille Bouton.'

The cogs had been whirring as my brain tried to get a grip, but now it was all starting to come together. Camille Bouton was one of the two names Sally had passed on to me after the posh party she'd been to.

'I was interested to hear from Camille about your bags,' Nadine said, 'and now she has shown me one, I am even more interested. So.' She took a Florentine biscuit from the plate. 'Then I knew you were a talented textile artist and a journalist.' She pushed the plate of cakes towards me. 'Quick,' she said, 'before I eat them all. And you write about what? Always art?'

'A real mixture,' I said. 'In the last few weeks I've written about a celebrity caterer and a New York talent agent.'

'So,' Nadine said, 'creative arts generally, from cooking, to acting, to painting. It is a nice mixture, and it must be so interesting.'

I was astounded. She was making the various things I had been dabbling in sound like a coherent career. Suddenly I was a textile artist and a creative arts journalist, giving up some of my valuable time to help out at the gallery. 'I do get to meet some fascinating people,' I said.

'Well,' Nadine said, after draining her coffee cup, 'I would love to exhibit your bags.'

I paused for a second, caught on the back foot once again.

'I run a crafts gallery you see,' she said, 'in Chelsea. Your bags would be a great success I know.' She reached into her own bag and pulled out a card. 'Could we meet to talk about it some more? You could come to my gallery and have a look round.'

'I'd love to,' I found myself saying. It would be fine so long as she didn't actually sell any. If someone really wanted to buy one I wasn't quite sure how I'd find the time.

'Perhaps you could come over after you finish here one evening next week? We could say Wednesday? Maybe six-thirty and we can have a drink?'

I nodded, making a note of the date.

'The other thing is,' Nadine went on, getting ready to walk back to the front entrance, 'I think I can introduce you to a lot of interesting people; you could interview them for your freelance work.' She looked at me. 'If that would be helpful?'

'It sounds wonderful. Thank you.'

She beamed again. 'Well, I look forward to returning your hospitality when you come and see me.'

I took the stairs back up to my office in a trance-like state. If it hadn't been for everything that was going on with Darrick, I would have felt extremely happy, though where it left my work for Seb, I didn't know. Of course, I had told Darrick I was intending to leave. Now I might have to find out if I'd really meant it.

Chapter Thirty-Three

By lunchtime I was still full of cake, so I worked through until Baz called up to say that Lawrence Conran had arrived. I found I was nervous about meeting him and, more specifically, about what he might say.

The man standing at the front desk was tall and broad like Darrick, but where Darrick was dark, Lawrence Conran was blond. I saw Baz indicating my approach and he turned to shake my hand.

He had a ready smile, reminding me for a moment of Alicia's Lester, and his handshake was warm and firm. I concluded that he must have come by car, or else have very good gloves. Outside, mist was rolling over the ground and the people coming in off the street were shivering. They had their coats pulled closely around them, only gradually letting them fall open as they reached the gallery interior.

'Would you like to go straight on up?' I said. 'Or you might prefer a coffee first?'

He shook his head. 'Straight on up's fine thanks. I've just had lunch.' He followed me to the stairs. 'No Seb today then?'

'He was very sorry not to be able to make it. He'd blocked this morning out of course, but this afternoon he's got back-to-back meetings. If it hadn't been for the change of plan ...' I let the sentence trail off and saw that Lawrence was looking at me, grinning.

'Of course,' he said, and I had a feeling he saw right through that little excuse.

On the second floor, where the general exhibition was,

there were several groups dotted around. 'I do hope you don't mind seeing it like this,' I said, indicating them. 'At least it's not too busy yet. We tend to get more people later in the afternoon.'

Lawrence shook his head, his shaggy hair falling over his eyes. 'It's no problem,' he said. 'Seb always wants me to come in the morning for some reason. Maybe it makes him feel less self-conscious about his sales pitch.' He laughed. 'I actually like being here with other people. I have my own ideas about what I want to buy anyway and, try as he might, Seb seldom changes them.'

He walked towards the far wall to begin his inspection. 'What might sway me is overhearing the comments the visitors make. That tends to be more significant.'

As he went quiet the conversation of a couple next to us came into focus. 'Just lovely,' the woman was saying. 'So pretty. And look, Jack! Doesn't that dog remind you of Auntie Bettie's spaniel?'

I looked at Lawrence and raised an eyebrow.

His stifled laugh came out as a snort. 'Well all right,' he said, 'I must admit nothing, not even a comment like that from a potential buyer, is going to make me put an offer in for that one. I hope Seb's not losing his touch.'

A moment later though he was looking very closely at a painting of the sea by someone called Zara Thomas. 'It's all right,' he said. 'The spaniel painting was clearly just a blip. I'd heard he'd got some of Zara's in. She's not selling for much over five hundred at the moment, but it's my bet that will rise a huge amount in the next couple of years.' He scribbled a note on the list of pictures I'd given him.

I was trying to concentrate on what he said, but at the same time Seb's words rang in my ears. *Lawrence might give something away about what was behind Darrick Farron's unorthodox visit.* He was hardly likely to do that unless I said something to lead him in the right direction. But did I want to? That was the question.

Although I didn't necessarily like the idea of having to report back to Seb, I wanted to know on my own account. As Lawrence worked his way round, passing some paintings without a second glance, whilst scrutinising others, I wondered how to broach the subject.

Lawrence was very efficient. I didn't feel I made any significant contribution to his spending spree at all. When he'd looked around the whole collection he went through what he was interested in, showing me the items on the price list.

'Seb's asking over the odds for this Bennett-Jones,' he said, leaving me feeling lame. Negotiating on price wasn't something I had the authority to handle. 'Would you tell him I'll take it for seven-fifty? Nine hundred's way more than it's worth at the moment. I'll take each of the others for the prices I've itemised.'

I could see he'd marked them all down, at least a little.

'Don't worry,' he said, seeing my face, 'the price list is just for the tourists really. Seb won't be expecting me to offer as much.'

As we left the room I was feeling rather green and inadequate. I obviously hadn't picked up on the protocol. 'Would you like to come to the cafe for a drink now?' I asked.

I knew it was probably more appropriate to take him to one of the plush meeting rooms upstairs, but I hadn't discussed this with Seb. If we went up now he might be busy wandering round, obviously not in back-to-back meetings, so maybe the cafe was safest. Besides, if I was going to probe about Darrick, I'd rather hear what Lawrence had to say on my own first.

'That would be very nice,' he said. 'Thanks.'

On our way downstairs I ran off a photocopy of Lawrence's list of planned purchases and handed it in at the front desk. 'The marked ones are sold,' I said, 'just in case anyone asks after them.'

Debbie mouthed, 'Wow,' and took the list from me, grinning.

At the cafe I was worried I might try the patience of the waiting staff, so once again I nipped up to the counter, having invited Lawrence to take a seat. 'I'll take everything over,' I said quickly.

'If we'd known you'd be bringing him down here ...'

'I know. I'm sorry – it was a spur of the moment thing.'

But Lawrence seemed very happy with the situation. He sat back in his chair – the picture of contentment – and watched the world go by, smiling broadly, until I returned with the same coffee and cake offering Nadine had been treated to that morning. I put down the tray and arranged things.

'So,' he said, when I'd laid the tray back on its stack, 'you've just started working here?'

Now was my chance. 'That's right,' I said, 'but although I've only been at the gallery just over a week, I did pop in to see Zachariah Shakespeare's private view.'

Lawrence grinned and took a sip of his coffee. 'You did, did you?'

I nodded. 'Funnily enough, I met a friend of yours there.'

He was laughing quietly now.

'Only he seemed rather confused. He told me at first that he was your brother.'

At this Lawrence laughed outright. 'Is Seb still furious with me?' he said. 'I assume that's what all this not-coming-down-to-see-me is about.' He looked at me. 'Though I'd far rather have you show me round than Seb any day. He always says far too much.'

'Well he'd probably have had quite a bit to say to you today,' I said.

'I knew it.' He relaxed back in his chair again, not looking at all disconcerted. 'Normally he takes me upstairs for a horribly formal cup of coffee in one of his trendy little meeting rooms instead of letting me in here. When you suggested coming to the cafe I knew he was seriously avoiding me.'

'I suppose he does have the right to be a little bit annoyed,' I said, taking care not to sound too judgemental.

Lawrence laughed again. 'Oh I suppose you're right. He's got no cause to take it all so seriously though. I've known Darrick for years and when he said he needed to come in privately to investigate one of his cases I was confident he'd be discreet.' He picked up his coffee. 'He's a professional. He can see trouble at a hundred paces and he's quite capable of dealing with it very efficiently without upsetting the apple cart.'

I felt a huge sense of relief that Darrick had given Lawrence the same explanation as he had me for coming to the private view. 'You're good friends then?' I asked.

He nodded. 'I've known him since school. Not that he's always that easy to keep track of. I guess that goes with his type of business.'

What he was saying was adding to my general impression of Darrick, but I really wanted to know more. If I didn't chance my arm he would finish his coffee and go, without me working out what to do.

The thought made me bold. 'It's an amazing coincidence that Darrick knew Seb's old girlfriend, Julia Thorpe.' I felt my cheeks flush, but it was too late, I'd said it. There was no going back now.

'You knew her too?' he asked.

I nodded. 'I was friends with Seb back in our university days, so I met her quite a few times when they were going out.'

'I see,' Lawrence said, picking up a brownie. 'Now you come to mention it I suppose it is a coincidence. Although there's the art world connection of course.' He looked across at me. 'Once you've been in the business for as long as I have, you start to feel it's a very small community indeed. The same people keep cropping up again and again.'

I was puzzled. 'Well, I know Julia wanted to study art,' I said. 'I remember her coming down to London to look round the various schools, but ...'

'Oh, I didn't know that,' Lawrence said. 'No, I was thinking of the artworks she owned.'

I felt my skin prickle. Here was something I hadn't been aware of. I knew I had to keep on acting my part, so I laughed, but even to me it sounded slightly shaky. 'Well I didn't know about those.' I paused for a moment. 'She was always quite shy you see. She didn't like to draw attention to herself and sometimes I feel I didn't know as much about her as I should have.'

Lawrence munched on his cake and then said, 'Yes, I remember Darrick saying she was quite reserved.'

Maybe he didn't get her into bed then, I thought.

'I suppose she talked to him about the pictures because she knew he was in the business,' Lawrence went on.

'Where on earth had she got them from?'

'Oh she hadn't collected them herself,' Lawrence said. 'They must have come to her via her family I suppose. I understand she didn't see a lot of her parents or spend much time at home until after they'd died. Darrick said it was only at that point that she came back from boarding school. It seems likely that she found out about the existence of the art collection then, when she started going through all the things that had been put into storage.'

'And what did Darrick think of what she'd got?'

'Oh he never saw any of the pieces, but he told me what she'd said about them at the time.' He took up his cup. 'He was quite excited by it.'

'Really?'

Lawrence nodded. 'Most of the pieces sounded like amateur works by family members. But a couple didn't fit. She had some photos of them, though they weren't very clear. Nonetheless, Darrick reckoned she could have been sitting on a real find. I must admit, I was more sceptical, but she'd done some investigating herself apparently. Don't laugh, but she'd come to the conclusion that the two in the photographs were lost works from one of Goya's Private Albums.'

'Blimey,' I said.

'Blimey would cover it very nicely, if it had been true.'

'Wasn't it then?'

'I don't think it can have been,' Lawrence said. 'To be fair on the poor girl she was only twenty or something, and not experienced in assessing works of art. The one thing that gave the story some credence was that Darrick looked into it and found her account of the drawings tied in with old descriptions of Goya's untraced works. I think Julia might have trusted him enough to let him take a look, only of course, you know what happened next.'

219

I nodded and he looked at me with kind eyes.

'Poor girl. She killed herself shortly after they met and so I presume the paintings all went off to some relative.' His gaze drifted across the room, but not as though he saw what was in front of him. 'Now either that relative never looked into their value, and they're still sitting in an attic somewhere gathering dust or, more likely ...' He faced me again. '... they investigated their provenance properly, found they weren't as exciting as Julia had hoped, and sold them at a jumble sale.

'One thing's for certain,' he added, 'if whoever inherited had knowingly found a couple of Goya's drawings we'd have read about it.'

Chapter Thirty-Four

In the stairwell I stood for a moment, thinking of everything Lawrence had said before he'd left. Had Seb known about the artworks? It was unthinkable that Julia wouldn't have told him, particularly given that it was his area of expertise, and yet if she had let on, he'd certainly never passed the information on to the rest of us.

I tried to work out what might have happened. Maybe she had shown him and he had spotted them straight away as lesser works. He could have broken the news to her, but she might have been disappointed, and wanted a second opinion.

And then, perhaps, she'd met Darrick by chance, found out about his expertise, and decided she might check to see if he reached a different conclusion. That seemed possible. But what was Darrick up to now? There were too many things I didn't understand.

Up above me I could hear someone else entering the stairwell. After a moment I identified the voice as Radley's; her familiar, sour tone echoed down the concrete descent towards me. I caught the second half of her sentence: '... you'd just be honest with me in the first place.'

Then I realised it was Seb she was with. I didn't manage to catch his reply, but whatever it was, it was short. By the time they rounded the corner I had started walking up towards them, so as not to look peculiar.

I could see Seb consciously relaxing his frown when he saw me, and he stepped away from Radley. 'All right, Anna?' he said. Then he spotted the list in my hand and sighed. 'How much has the old bugger tried to knock off this time?'

When I showed him the paper he raised his eyebrows. 'He's bought more than usual.'

'Well it must be down to your taste then,' I said. 'I didn't say a thing. He seemed to want peace and quiet.'

Seb smiled.

'But don't go getting all smug,' I added. 'He hated the one with the spaniel.'

'Ah yes,' said Seb. 'A bit of a wild card, that one, but I bet someone'll buy it. Not everyone shares Lawrence's high-brow tastes.'

I thought of the woman we'd overheard and wondered if he might be right. 'Seb,' I said. 'I wonder if I could have a quick word later, when you're back upstairs.'

He nodded, gave me a look that told me he knew I wasn't going to ask about my holiday allowance, and then carried on his way. Radley nipped down just behind him, the friction between them palpable.

In the end we arranged to go round the corner to the pub for a drink after work. 'By the look in your eye, Anna Morris, I have a feeling I don't want to have this conversation in the office,' was all he said.

He looked concerned when I met him by the front desk and, as we walked along a side street next to the gallery, he put an arm around my shoulders.

'I'm going to buy you a stiff drink,' he said, 'and you're going to tell me all about it. Agreed?'

I nodded. Whatever was behind all this, it was time for a bit of honesty on my part. I just hoped what he told me in response would be reassuring. Something was making my insides feel taut as a drum.

He drew me in closer and gave me a Seb-like hug.

At that moment, the lights of a car, parked right next to us, flashed on. A window descended smoothly and Lawrence stuck his head out. 'Seb old man!' he said in a delightfully hearty tone. 'You've managed to escape all those awful meetings at last.'

Seb looked at me and raised his eyes to heaven. 'Caught,' he said. 'I thought you'd gone hours ago.'

'I had another appointment round the corner so I thought I'd make the most of the permit your lovely receptionist gave me and leave the old banger here.' It was a Jaguar. 'So, how long are you going to make me sit on the naughty stair?'

At last Seb laughed, releasing me from his grasp to walk nearer to the car. 'Oh all right,' he said. 'I forgive you. Nice choice of paintings by the way.'

'She's a great saleswoman, your Anna,' Lawrence said, giving me a mock salute. I was glad it was too dark for him to see me blush.

'We're just off to The King's Head,' Seb said, 'if you want a quick drink before you head off?' I could tell he didn't want extra company, but felt he ought to ask.

'No, no,' Lawrence said, 'I'll let you two get on with it, thanks all the same.' And he drove off up the road, the car's engine purring like a pedigree cat.

In my bag there came the sound of a text coming in. I peered in at my phone for a moment. Darrick.

Seb seemed to hear my intake of breath. 'Trouble?' he said. 'Do you want to deal with it?'

I shook my head. 'It doesn't matter,' I said. 'I'll leave it until later.'

Chapter Thirty-Five

'You're very quiet,' Seb said, looking at me as we went through the oak swing door and into The King's Head. It wasn't too busy and we found a place in the snug to the left of the bar. I opened my mouth, anxious to dive in and get it over with, but Seb said, 'Drinks first,' holding up a hand, and so I waited until I'd got a gin and tonic in front of me before I started. As I worked out where to begin, Seb picked up his whisky. I noticed the whiteness of his knuckles as he clutched the glass.

'So,' he said, looking up at me at last. His eyes were wary, his face pale next to the black shirt.

So. I took a deep breath. 'I ended up seeing Darrick again. It's already several days ago now, and I haven't contacted him since.' I pushed out my words in a rush and waited for him to say something, but he just looked back at me, his jaw set.

'I wasn't intending to deceive you, or let you down,' I said, 'but I really did like him. I thought if I saw him one more time it would help me make up my mind. I took what you said seriously, so I knew I had to decide whether I wanted to give him up, and stay on at the gallery, or whether ...' I took a large swig of my gin. '... I actually liked him so much that I'd have to hand in my notice. It wasn't a judgement I could make without seeing him one last time.'

Still Seb said nothing. It was almost as though I was alone in the room, talking into a vacuum. 'Seb?' I said at last, wanting some kind of response before I carried on.

Eventually he said, 'So, did it help you to decide, being

with him again?' He seemed to have to drag his mind back from somewhere far away to form the question.

'That's not really what I came to discuss with you,' I said. 'It's what I've found out that's important.'

Seb took a mouthful of whisky. 'I see,' he said. Then after a moment's pause he went on, 'Though I don't understand why you've waited until now to tell me whatever it is that you know.'

'At first I wasn't sure that I had to, but after what Lawrence said to me today, I knew there was no getting away from it.'

Seb's eyes flicked away from mine. 'So what is it, then, this thing that can't be avoided?' he said at last.

So bit by bit I explained – without admitting how far our relationship had gone – about how I'd come to find the photograph of Julia at Darrick's flat.

For a second he was silent, and I was momentarily conscious of the noise around us: the clinking of glasses, the laughter, Ruby Tuesday emanating from a jukebox, all permeating the small, private space we shared.

At last he said, 'What sort of a picture was it?'

And I knew what he was thinking. 'Perfectly innocent. It was taken at a wedding, by the look of it. Julia was wearing a waitress's outfit so I think she must have been there to earn some extra cash. There were several other guests in the photograph too.'

His expression was still guarded.

'You can see why I didn't come and talk to you at that point, can't you, Seb?' I said, leaning forward. 'I mean, what good could it do? Okay, so Darrick had had some kind of fleeting connection with Julia at some stage, but I felt bringing it up could only hurt you.' I sat back again and took up my glass. 'I wouldn't have come to you at all, except that what Lawrence told me today makes me think you do need to know. Have a right, even.'

Seb's eyes seemed to sharpen their focus and at last I felt I had him with me. He sat back suddenly, his shoulders sagging, and let out a long breath.

'I'm sorry,' I said. 'I can understand if you think I should have come to you sooner. I just did what I thought was best at the time.'

'I can see that,' he said, draining his whisky. 'It's just so extraordinary to think of Julia knowing Farron. I knew she'd done the odd stint of waitressing at events, to bring in some cash, but I didn't know she'd made any friends through it.' He paused and looked up. 'Do you think they were more than friends?' His eyes were still tired, but a flash of anger brought back some of their usual vitality.

I shook my head. 'I wondered, just for a moment, when I first found the photo,' I said, 'but Julia wasn't the sort, Seb, was she?'

'No,' Seb said, letting out a breath, 'you're right. So what was it that Lawrence said, then, to make you feel you had to talk to me?'

I felt my stomach tense. 'I pretended Darrick had been quite open about knowing Julia,' I said. 'I got Lawrence into conversation about it that way, saying what a coincidence it was.'

'God, Anna, when I said you might be able to find out a thing or two, I didn't know just how adept you'd be at it.'

'It was a spur of the moment thing,' I said, taking a sip of my drink. 'Anyway, Lawrence said that it wasn't such a coincidence really, given that you, Darrick and Julia were all involved in the art world.'

Seb raised his eyebrows.

'I was surprised too,' I said. 'I told Lawrence I'd known Julia wanted to study art, but I'd thought that had been the extent of her interest.'

'And?' Seb said.

'And then Lawrence mentioned her collection of artworks ...'

Seb frowned. 'What?'

'Exactly. I asked about them, and Lawrence said she'd described them to Darrick in great detail and shown him photographs of a couple. Apparently Darrick had been quite excited about the whole thing.' I paused. 'Seb, Lawrence Conran says that Darrick and Julia both thought a couple of them might have been missing drawings from Goya's Private Albums.'

Seb brought his glass down hard on the table, his eyes fixed on mine now. After a minute he said, quite quietly, 'No, Anna, that can't be right.'

'Lawrence didn't reckon it was,' I said quickly. 'He was quite sceptical about the whole thing. Darrick never got to see them apparently, although Lawrence thought Julia might have shown them to him if she hadn't died.' I could feel the implications of all I was telling Seb hanging heavy in the air between us. I wanted Lawrence to be right and the works by Goya to have been a fiction.

'That's not what I meant,' Seb said, his voice so soft I could hardly hear the words. 'She would have told me, that's my point. She can't have had those drawings, because if she had, I would have known about them.'

His hand shook, and I waited for him to compose himself. Eventually I said, very quietly, 'It really does look as though she had some kind of collection though. Lawrence remembers Darrick telling him about Julia's description of them at the time, and Darrick went so far as to check old written descriptions of some of Goya's missing works.'

'And did they match?' he asked.

I nodded.

For some moments Seb sat with his head sunk onto his upturned hands. When he looked up at me his face was devoid of all colour. 'I know why she didn't tell me,' he said, and once again now, his eyes had that faraway look.

'Why?'

His voice cracked as he spoke. 'What do you think I'd have wanted her to do, Anna, if I'd found out she had some major works of art stashed away?'

I was at a loss. 'I don't know. Display them maybe, perhaps at the gallery you were planning to open, to draw people in?'

He shook his head. 'I'd have wanted her to sell them. That's what I would have tried to persuade her to do. To me, art's business. I make my money out of people who want to own something they regard as beautiful, but I don't necessarily see it myself. I know what other people will love, but without ever experiencing the same emotion they do. I would have had no patience with her hanging onto something that could have made us a fortune. No.' He paused to drain his drink again. 'I would have been a shit about it. Maybe, once I'd had the gallery all set up, I'd have wanted her to have the sale there. Think of the publicity.'

'Would you really?' I reached over to touch his arm. 'I think you're still punishing yourself, Seb. You always seem to take the blame for what happened to Julia, but what she did was beyond your control.'

'Whatever. If I'd known about the drawings I wouldn't have left the decision up to her. I'd have bullied her and made her life a misery. I wanted her to let go of her parents' possessions, you see, to make a clean break of it.'

'Well, she seemed quite interested in finding out the value of the drawings,' I said. 'Maybe she wanted to sell them.'

Seb shook his head. 'She didn't want to part with anything that had belonged to them. That was one of the reasons she was so short of money.' He looked up at me, his eyes dry. 'I wasn't very understanding about her approach,' he said. 'I mean, I pretty much hated my parents. They never had any time for me, only ever cared about making money and, to me, Julia's parents seemed to have been from the same mould. They'd packed her off to boarding school, mostly not even been in the same country as she was.

'I wanted her to think the way I did: that parents like that are no parents at all. It would have made me feel less alone if she'd shared my feelings. But she didn't. She'd adored them and she clung on to all their old things as though nothing else mattered.'

He slumped in his chair. 'I'd hoped she'd sell everything and come south to be with me; I knew I needed to be in London. But she never would have. She just wanted to stay up in that old house with the walls crumbling round her.

'I feel awful about it now,' he added, 'but I was actually jealous of the things she'd been left. It was as though she loved them more than she loved me. That was why I wanted her to get rid of everything. What was left over just tied her to her past and kept us apart.'

'I guess she was still grieving,' I said. 'I suppose she might have come round eventually, if …'

'If she'd been allowed to live long enough,' Seb said, cutting across me.

If she'd been allowed … Seb's words echoed in my head as I went to the ladies'. I bought us another round of drinks on my way back. In the snug, Seb had gathered himself together, sitting up straight, his eyes clear.

He took the whisky from me. 'Thanks.' His tone held new purpose. 'My turn to tell you some things, Anna,' he said and I waited for him to begin.

'How do you feel about Farron now?' he asked.

I shrugged. I still couldn't think of him without remembering the sensation of our bodies together – and me deciding to give up my job, and placing my total trust in him – but Seb's tone made the hairs on my neck prickle. 'I don't know what to think,' I said at last.

'Let me tell you some things that might influence you then,' he said, taking a large slug of whisky. 'After Julia died, all her possessions went to her only living relative, an elderly aunt up in Aberdeen who had no family.'

I didn't know exactly what was coming, but even at this stage I knew I didn't want to hear it. As Seb spoke, Darrick's face filled my mind, his laughing eyes and sensuous mouth.

'The aunt, Dorothy Mackay, had no room for a load of heirlooms in her house, and no children or grandchildren who might feel sentimental about family belongings. That being the case, she decided to sell off all Julia's things: everything she had owned, her parents' house, the lot.'

He looked at me with steady eyes. 'Despite being elderly and alone she spared a thought for me, and invited me up to see what was in the sale, in case I wanted to pick out something as a keepsake.' He let out a hollow laugh. 'It was ironic really. At last there was a grand letting go of all the items that Julia wouldn't part with, but for that to happen I had to lose her first.'

'So did you go up, before the sale?'

Seb nodded. 'I suddenly found that Julia had been right after all. It does help to keep something. There was a pendant she used to wear, with a little Gaelic knot on it. I took that and I still keep it in a box in my bedroom.' He looked at me. 'In the way of artworks, there were several watercolours painted by Julia's mother and a couple of oils by a family friend.' He sipped his whisky. 'And that was it. There were no drawings at all. And nothing that Julia could possibly have thought was by Goya.'

I felt my insides go cold, as though someone was slowly dripping meltwater from an icicle into my stomach.

Seb looked me in the eye with that cool blue gaze of his. 'Between Julia telling Farron about those drawings and the sale, two things happened. Julia died, and the works disappeared.'

Chapter Thirty-Six

Seb was oddly calm now, and measured. 'If they were genuine, and Farron took them, he could never have sold them on the open market of course, but he wouldn't have needed to. He had the perfect connections to arrange a private sale; the sort that no one ever hears about. Maybe someone put in a bid for them before Julia was even dead. I told you some of the people he deals with are ruthless. With a prize like that he wouldn't have had to look too hard for a buyer.'

'But, Seb, it doesn't make sense,' I said. 'I mean, I hear all you're saying, but if it's true, why on earth would Darrick be on the scene now? Who carries out a theft like that and then risks coming back years later to make himself look suspicious?'

Looking up at Seb I was shocked to realise he was about to give me an explanation. I didn't want to know. Everything inside me was in denial, pushing away the evidence he was giving me.

'When Julia died,' Seb said, 'I was just as sure as anyone that it was suicide. She'd been through an awful time, and she was young and often alone. God knows I hadn't given her enough support. I was convinced it was at least partly my fault.' He rubbed his forehead. 'Apart from anything else, the police believed she'd killed herself too. I was younger then and of course I thought if they were satisfied with that conclusion then they must be right.'

I clutched my glass and waited for him to continue.

'It was only later that I began to wonder,' he said, staring into space, not seeming to see the room around him. 'Just before she died, Julia called me and she was actually quite upbeat. I started to think about that call, and to wonder if she'd been coping better than I'd thought.'

He looked at me. 'It was one of those feelings that gradually built up, until after a while I really convinced myself that she hadn't taken her own life. We'd had plans,' he said, 'and in fact …' A look of realisation suddenly came into his eyes. '… one of the things that she mentioned during that last call was that she had something to tell me. She seemed quite excited about it.'

He paused for a moment and then went on slowly, almost as though I wasn't there, 'I wonder if she'd decided to let me in on the existence of the drawings after all. Anyway, her excitement and apparent happiness then jarred with the verdict of suicide. Or at least I started to think so. I didn't know enough about it, but I kept wondering whether I'd let her down by accepting the official version of events. I never questioned it at the time.'

'I'm sure it's only natural to look back and worry about these things,' I said. 'But maybe she was up one minute and down the next.'

'Possibly,' he said. 'That could have been the answer. But I went through a patch where I was sure it hadn't been as they'd thought. I'm afraid I allowed myself to get a bit obsessive about it. You know how these ideas can fester, whether they're right or wrong.'

'It's understandable.'

'Anyway, one day when I was feeling especially low – about six months ago it must have been – I sounded off about it at a bar in town. I'd had a few too many.' He grimaced. 'Well, a lot too many to be honest. So I told anyone who would listen that I didn't believe Julia had killed herself.'

I looked at him blankly, not seeing where this was leading.

'The point is, Anna, one of the people with me was Lawrence Conran.'

I still hadn't caught up.

'You're absolutely right about it making no sense for Darrick Farron to come back here after stealing those drawings – if he did take them,' Seb said. 'But, Anna, what if word got back to him via Lawrence that I didn't believe Julia had committed suicide?'

I was silent, staring into my glass.

Seb rested his hands on the table. 'What if Farron killed Julia? He had a damned good motive. Then he hears, via some general chit-chat with Lawrence, that I'm saying I don't believe the suicide verdict. What then?'

I waited, not wanting to admit I even understood what he was saying. 'I still don't see why he'd be hanging around,' I said.

Seb sat there necking his whisky. I think he was hardly aware of how much he'd drunk. His attention was wholly focused on his idea. At last he said, 'Maybe what he heard got him worried. Could he be checking for loose ends that might give him away, or provide proof against him? He'd want to find out why I'd stopped believing Julia had killed herself.'

He waited for me to reply.

'It's all very speculative,' I said at last.

'Even if he didn't kill Julia I'd bet my life he knows where the drawings went,' Seb said. 'And the timing of her death was very convenient for him. Think of all that secrecy. If things had gone his way we might all still be sitting here thinking of him as Max Conran.'

His thoughts echoed Sally's so closely that I shivered for a second.

'Try to remember what you talked about,' Seb went on. 'Did his questions make any sense if what I'm saying's true?'

I didn't reply. I'd already been mentally running through everything Darrick had asked me about the old days. He'd wanted to know how well we all knew Julia, how often we'd gone up to see her. Was he trying to find out if the rest of us had had any idea about the drawings?

'Well, Anna?' He wouldn't let it go.

'Possibly, Seb,' I said. 'But think about it. What you're saying doesn't hold water. What about Lawrence Conran for instance? Darrick hadn't kept the existence of the drawings a secret from him. Wouldn't he have, if there was anything underhand going on?'

I seized on this point and held on to it for all I was worth. He might not worry about what Lawrence said to people these days, given that he had been sceptical about the provenance of the drawings anyway, but surely Darrick would never have mentioned them to him in the first place if he'd seen a way to make money out of them.

Seb paused, but only for a second. 'The attack on Julia might not have been planned,' he said. 'What if he suddenly had the opportunity to get rid of her? It would have been too late to take back what he'd said to Lawrence then, but he might have risked it anyway, for the sake of such a valuable reward.'

Would he have? But even as I decided I couldn't believe it, my mind ran through the few indisputable things I knew about him: he was assuredly a liar and an adventurer; rich and with a penchant for taking risks …

'Anna, you must keep away from Farron now,' Seb said, breaking into my thoughts. 'If he thinks you're onto him you could be in danger. Will he know you've seen the photo of Julia?'

'Probably not,' I said. 'I put the album back where it was, so unless he talks to Lawrence and they discuss what I said, it should be okay. And I think Lawrence just saw the conversation we had as general small talk, so he probably wouldn't refer to it.'

It really depended on how often they were in touch, I reflected. If they went out for a drink tomorrow there was a ninety per cent chance Lawrence would recount our conversation, whereas if they didn't see each other for a month or so, he would probably have forgotten all about it.

'What are you going to do?' I asked Seb.

He shook his head slowly. 'I'm not sure. I need to work out what we've actually got in the way of evidence.' He looked up at me. 'I can't let this lie, Anna, that's for certain. I've got a friend whose sister's CID. Perhaps I could run it past her and see what she advises. But in the meantime, so long as I know you're steering clear of him, at least that will be one less thing to worry about.'

But then I suddenly remembered Darrick's text. He was bound to try to contact me that very evening, and I was going to have to work out what the hell to say.

We walked to Waterloo and went our separate ways so I could take the Northern Line back to Hampstead. 'Keep your distance from him now, Anna,' Seb said again, as we parted in the crowds. 'I really mean it. He may not know where you are now, but he knows where you go to work each day.'

And he knows where I live, I thought.

It was on the platform that I felt someone clutch at the back of my coat.

The area was crowded with people and Darrick

236

manoeuvred me round so that he had tight hold of my shoulder, between my collar bone and my neck, leaning in to push me back against the tiled wall. I guess to outsiders it might have looked as though he was about to kiss me, but the fingers that dug into my flesh were anything but gentle.

'As a matter of fact I do know where you are *now*,' he said, 'as you can see.'

The implication of his words hit home. How had he been able to follow me so closely?

'It's always been rather hard to know whose side you're on,' he said. 'But I think the matter's becoming a little clearer now.' His fingers tightened painfully and I held my breath.

I knew he couldn't do anything. We were surrounded by people – the noise rang in my ears – and, if I wanted, I could shout and make a fuss. I suppose it was only shock and disbelief that stopped me from doing just that.

'No one likes being spied on, Anna. You should remember that. At least I know how the land lies now.' His eyes flashed with anger.

And then suddenly he let go of me, and disappeared into the crowds as quickly as he had come.

Chapter Thirty-Seven

'Are you sure you're all right?' Sally was horrified when I told her what had happened and all that Lawrence and Seb had had to say. She was up in my room, pacing around and wanting to do something. 'You really ought to go to the police, Anna. That's what Alicia would say.'

'Don't tell her for God's sake,' I said, sitting down on the chair by my desk. 'I don't think I could stand a dose of Alicia right now.' Although I'd held my nerve at the station, and had known I wasn't really in danger, I hadn't stopped shaking since, and felt as though I'd gone down with the flu.

Sally was putting the kettle on. 'Have you got milk and sugar up here?' she asked.

I laughed, but the sound was shrill and anxious. 'You're not thinking hot, sweet tea are you?'

'It's not just a rumour. It really does work,' Sally said, heading for the door to go and fetch what she wanted.

It was only at that point that I remembered the text from Darrick again. I took my phone out so that I could read it before Sally came back. 'Did u get my text on Sunday?' It read. 'Back in London now. Can we meet?'

I thought of the sequence of events. He'd called me the night after we'd been together and I hadn't picked up. Then later he'd texted me and I hadn't replied. He'd tried again after work today and instead of reading what he'd written, I'd gone off to the pub with Seb. I wondered what had happened then.

Perhaps he had known that Lawrence had been due to visit the gallery. Maybe, when he hadn't heard from me, he'd called him and asked if I'd been around. Lawrence would have been able to tell Darrick exactly where I was. After all, he'd seen me go off arm in arm with Seb, and Seb had even told him the name of the pub where we were headed.

Small matter for Darrick to follow us there, and tail me to the tube station, especially given the line of business he was in. I wondered if there was any way he could also have heard our conversation in the snug, but I thought not.

'Here we are,' Sally said, bustling back in and making her sugary concoction. 'Now drink that and tell me you don't feel better.'

I sipped the tea and felt sick. 'Thanks, Sally,' I said.

'So, what are you going to do about all this then?' she asked. 'If Seb's right about Darrick you can't just carry on as normal.'

'I'm certainly not going to turn my back on people at tube stations any more,' I said, experimenting with a laugh.

Her eyes narrowed. 'It's no joking matter.'

'No,' I said. 'I know. But …' I knew what she'd say if I said I still thought Seb was wrong.

'You're not going to tell me you need more convincing are you?'

'Not everything adds up,' I said. 'For a start, Seb feels it's terribly incriminating that Darrick found out all about these drawings just before Julia died.'

'Well, don't you agree?'

I could tell she was losing patience. 'It looks awful, of course I agree,' I said. 'But what makes him think it has to be Darrick that's involved? After all, Lawrence Conran knew all about the drawings too. It could just as easily have been him. I mean I'm not saying it was. Lawrence seems like a nice guy. But if you take first impressions out of it, they each of them had enough knowledge to give them a motive.'

'Yes, but it's not Lawrence who's been lying about his identity and keeping his friendship with Julia a secret, is it?'

I sighed. 'It's not just Lawrence. Several things have struck me as odd lately.'

'Like?'

I tried to pull together the various incongruities in my mind, but felt sure they wouldn't be enough to convince her.

'Like why Radley's meeting with Seb's old professor behind his back, and why Seb's ex-wife cut me dead in front of a restaurant full of people.'

She perched on my bed. 'Yes, and weirdest of all, why you still feel sympathy for a guy who makes a habit of stalking you and has now added threatening behaviour to his repertoire. Look, Mel's probably jealous of you and Radley's a schemer. Ours is not to reason why. It's got nothing to do with this business.'

'Except ...' I tried to argue my way out of her logic. '... except that Maxwell-Evans and Mel are both contacts from the old days, just like Darrick is.'

Sally shrugged her shoulders. 'Mel's current. You only bumped into her because she's still friends with Alicia. And as for Maxwell-Evans, he's an arts contact, right, if he's Seb's old professor?'

I nodded.

'So maybe Radley's after a job with him, and doesn't want Seb to know about it until after it's all fixed up. You might try looking at the most plausible explanations for a change – particularly when it comes to the most plausible explanation for Darrick's actions, viz, he's a crook.'

She looked at me for a moment, obviously noting I was about to say something else, and let out a heavy sigh. 'What is it now?'

'Well, it did occur to me that if Seb's barking up completely the wrong tree, Darrick's behaviour this evening could still be explicable.'

Her eyebrows shot up. 'Well this I have to hear.'

'He'd been trying to get hold of me ever since we saw each other last week and I hadn't taken his calls or replied to his texts. He was already a bit jealous of Seb and then, lo and behold, he finds out from his friend Lawrence that I've gone out on the town with him, when, in the normal way of things, I should have been his date for the evening.'

'Anna, did the feminist revolution somehow pass you by? It is not all right to ram someone up against the wall of a tube station just because you don't like their choice of companion.'

My head was starting to ache. 'No, no,' I said. 'I know that.' I knew I was going to start crying in a minute. The numbness that had enveloped me was wearing off. 'But I'd rather he was jealous than a murderer.'

Before she left my room that night Sally said, 'Just promise me you'll take care on your way to work tomorrow. If he comes within fifty metres of you, you're to call the police.'

After she'd left me I flipped open my laptop and sat there for a moment, irresolute. Of course, Sally might well be right about Radley schmoozing Maxwell-Evans in the hope of landing a new job. She was just the sort to do all her manoeuvring in secret, and also not the type to stay second in command for long. I Googled Maxwell-Evans to see if he might be in a position to further her ambitions.

He'd done well for himself. He was tipped for a peerage, according to a piece I found on the BBC News website. The article also revealed that he was on the boards of several top art institutions and there was a photo of him alongside a couple of minor royals. I paced up and down my room. He would certainly have it in his gift to find Radley some nice high-powered role. On the other hand, it was possible Radley and he were meddling in Seb's affairs in some way behind his back. If either of them had something to hide – even if it was unrelated to Darrick – I wanted to know about it.

In the end I emailed Seb. I didn't want to come across as a bitch, all eager to drop Radley in it, so I tried to be subtle, dressing the message up with some other queries about work. Then, in a cheery little aside, I added, 'By the way, are you and Radley working on any new projects with Professor Maxwell-Evans?' This way I might be able to find out the background to the situation without stirring things up.

The following day I looked around very carefully on each stage of my journey to work but saw no one I recognised.

For some reason I couldn't account for, I didn't want to tell Seb about my run-in with Darrick. It didn't make any difference to what had been said the night before.

So instead of dropping by his office, I went straight to my own. I tried to focus on normality and shut out everything else, going through the motions of a catch up with Elsie and Sinem and then getting down to the business of the day.

'By the way,' Sinem said, 'Monica wants to see you.'

She saw my face. 'Sor-ree! More about budgets I think. Something to do with the brochure you've proposed for the Jabez Clark exhibition.'

'Oh yes. I was trying to get away with some silver on it, to tie in with his work, but it did come up rather expensive.'

'Well, it's caught the attention of her mean little mind,' Sinem said. 'And she's around all morning, so whenever you want to go down you can bask in the warmth of her company.'

'Lucky me.'

I decided I might as well get it over with. It would only occupy my headspace otherwise, and I had enough things doing that already.

Monica was hunched over her laptop when I went in. 'Ah!' she said, looking up.

'I gather you're not keen on my use of silver in the Jabez Clark brochure,' I said.

'It's not the silver per se,' she replied, looking at me over the top of her reading glasses, 'but the cost.'

'If it's too expensive then I can change it,' I said, 'but sometimes you have to pay a little more to get something to look really good. And, after all, if that draws in twenty more buyers, the costs are quickly covered.'

'It seems like a big if,' she said. 'As a matter of fact, Melanie Rice did the publicity for the first Jabez Clark exhibition we had here. She used flyers, not brochures, and they were printed in black and white.'

I sighed. That's what all this was about: Monica's old, old connection with the gallery and the fact that I wanted to try something different, even though I was the new girl.

'Back in those days a Jabez Clark was a lot cheaper,' I said, 'and I bet Mel was trying to draw in the young arty set.' I wanted to meet Monica halfway. It would be hopeless if we were always at daggers drawn like this. 'Look, I know it was Mel that first had the idea for this gallery, and I'm sure she was a true professional, but things do move on.'

She looked up at me. 'And I know it was you who put Mr Rice on to this place, even though Melanie already had her name down for it. You did her a bad turn that day.'

'They seemed like a dream team for a long while,' I pointed out. 'And when I put Seb on to Sir Anthony's agents I didn't know anything about Mel. Anyway, I thought Seb's involvement solved all her problems. Didn't he come up with the money she needed?'

Monica made a face. 'Sir Anthony was a friend of Melanie's family. He was holding the lease for her as a favour; she'd have come up with the finance sooner or later, with or without Mr Rice's help.'

'Still, it clearly suited them both to go into business together.'

She rolled her eyes. 'Her judgement was clouded. Mr Rice had got his hooks into her even before they made the gallery deal official.'

'What do you mean?' I asked. I didn't want to encourage her, but if there were undercurrents I didn't understand I wanted to know.

'The first time they turned up to discuss matters with Sir Anthony it was quite clear that Mr Rice had already become Melanie's lover.'

And this coming from the woman who also thought Seb and Radley were having an affair. 'How could you be sure?' I asked.

She had the grace to lower her eyes a little. 'I was there

don't forget,' she said. 'I still worked for Sir Anthony then and I just happened to see them waiting in the corridor. They hadn't noticed me, but their behaviour made it all quite obvious.' She shuddered slightly. 'I suppose they were excited about what they were planning. Anyway, they were all over each other.'

She took her glasses off, folded them and put them on the desk. 'It was an awful shame that she let him steal her ideas, and then ultimately push her out, so he could carry on as he pleased. I wonder if he'd planned all of that, right from the beginning.'

'Oh, Monica,' I said. 'I'm sure he hadn't. He really seemed to care about Mel and they were together for quite a long time.'

'But I imagine you didn't know how quickly he'd made his move towards her, did you?' She caught my look. 'No, I thought not. He had that other girlfriend, didn't he, up in the Lake District? That'll be why he was keeping his affair with Melanie quiet.'

She sat back in her chair. 'I expect he was too ashamed to tell his friends.' She spat out the last words and I thought back to Seb's constant insistence that he had let Julia down. Was this what had been on his mind all these years? When he had stayed in London rather than going to Julia the weekend she died, had it really been Mel that had kept him down south, rather than the pressure of work? I knew they were meant to have been together during those crucial hours when Julia had given up hope, holed up in a room somewhere …

'I'm surprised at Mel, too,' I said eventually. 'I presume she must have known about Julia, in which case you wouldn't think she'd have wanted to get involved with Seb.'

'Oh it was the usual story,' Monica said, her tone exasperated. 'I asked her, point blank, about that. I thought it was my duty to show her what he was up to. He'd told her that it was all but over between him and the girl in Cumbria, but that he had to be kind and handle the break-up carefully, because of everything she'd been through. Mel felt sorry for her and swallowed that one hook, line and sinker. I'm afraid I thought she was being a fool. I told her I was quite sure the Cumbria girl would remain on the scene, unless she did something to make it clear she wasn't going to be part of a threesome.'

Chapter Thirty-Eight

I'd brought in my own sandwiches for lunch but now I found I couldn't face eating them. The conversation with Monica had sent adrenaline coursing through my body and this was layered on top of the constant tension that had been with me since the evening before.

Shortly after one, Seb called and asked me to go to his office.

'Thanks for coming,' he said as I closed the door behind me. 'Just a couple of things. Firstly, I'm afraid I've got more news on Farron. The logistics guys are downstairs getting those paintings for Lawrence Conran packaged up. One of them noticed a man hanging round in the back lane. From the description I think it's him.' He looked up at me. 'The lads went and told him to get lost, and now he knows he's been seen he'll probably leave it. All the same, I think you should take a taxi back tonight. Just use the company account.'

'I can't do that.'

'Yes you can, and I'm telling you to. I don't want him anywhere near you.'

I drew in a breath. Perhaps it was simpler just to agree, and maybe it would give my nerves the chance to settle. 'Okay then,' I said. 'Thanks.'

'And if you notice anything out of the ordinary, you're to call me, okay? I may have failed Julia, but I'm not going to fail you.'

'Okay.'

His talk of failing Julia suddenly made me think of Mel again.

'Seb,' I said and he looked up. 'There's something I forgot to ask you. In amongst everything else that's been going on it seemed unimportant, but now it's come back to me.'

'Sure,' he said. 'Take a seat and tell me what it is.'

I dropped into a chair. 'I almost had dinner with Mel the other night.'

He raised his eyebrows. 'That wasn't something I was expecting to hear.'

'Alicia was due to meet up with her and she let on that Mel had an exciting new project in the offing. I was quite keen to interview her about it and Alicia, in her own sweet way, decided it would be absolutely fine for me to just muscle in on their evening and ask about the interview then and there.'

'You've got to learn to stand up to her one day you know, Anna.'

'I know,' I said. 'It's a bit sad really. But anyway, I went along to see what Mel had to say.'

'And she was cagey?'

'Not just cagey, Seb. It was really embarrassing actually. She cut me dead. Saw me across the crowded restaurant, stopped in her tracks and refused to come any closer.'

Seb frowned. 'Really? I'm sorry. That must have been awkward.'

I nodded. 'She ended up asking Alicia to get me to go home and effectively hid in the ladies' loo until I'd complied.'

'And you wonder why we divorced?'

I grinned. 'I was at a loss. I haven't done anything to offend her, have I?'

'Certainly not that I know of,' he said. After a pause he added, 'I suppose it may not help, the fact that you're working here.'

'How d'you mean?'

Seb wasn't meeting my eye. 'I think Mel always felt a bit left out when you and the rest of the gang were around. It was almost as though she thought I was closer to you lot than I was to her, at least at the beginning …'

My mind went back to the time just after Julia had died; a time when it now seemed likely Seb was already in a relationship with Mel. 'She didn't ever know,' I began. 'I mean, well, she didn't ever know about what happened with us, did she?'

There was a long pause. 'She might have had some idea,' Seb said.

I looked across at him and he sighed. 'I'm sorry,' he said, 'I'm being evasive, aren't I? The truth is she did make some comment that made me think she was jealous of you in particular, yes. She noticed I spent a lot of time with you just after … Well, you know, just after Julia.' He paused for a moment. 'Obviously that was before Mel and I got together, but it doesn't mean she wasn't already interested. I think later on she wished it had been her I'd automatically turned to.'

I watched him as he spoke, watched him as he told me he and Mel weren't together when we'd had our affair. He wouldn't admit anything to me, not even now.

And why had Seb turned to me, rather than Mel, when they were already an item? Guilt, perhaps? Maybe, just after Julia's death he couldn't face revisiting the woman he'd been cheating with when his regular girlfriend had topped herself. I found myself shivering.

Seb hadn't noticed my reaction to his words. 'The other reason I wanted to see you,' he was saying, 'was about your email.'

For a second I couldn't think which email he meant.

'I'll get back to you on the various queries you had,' he went on. 'I just need to have a quick word with a couple of people first. But I wondered what made you ask about Maxwell-Evans? I haven't seen him in ages.'

I paused for a second, wrong-footed. I must have been mistaken about the man I'd seen going into his office then. I'd been quite convinced it had been him, but then again, I'd only seen him for a short time that day, in the foyer and the corridor. And if Seb hadn't seen him recently then that, in turn, meant Radley had definitely lied to me, making her secret meeting all the more odd. It was probably time to tell Seb I'd seen them together.

I took a deep breath, but as I opened my mouth I happened to look up and realised that Radley was standing right outside Seb's glass-walled office, clearly waiting for us to finish so that she could nip in for a word. If I dropped her in it now, he'd have an immediate opportunity to tax her with questions, and it would be quite clear I'd been telling tales.

After an awkward pause, I came to a decision. 'Oh, nothing. I just thought I saw him the other day. I'd almost forgotten he existed.'

I didn't quite manage to meet his eye as I spoke, and I was sure he knew there was more to tell.

Radley pushed past me as I left the room.

I took a taxi home as Seb had instructed, and we were driving through Bloomsbury when I realised how close we were to Mel's place. I had the sudden, possibly mad, urge to go and see her. I hated the idea of her thinking I'd knowingly had an affair with Seb when she was already on the scene and the solution of having it out with her presented itself. It was the one part of the many things that were happening that I might be able to sort out. I didn't like having bad blood between us. Also her extreme reaction still seemed odd. If there was more to it than simple jealousy, then I wanted to know.

I looked up her address on my phone. 'Actually,' I said to the driver, 'could you just take me to Sutton Square instead? Number eleven please.'

As he turned the corner I peered for the right house, but he knew the square better than I did. 'It's over there,' he said, 'next to the postbox.'

We drew nearer and, at that moment, I saw someone coming out of her house. 'Hang on,' I said. 'Could you just pull over here a second please?'

The driver sighed, obviously losing patience with my whims. I sat and watched from the car as Darrick slid into his coat and walked off down a side street.

'Do you still want number eleven?' said the driver, yawning. 'Or is it back to Hampstead after all?'

I could see Mel at one of the front windows, looking out at Darrick as he moved away. She was impassive, just standing still, staring into the night. What the hell had he been doing there?

'Back to Hampstead after all please,' I said, and the driver sighed again and put the car into first gear.

Chapter Thirty-Nine

I stayed in my room for most of Saturday, wanting to be alone with the thoughts of all that had happened that week.

No wonder Seb had latched onto the idea of Julia's death being murder rather than suicide. It let him off the hook if it had been. The guilt brought on by staying in London with Mel, in preference to seeing Julia, must have been almost overwhelming. But was he right about someone having killed her?

If the artworks she'd had were genuine it would certainly have provided a motive. I flipped open my laptop lid and Googled Goya. I found a set of three of his drawings had sold at Christie's for over £2m. It was a tidy sum, but would seem more substantial to some people than to others. My mind flipped back again to Darrick's flat.

The fact that he appeared to have thought the works were the real thing threw suspicion on to him, but then someone else could have come to the same conclusion too. Julia might well have talked to other people about them – or someone could have stumbled across them after she'd died.

I tried to think who might have had cause to go into the house. The police certainly and then, at some stage, whoever was put in charge of clearing the place. Surely there was an opportunity there for some underhand worker to spot the undiscovered goldmine in Julia's attic.

My mind spooled back through what Darrick had said to me: *it's always been rather hard to know whose side you're on*. What had he meant by that? If he'd murdered Julia and thought I was onto him, he'd hardly expect there to be any question about me being on his side.

And what had he been doing at Mel's? If Seb's theory was right he'd be finding out if she knew anything that might prove his guilt. Well, that made no sense at all. He'd hardly be rocking up at her house and barging in there, if that was what he'd been up to.

By six, I still held the same basic opinion that Seb was wrong. And I didn't buy what Sally said either. I wasn't just going back for more, like a glutton for punishment. I needed to know more, because there was more to this situation than I'd understood.

I looked at my mobile. Should I call him and tell him everything that had happened? I had a feeling that was the only way I'd find out what was going on for sure.

I picked the phone up, ready to dial, when suddenly it rang, almost making me drop it. For a second I thought it was going to be him but, looking at the screen, I saw it was Terry.

'Anna, I'm glad I've got you,' he said.

'What's wrong?'

'Hopefully nothing. I'm not sure. Did you tell Seb about the photo of Julia in Darrick Farron's flat in the end?'

'Yes,' I said, leaving out the fact that I'd left it several days. 'Seb's got his own ideas about why Darrick's interested in her.'

'Oh?'

'He believes he had something to do with her death, and that he's snooping round, trying to check for any evidence that might still incriminate him.'

'Bloody hellfire,' said Terry. 'That's quite an accusation.'

'I had much the same response,' I said. 'But a contact

of Seb's says Darrick knew Julia had some potentially valuable artworks stashed away somewhere: ones that belonged to her parents. Seb thinks theft was his motive.'

Terry let out a long breath. 'Well I would have said it all sounded crazy – especially after all these years – except what I'm going to tell you might add weight to Seb's case.'

I was suddenly conscious of the beat of my heart, pulsing against my ribs, and sank down onto my bed. 'What is it?'

'An hour or so ago a man came round to our place. I wasn't there – I'm still at the restaurant on Fitch Street now – but Steve let him in and called me after to let me know.' He paused. 'Anna, this man told Steve he was a relative of Julia's.'

I caught my breath. 'What did he look like?'

'Tall, broad, dark hair, blue eyes. Darrick?'

'It does sound like him.'

'He said he was visiting from overseas, and was hoping to talk to people who'd known Julia.' He sighed. 'Steve was sympathetic of course. He explained I'd known Julia but that I was working and wouldn't be back until late. So this guy asked if there was anyone else he could call on to fill in time. Steve suggested Jez and gave him his mobile number.'

'He'd be lucky to get Jez,' I said.

'He was lucky,' Terry said. 'I called Jez as soon as Steve told me, and he'd already spoken with this guy on the phone. Said he'd passed on what he could remember, told him what a nice girl Julia had been and all that kind of thing. And then the guy asked if Jez had ever met any other friends of Julia's.'

'And had he?' I asked, thinking back to what the shopkeeper at Henley's had said.

'When Jez and I went up there that time there was a bloke Julia had made friends with. Sort of friends, anyway. She liked to go out on Derwentwater and this man owned a couple of boats and had taught her a bit of sailing. When Jez and I were there he let us have the boats again and taught us a bit too.'

I could hear him let his breath out for a moment as he smiled at the memory. 'Jez was crap. He kept falling in. Anyway, when I called Jez he told me he'd told this guy about him. His name was Toby and he was based by the lake. That was all Jez could remember. I'd almost forgotten his existence honestly. It was such a long time ago, but when Jez mentioned him to me this evening the memories came back.

'I've got a feeling he was one of the few locals at Julia's funeral. I seem to remember Seb mentioning some bloke, and at the time, I wondered if he was a bit jealous.'

'So Jez put this guy – probably Darrick – onto Toby?'

'That's right,' Terry said. 'And Jez said he seemed very grateful. I don't know what this man Darrick's up to, Anna, but I'll let Seb know, for what it's worth.'

I paced around the room for a while, wondering what it all meant. Julia certainly hadn't had any living relatives apart from the aunt in Aberdeen, a detail I'd remembered but Jez clearly hadn't. It seemed quite obvious really that it had been Darrick who had called on Steve and that, once again, he'd been lying.

I picked up my phone again, but I was far more hesitant now than I had been. Could it really be that Darrick was dangerous? But even if he was, I could still find out more by seeing him again than by holding back. And, after all, if I didn't go to his flat, but stuck to some kind of public venue like The Midnight Hour, I couldn't come to any harm.

I debated for another ten minutes before I keyed in the text. 'Need 2 understand what u meant when u asked whose side I was on,' I put. 'Can we talk?' I sent it off into the ether, thinking he probably wouldn't even get back to me.

In fact, I'd only got as far as putting the kettle on when my phone let out a double beep. I opened the message.

'Have something 2 deal with,' he'd written. 'That should round off a job & then we can talk.'

I felt a shiver run through me and goosebumps rise on my arms. After Terry's call I had guessed Darrick's next move would be to try to talk to Julia's old sailing instructor, but the words he used chilled me. Why put "something to deal with" rather than "someone to see"?

And now Sally's words circled in my head. I was going to go back for more when any normal person would turn away.

Chapter Forty

Darrick's text made me look again at what I was planning. On Monday, he would probably call me and off I would go with him and, whatever he said, I still wouldn't really know if I was being fed a line. And then what? How could I go on seeing him with something like this hanging over us?

Sally had certainly been right in one sense: whenever I'd tried to find out what Darrick was up to by asking him, I was left with more questions than answers.

Of course, the simplest thing would be to do what Seb said and keep well out of it. But however much reason told me to forget it, instinct kept drawing me back. The text was another matter though. For the first time I genuinely wondered if Seb could be right.

Before I went any further I needed to find out for certain, and that meant discovering the truth for myself.

Seb's ideas had seemed far-fetched – and they jarred with the facts – but I could still believe there was something for me to find out that would cause me hurt. If that was the case, I had better face up to it. At least I'd know the truth and could lick my wounds and then get on with my life, rather than obsessing about Darrick.

The most obvious port of call was Mel. He'd been with her, and I had wanted to make contact with her anyway. It was really a question of whether she'd talk to me; I wondered what would give me the best chance of a hearing. In the end I decided to text first and then call. If she read my message at least it would put my approach to her in context.

'Wd like 2 call u soon 2 straighten out a misunderstanding.'

I put. 'Also I badly need yr help.' I decided not to give more detail, hoping that I'd raise enough questions in her mind to mean she'd hear me out.

It was time for supper and I decided I'd eat first and then call but, predictably, I wasn't very hungry. In the end I had a sandwich, chewing mechanically, the bread feeling dry in my mouth. I knew I was stretching it out; not wanting to pick up the phone. I was only halfway through it when I heard a text come in.

'Don't call, Anna,' Mel had typed. 'If u do I won't answer. I'm sorry.'

But if she was sorry, why wouldn't she talk to me?

I went up to my room, still with the plan of looking into Darrick's actions hot in my head. My only other lead was in Cumbria. If I really wanted to take matters into my own hands I needed to follow him up there and talk to Toby too. If I could find him.

I sat in my room thinking, but only for five minutes. Either I could hang around for the rest of the weekend with my stomach in knots or I could go for it, and I'd already decided I'd had enough.

Within fifteen minutes I was packing. It was far too late to set off that night, but I wanted to make an early start on Sunday morning. For a moment I wondered about getting back in time for work on Monday, but if necessary I would call the office and explain. When it came down to it, this was more important.

By 6 a.m. I'd got all the clobber I might need into Alicia's hallway. It mainly consisted of jumpers and waterproofs, although I had also taken my overnight stuff and packed a pair of walking boots in a carrier bag, just in case. The weather in London at least was crisp and sunny.

I'd had my car parked in a residents' bay, since Alicia had given me a permit. I was just opening the front door to start ferrying my stuff out onto the street when I dropped the bag with the boots in it, knocking the umbrella stand and letting out a clatter loud enough to wake the whole house.

I set things to rights and was about to dash out to avoid any questions when I heard Sally's basement door open. 'Good grief,' she said. 'You're up early. I thought we had burglars.' She clutched her dressing gown around her. 'Where are you off to?'

I pushed the door shut again. 'I've been feeling restless,' I said. 'I thought I might get out of London for the day. Just to give myself some space.'

She pushed her hair back from her sleep-crumpled face and looked at me. 'That actually sounds like a really good idea. You've been under a lot of strain recently.' I saw her glance at the map in my hand. 'Oh God,' she said. 'Penrith and Keswick? Anna, that's a heck of a day trip.'

'I thought I might even take tomorrow off work,' I said, 'if I feel like staying up there. And I used to go to the Lakes when I was a child, Sally. It's not just the place where Julia died.'

Obviously, I knew my lie was blatant. As I packed my belongings into the boot of my Mini I wondered why I'd even tried to pretend. What made me more depressed was that Sally hadn't attempted to prise the truth out of me either. She knew damn well what I was up to and had probably lost patience with trying to make me see sense.

As I drove through London the worry stayed with me, and only when I got onto the M1 did I finally start focusing on what lay ahead, rather than what I'd left behind.

I was supposed to be able to investigate things; that was all part of what I'd trained for as a journalist. Now it was time to put my skills to something more useful than finding out the favourite underwear of up-and-coming artists.

I put Arcade Fire on the CD player and drove on towards Birmingham.

By eight-thirty I was already desperate for a break and breakfast, and I was still less than halfway there. I stopped at a services. The weather had turned even as I reached the outskirts of London and it was spitting with rain when I dashed indoors from my car.

I went into the cafe and sat there, stoking up on caffeine. I would need to go to Derwentwater first and try to find someone who knew Toby. If he was still around. Of course he might be anywhere by now. It was fourteen years since he'd helped Jez fall off a boat. And it wasn't as though it was the best time of year to look for leads. I imagined a lot of the outdoor pursuit centres would be shut up for the winter. Suddenly I felt very tired. The whole venture was crazy.

By eleven o'clock I was nearing the end of my route. You'd never have guessed it was still morning. The sky was dark, thanks to the weather, which had got much worse as the journey wore on. Driving rain lashed my windscreen and even with the wipers going full pelt it was only just sufficient to clear my view.

Mountains rose up on either side of me: the Lake District to my west and the Yorkshire Dales to my east. The motorway sliced through the prehistoric setting, presenting a bizarre mixture of speed and stillness. I was conscious of the massive bulk of rock. Unlike London where the city danced to the tune of its inhabitants, the people in the Lakes had to work their way round the landscape, threading through corridors etched by the forces of nature.

I turned off at Penrith, and as I neared Keswick the great masses of Blencathra and Skiddaw sat on my right. The fact that they were masked by a thick layer of cloud did nothing to diminish their awe-inspiring presence.

I made for Lakeside at first. I remembered there had been a boat company operating a ferry service there, and I thought they might know where to find Toby. I parked outside the Theatre by the Lake and walked on down the lane that led to the waterfront, pulling my hood up to fend off the wind and rain. There were very few people around, but the ticket hut for the Keswick Launch was open.

'I'm sorry,' I said to the man on duty, 'I don't really think I'm in the right place. I wanted to find out about sailing tuition.'

He shuddered. 'At this time of year?'

I shook my head. 'I'm just here for the weekend, but I was planning to come back in the summer and learn. A friend of mine had lessons on Derwentwater from a guy named Toby, but I couldn't remember his surname.'

'He'd most likely be based over in Portinscale,' the man said. 'Follow the main road and try at Nichol End Marine.'

I found the place all right, at the end of a long track leading towards the Lake. There was no one about when I walked in, but I could hear voices from the basement and followed some stairs down to find myself in a cosy cafe with deep red walls. The smell of carrot soup and freshly baked bread made my stomach rumble. Suddenly,

I felt getting warm, and fed, and travelling home again was probably the best I could hope for. I'd driven a very long way on a whim.

A boy I guessed to be in his mid-teens grinned at me from behind the counter. 'Didn't expect to see anyone else in here today. Sorry there was no one upstairs; we're a bit short handed. Did you want to hire a boat?'

I shook my head. 'Just some soup and a roll thanks.'

'Fair enough.'

'I might want sailing lessons next summer though,' I said, ploughing on with my preferred backstory. I told him I'd heard a man called Toby was a good instructor.

'Toby?' he said. 'Don't recognise that name I'm afraid.'

'He may not even be teaching any more,' I said. Might be in New Zealand or the Outer Hebrides for all I knew, but I decided not to admit that.

'Dad?' The boy called out over his shoulder, into a back room, somewhere behind him. 'Heard of someone called Toby, teaching sailing on the lake?'

'Toby?' A man in a navy sweater and jeans, his face outdoor lined, appeared behind the boy. 'Name does ring a bell actually.' He rubbed a stubbly chin and grinned. 'Might be one of our rivals. No wait, I've got it. There's a guy called Toby does outward bound stuff for schools out Lodore way. Not sailing, but raft making, things like that. He probably sails too though. If he has his own boat he might do lessons for people who want them. Then again,' he said, 'it might not be the same bloke.'

'It could be worth a try,' I said.

'Not many Tobys that I know of, at any rate,' the man said. 'I'm just trying to think of his surname …'

His son handed me my soup and bread, and I paid up.

'You tuck in,' his father said. 'Leave it with me.'

I went and sat at a table next to the window and stared out at Derwentwater. A handful of boats scudded past, leaning at precarious angles.

I was halfway down my bowl when the man in the navy sweater came over.

'Got it,' he said, tapping the side of his head. 'Toby Mason. Don't know his number I'm afraid, but Dan's back in the shop now and he's shared a pint with him in the past. Lives in Thorneygarth apparently.' He picked up the map I'd put down on the table and unfolded it to show me.

'It looks like a tiny place,' I said.

He nodded. 'As remote as it gets. There's only a farm there, and a couple of cottages. They get cut off for weeks in winter sometimes. The road's narrow and steep, so watch yourself.'

Back in my car I looked again at the route to Thorneygarth. Suddenly, driving over the fells in the rain to a remote cottage belonging to someone I'd never met didn't appeal. The guy was probably some other Toby altogether. But then again it would be crazy not to investigate now, after coming all this way.

If Darrick had found out about him late afternoon yesterday he would hopefully have had time to contact him by now, so I should be able to go and quiz him in peace. I put my key in the ignition and then paused again. Oh God. What was I doing? He'd probably call the police or get his farmer neighbour to come and see me off. But I wasn't going to back out now. And if it all came to nothing and it was the wrong Toby, or I couldn't get anything out of him, I would be tired for work the following day, but that was the worst that would come of it.

* * *

I wouldn't have enjoyed the road to Thorneygarth on a bright summer's day. In this weather it was horrible. It was now well on the way to becoming dark and the road was so narrow I had to reverse each time I met something coming the other way. In some places the lane descended sharply on one side to a river valley below. Inaccuracy was not an option. I wove my way carefully past streams and ditches and hoped the car had what it took to cope with the steepness of the roads. At last I came to the hamlet.

As the guy at the cafe had said, there was only the farmhouse – a long walk down a muddy track – and two cottages. I didn't see how Toby could be a farmer as well as an outdoor pursuits professional, so I tried one of the cottages first. The windows were dark and, although there was a car in the driveway, I was sure the owner was out. I walked a hundred metres or so up the lane to the other, where I could see a woman with a baby through the window.

I knocked. The woman looked up and the baby started to cry. In the end it was a man who came to the door.

'I'm so sorry to bother you,' I said. 'I was looking for Toby Mason, but I wasn't sure which of the two cottages he lived at.'

The man's expression changed suddenly. 'You're a friend of his?'

I shook my head. 'Someone said he organised outdoor pursuits and sailing and things like that. I'm only here for the weekend but I wanted to ask him about booking something up for the summer.'

The woman had appeared in the hall behind the man now, the baby on her hip. 'She's after Toby?' she said, her eyes wide, face pale.

The man nodded.

I felt my insides go cold. 'What is it?'

The woman had tears in her eyes. 'They'd ... someone had ...' She didn't manage to go on.

'Go back through, Tina,' the man said, waving her towards the living room door. 'Put Mary in her bouncer and stick the kettle on.' He turned back to me. 'He was found dead, out in the lane, early this morning. He'd been strangled.'

Chapter Forty-One

'It looks as though someone had caught him from behind and put a cord round his neck,' Toby Mason's neighbour went on. 'My sister's husband's in the local police and he says they reckon someone maybe knocked on his door and asked for help, late last night. There are signs that there was a car parked next to where his body was found, and he'd been holding a can full of petrol. It was spilled all over the road.' His words came out in a rush, his eyes dry, but wide with shock.

I felt sick. Little pricks of light danced round me and my head swam.

'Are you all right?' the man said. 'Here. Sit down.' There was a chair by the coat hooks.

'I'm okay,' I said, leaning for a moment against the wall. 'Thank you. But I must go.' And I backed out of the house, hardly knowing what I was doing. I went to sit in my car but I couldn't drive anywhere. I lowered the window and let the wind and rain blow in, attempting to pull out of the feeling of unreality and horror that threatened to swallow me.

I tried to absorb what the man had said, his words rattling round and round in my head. I had to get back to Keswick, get into the centre of town where I was surrounded by people. Mechanically I looked at the map. I needed to find the quickest way. It seemed as though going ahead and then cutting through the next valley might be faster than going back.

I turned the ignition and drove at what was probably about five miles an hour, my hands shaking on the wheel.

Of course, if I'd had my wits about me I might have realised that they'd have closed the road. As it was, I drove almost all the way up to the police cordon before I came to and realised that going ahead wasn't an option.

The murderer had picked their location with care, luring Toby Mason well away from help before striking. The police had erected a screen, so that I couldn't see the spot where he had been found, but this meant my imagination ran on without check. In my mind's eye I saw the body sprawled, the face contorted, the cord lying loose now, on the ground. I realised I was crying when a police officer knocked at the window and told me I'd have to turn around.

In the end, after I'd explained that I'd come specifically to look for Toby and was feeling the effects of shock, the officer made me get out of my car so she could back it round for me.

'You shouldn't really be driving in your state,' she said, frowning as she handed back the keys. She pointed the way I'd come. 'After a mile or so you'll see a pub: The Ram. It's at the crossroads. You might have noticed it on your way here.' She glanced at her watch. 'They should still just be open. Stop there, get out, buy yourself a Coke and sit down for fifteen minutes before you think of going anywhere else. Promise?'

I nodded but she still looked concerned as she let me go.

I made my way back as she'd said, crawling along, gripping the steering wheel tightly now, as though it would help me hold my panic at bay. Although I didn't want to see anyone else, by the time I got to the pub it did seem sensible to follow the officer's advice. The effort of having to concentrate on driving the car was too much with all the frightening thoughts filling my head.

The car park was almost deserted so I thought I should be safe from small talk. I pulled up near the entrance, allowing myself a bit of a walk up to the pub to calm down. Even then I paused for a moment in the doorway, taking a deep breath before I went in.

It was only a second before I registered Darrick.

He was standing at the bar and I heard him say, 'God, how horrible. That's tragic,' before taking a sip of his drink. Putting it down, he added, 'And have they any idea who would have wanted him dead?'

Through my panic it struck me that the shock he'd injected into his tone didn't sound natural. In that instant I knew that the news of Toby's death hadn't come as a surprise.

As that thought sank in, the barman looked up and saw me. I caught sight of the split second his expression transformed into one of welcome before I backed out again, running for the car, my legs turning liquid.

The barman must have expressed his surprise or something. Whatever he'd said, it brought Darrick to the door and he saw me, shouting my name as I slammed the car door closed.

I tried to start up, but in my panic fluffed it. He was running over, still shouting my name. It must have only been a second before I managed to fire the engine, but it felt as though everything was happening in slow motion. Darrick got between me and the exit but I put my foot down so sharply that he had to jump out of the way.

I caught the look on his face as I swung past: pale and shocked.

Chapter Forty-Two

I drove at random, my only conscious thought being that I had to put as much distance between us as possible. After a little while I realised I had no idea where I was. I paused in a passing place, shaking and – only then did I even realise it – crying.

I didn't have a satnav. It had never seemed worth it; I spent most of my time on public transport.

I wanted to call Seb but there was no mobile coverage. I drove on again, glancing down at my phone in its holder every few metres to see if it had picked up a signal. Eventually I went past a footpath that was signposted High End Tarn. I paused for a moment to try to locate it on my map, but I could hardly focus on the images in front of me. The printed place names seemed to jump before my eyes as I tried to rein in my panic. It wasn't long before I gave up and drove on again.

At last the phone flickered into life. I tucked the car into the grassy bank as neatly as I could – not wanting to move an inch in case I lost the signal – and called. Seb answered on the third ring. 'Anna!' he said when he heard my greeting. 'What on earth's wrong? You sound dreadful. Where are you?'

'The Lakes,' I said.

'Shit! What are you doing there?'

'Terry called to explain that Darrick was on to the sailing instructor Julia knew: Toby Mason. I didn't believe you, Seb.' I was crying again. 'I thought you were wrong about him. Even though it looked bad I wanted to find out the truth for myself.'

'Oh, Anna, what's happened?' Seb said, his voice quiet.

'Toby was killed last night. Someone lured him out of his house and garrotted him.' I felt the nausea rise in my stomach again. 'And I've just seen Darrick. He was in a pub called The Ram, hanging round, asking questions … I think he was probing to try to find out what the police know.'

'Anna where are you?' Seb's tone was urgent now. 'Are you safe?'

'I don't know,' I said, trying to steady my voice. 'I drove away so fast when I saw him that I'm not sure what direction I took.'

'Did he catch sight of you?'

'Yes,' I said, shaking as I remembered. 'Oh yes, he saw me.'

'Right, now listen, Anna, I'm on my way up there too and I'm not far away. I can be with you in an hour.'

'You're coming to the Lakes?'

'That's right. Terry called me too. As soon as I got his message, and heard that Farron had been asking about Toby, I made up my mind to come up. I remembered him from the old days of course, but I don't think I ever knew where he lived, or even his surname. No one else seemed to know either, so asking questions in person was the only way.'

'It was the same for me,' I said. 'I only found out by asking locally. And then, when I finally discovered where he lived, I went there, and just up the road there were police and the lane was cordoned off. They'd put up a screen …'

'There there, Anna,' he said, as though talking to a child, 'we need to get you safe. I'm going to pull over and we'll talk about where you should go until I get there, okay? I'm just coming up to a junction now.'

And then there was a longish pause. Too long. I realised the line had gone dead.

I didn't know what to do. If I went any further I might lose the mobile connection again. I sat there, waiting, looking in the rear-view mirror, hunched in my seat.

Within seconds my phone rang and I snatched it up, my thumb pressing the green button hard. But just at that same moment, I registered it wasn't Seb's number on the screen, but Darrick's.

Chapter Forty-Three

I dropped the phone – my former lifeline suddenly as deadly as a cobra – and it landed in the passenger footwell, glowing. Distantly I could hear his voice and it was some moments before I plucked up the courage to reach down and disconnect the call.

I kept the phone well away from me as I pressed the red button; the very thought of hearing him made me shake.

Before he could try a second time I called Seb's number, but it came up as engaged. I tried again immediately with the same result. I kept at it, until at last, between attempts, my phone rang, and this time it was Seb's details on the screen.

'God I'm sorry, Anna,' he said. 'What a time to lose coverage. Thank goodness you had the sense to stay where you were. I tried you before but you were engaged.'

'Darrick called,' I said, stuttering. He was silent but I carried on, the words tumbling out, my teeth chattering. 'I answered, thinking it was you, but when I saw it was him I dropped the phone. I managed to cut him off, and then I tried to ring you.'

I heard him let out a long breath. 'I'm sorry,' he said, 'but it's all right now. He can't find you and I'm going to get you safe, d'you hear me?'

I swallowed.

'Anna?'

'Yes.'

'Right. Have you been past any landmarks that would help me find out where you're stranded?'

Thinking back gave my mind something concrete to

latch onto. The relief that he was on the line again was overwhelming. Just talking to him began to calm me. 'I went past a footpath to High End Tarn,' I said.

There was a moment's pause. 'I see it. Now listen, I've still got my parents' place up there. Not the main house but a weekend cottage they used to use once they'd sold up and moved down south. End House it's called. I let it out, but it's unoccupied at the moment. Why don't you head there?'

He gave me directions and I scribbled them down, my writing spidery, my hand still shaking. Although it was a little way, there were so few roads going in that direction that it sounded fairly simple to find.

'If you get stuck, drive to the top of a hill where you can get coverage and call me again, okay?' he said.

'Right.'

'When you get to the house there's a key under the plant pot to the left of the front door. It's not the type of place where you get burglars.'

The drive seemed to take forever. I went slowly, feeling scared about what I might find round every corner. Seb was right: Darrick couldn't possibly know where I was, but if I did come face to face with him I'd have no way of escaping. The road was so narrow and the mountains hemmed me in on every side. I hadn't seen any other drivers for miles now, nor passed any houses, and it was properly dark. The rain teemed on.

From Seb's directions I reckoned I must be almost there. There were few landmarks to see, but he'd mentioned a gateway and an old barn that I thought I'd spotted. At the same time the idea that I might have missed it was horrible. I wondered whether to call him to check, but my mobile had been out of coverage ever since I'd started to drive again.

At last I saw a turning up ahead. That could be it. And my mobile must have come back to life then too. There was the sound of a text coming in. The relief to be somewhere safe and back in touch with the outside world again was enormous.

I scrambled out of the car, grabbing my holdall, and went to the find the key.

Inside the cottage it was cold. I'd got slightly wet, fumbling with the plant pot outside, and I suppose reaction made me shake too. I flicked on a light and then went to find some way of getting warm. There was a fire in the living room, but no coal. I found a backdoor key and looked outside where I discovered a store, so I refilled the scuttle and found some matches in a drawer in the kitchen.

Once the fire was lit, I remembered the message on my phone. It told me I had voicemail. Someone must have tried to call me when I was out of coverage; probably Darrick, but I needed to check. It could have been Seb.

I went to dial to pick it up, but realised the connectivity I'd had briefly had gone again – maybe before I turned the corner towards the cottage track.

I wondered whether to go out and try to get back to the right spot so I could dial in and pick it up. I peered out of the window into total darkness. It wasn't tempting, but it might be important and, now that I'd found the house, I felt more confident. No one but Seb knew where I was. Light and warmth brought some return to sanity, and I pulled my coat around me, ready to brave the walk back to the lane.

The wind was strong, whipping my hair across my face and driving the rain sideways so it reached under my hood. I was relieved to see my phone come back to life, just under half a mile from the house. I dialled my voicemail and jabbed impatiently at the 'one' key on my phone to cut the instructions short. The voice was announcing message one, received at 4.50 p.m. when I saw the lights of the car.

I cut the call. Seb was the only person who might be ringing with anything urgent to say, and now he could tell me in person.

But it wasn't Seb.

The car was unfamiliar – sleek and black. The driver door opened, and out stepped Professor Maxwell-Evans.

Chapter Forty-Four

The Professor was holding a knife; its long blade gleamed in the car headlights. For a split second I considered running, but I knew I'd never outpace him; he was more than a foot taller than me. I found I was breathing hard and fast, trying to get enough air in. My legs were like lead; everything felt heavy. My heart lurched unevenly in my chest, but I was also just lucid enough to think that making any sudden moves might surprise him into lashing out sooner than he'd intended.

Even though I'd wondered about him recently, I still couldn't think how he came to be here. Panic made my mind slow and stupid.

When I spoke my voice came out dry and broken and my comment was pulled from the air. 'I saw you with Radley.'

He nodded, his smooth, dark hair flying in the wind, his silk scarf fluttering over his shoulder. 'She's got a sharp, nasty little mind. Just like you. She'll find out what happens to people who ask too many questions if she's not careful.' He made a move towards me, the knife point just inches from my chest. 'It's all self interest with her though. She doesn't give a damn about what happened to Julia Thorpe. She's just homing in on anything that might affect Seb. She's after his job, looking for chinks in his armour now their relationship's gone sour.'

I watched his dark eyes as he spoke.

'Seb will be here in a minute,' I said. 'He knows where I am. You'd better give this up; it's not going to work.'

Maxwell-Evans laughed now, the noise loud and harsh,

rising above the sound of the wind in the trees. 'Seb's in London,' he said.

I shook my head. 'I just spoke to him. He told me to come here ...' And it was only then that I realised what must really have happened. I felt hollow, my breath taken away from me. I remembered the time I thought I'd seen Maxwell-Evans going into Seb's office. But then Seb had denied having been in contact with him recently, and I'd believed him. Just like that. Trusted him above the evidence of my own eyes.

Maxwell-Evans was smiling lazily, shaking his head, and moving towards me. 'You see it now, don't you?' he said. 'Sebastian told me to watch out for you. He said you were quick. But frankly, you haven't lived up to your billing.'

Through the fear and shock his words reached my paralysed brain. When I spoke, I was just confirming what I already knew; trying to absorb the truth. The betrayal seemed too monumental to take in. 'Seb told you to come to me here?'

'Of course. Very easy for him to claim to be in one place when he's actually in another.'

'I saw you go into his office.'

'Shame you didn't make better use of the knowledge. That's what set Radley off too. She noticed Sebastian was going crazy trying to contact me just after Farron showed up at Shakespeare's private view. I was abroad and the fool let his desperation show.

'She pretended she wanted to have lunch to pick my brains about the wider arts world. It was all quite pleasant until she started dropping hints about my dealings with Sebastian, and what she might know. It was all bluster of course, but I think she hoped I might accelerate her career to keep her on side.' He laughed. 'She's got no idea what she's dealing with.'

I tried desperately to get a grip on the situation. My mind moved slowly, as though I'd just woken up out of a deep sleep. 'So Seb killed Julia?' I said. 'And now you're covering for him?' I remembered that he collected art. 'He sold you the Goya drawings?'

'B minus,' Maxwell-Evans said. 'I had her drawings all right, but Seb didn't kill Julia and sell them to me. You don't really think a pretty boy like him would get his hands dirty do you? He'd have ripped Julia off, no problem. He tried to in fact. Told her the artworks were crude copies, offered to flog them for what he could get.' Maxwell-Evans snorted. 'He would have taken the profit without batting an eyelid. He's a smooth and ruthless businessman, Anna, but he hasn't got the guts to kill.' He smiled down at me.

'You killed her?'

He nodded and there was an awful pride in his eyes. 'You need a combination of intelligence, strength and balls to go after what you really want,' he said.

And then he smiled, and took a step towards me.

Chapter Forty-Five

Maxwell-Evans towered over me, the knife clutched tight in his right leather-gloved hand. 'Give me your phone and the cottage keys, and then turn around, and lean forward on the car bonnet.'

As I handed over my mobile, my hands were shaking. If I'd picked up my message, if I'd talked to Darrick, if I'd left the house just a moment earlier …

'Go on,' Maxwell-Evans said. 'Waiting patiently isn't one of my strong points.'

I turned slowly and did as he said.

'Now put your hands behind your back.'

If he was going to tie my wrists he'd have to put down the knife. I tried to turn my head so I could watch for the crucial moment.

He paused. 'If you look anywhere but straight ahead I'll slit your throat without a second thought,' he said, yanking my hair with his left hand so that I had to face straight up the bonnet, towards the windscreen.

Within seconds he had secured my hands. As he pulled me up again and turned me round I tested his work; the knots felt horribly secure.

'What are you going to do?' I asked, my throat constricted with fear.

'I'm taking you back to End House.'

'But why kill me there?' I said. 'Surely Seb can't have suggested that, if it belongs to him.'

'It doesn't,' Maxwell-Evans said. 'It's no wonder you're in trouble if you keep believing everything everyone tells you.' His face was in shadow now, but I could hear from his voice that he was smiling. 'Seb pretended your call to him had dropped so he could work out where to send you.'

Once again I reeled at the thought of Seb, cold and detached, using his intelligence to work out how best to dispose of me. I felt my eyes fill with tears, at my own foolishness for misjudging his character, as much as at his total lack of feeling for me.

'End House is just another holiday cottage,' the Professor went on. 'He stayed there once, a couple of years ago, so it was a simple matter to check on the agents' website to make sure it was vacant. And of course he knew the drill: where to find the key and so on.'

'But if it belongs to someone else, anyone could come along at any time,' I said. 'The owners might employ a cleaner or something.' I could hear the rising pitch of desperation in my voice.

He laughed quietly. 'And you think the cleaner would be booked to come in on a rainy Sunday night in winter? I don't think so. And I'm not overly worried about passers-by.' He looked up the deserted road for a moment. 'This lane doesn't lead anywhere you know. Beyond the house there's only a barn and a farm track. That's why Seb thought it would be so convenient.'

He looked back at me. 'Once you're dead, I'm going to send a text using your mobile to get Farron here,' he said, 'and then I'll kill him. Only I'll remove his body of course, once his DNA and prints are all over the house, so it'll look as though he killed you and then ran for it.'

He was holding the knife very close to my chest, his face inches from mine, and I could see the fire in his eyes. He was pleased to be running with this plan, glad to be the one putting it into action.

I knew I needed to delay him. 'The text won't work,' I said, trying to think. 'The police are bound to check my mobile records. It'll look as though I sent the message after I was already dead. They'll know someone else was involved.'

Maxwell-Evans smiled. 'I don't think so. I'll be texting within seconds of your demise. Time of death won't be that accurate – especially given that it'll probably take some while to find your body. I don't think people are here that often in winter. Seb said the next booking he found on the internet wasn't until Christmas.'

He drew in a long breath that conveyed complete relaxation. 'And think of what your mobile records will show. Conversations with Farron, as well as with Sebastian. You remember you told Seb you actually picked up Farron's call, but then dropped the phone when you realised it was him? No one else will know you didn't actually talk.

'Seb will tell the police he was convinced Farron had killed Toby Mason, and was trying to talk you out of seeing him, but that you wouldn't take any notice. After all, it's what everyone's been trying to do all along: make you see sense and give him up. And everyone knows you haven't been listening. Seb will tell them that you were insistent on texting Farron to give him the chance to explain, face to face. And when they check they'll find the record of the SMS sure enough, and that you took a call from him as well.'

Maxwell-Evans put up his left hand to touch my cheek. 'The first thing Farron will see as he comes through the door will be your body. Quite enough of a distraction to let me get the upper hand.'

Chapter Forty-Six

He paused for a moment and turned to face me. 'Disloyalty, Anna,' he said. 'You've only yourself to blame for this. If you hadn't carried on seeing Farron and believing in his innocence, none of this would be happening. Sebastian did try to warn you. And it's only because of Farron's meddling that Toby Mason had to die too. You've both got a lot to answer for.'

'So you made it up here before Darrick did, and killed Toby?' I was still trying to order the facts in my mind.

'Not before him,' Maxwell-Evans said. 'Very shortly afterwards. As soon as Sebastian told me Farron was onto Mason I knew I had to get up here fast. But time was on my side. Farron was just coming to ask questions. He'd be unlikely to knock on Mason's door at one in the morning, and he couldn't manage to arrive any sooner, even if he drove like a maniac.

'No,' he went on, raising the knife up now so that it was inches from my throat. 'I knew he'd have to wait until morning. But if you're planning a murder there's no need to wait for daylight. I said I'd run out of petrol, and Toby was terribly helpful. Came out with me to top my car up again and everything. A silk scarf makes one look so respectable. It was an easy matter to silence him before Farron got a look in.'

My mouth was so dry I could hardly talk. 'So Toby Mason knew, then, about Julia's drawings?'

Maxwell-Evans nodded. 'She'd told him, and Sebastian says Mason even knew I was aware of them too. Shame really: he could still have died an old man, never having thought more about it, if no one had interfered. But there was no way I could let him talk to Farron.'

'But if Darrick never got to talk to Toby Mason, why does he still have to die?' I said. 'And why come after me?'

Maxwell-Evans raised an eyebrow. 'I'm surprised you ask,' he said. 'You haven't been very discreet. Of course, when you asked Sebastian if he'd been in touch with me recently, alarm bells rang so loudly you could have heard them in Brighton. He got straight onto me. It was quite clear something had told you I was up to my neck in this business.'

The sequence of events replayed in my mind in awful slow motion. I remembered how I had questioned Seb about Maxwell-Evans, and how flimsy the excuse for my curiosity must have sounded to him. To think that, at the time, I'd seen it as a matter of office politics. I'd been economical with the truth to avoid a row with Radley, little knowing I was signing my own death warrant. And now it was too late to go back.

'You certainly frightened Sebastian,' Maxwell-Evans was saying. 'Predictably, he wanted to save his own skin. The moment he knew you were up here he was all for taking the opportunity to get rid of you and I was in complete agreement. Neither of us could risk you being that close to the truth without joining all the dots.

'As for leaving Farron alive, that would never do. He's no fool. He may have thought Seb killed Julia to start with, but it's my bet he'll have kept tabs on him. He probably already knows he's still in London and he'll be rethinking the whole matter. I have reason to believe he has me down as a second suspect on his list. Rumour has it he's been sniffing around my affairs.

'On the other hand, if Farron dies, my problems over Julia die, and he can take the rap for killing Mason.' He smiled down at me. 'And you, of course.'

Chapter Forty-Seven

He put an arm around my shoulders, turning me towards the house. 'Time to walk back now, Anna,' he said, and he held the knife in front of me in his right hand, hard up against my stomach, pointing towards my heart. I couldn't even afford to stumble.

All the while we walked one part of my mind was there with the knife, but stray thoughts still managed to gather themselves. 'So how did you find out about the drawings?' I asked.

'All Sebastian's doing,' he said. 'He knew I'd buy them, if he could only persuade Julia to give them up, thinking they were imitations. Part of his plan was to take me up to meet her one weekend. She wouldn't trust his judgement on the matter, but he thought if I went up too, and told her, as a professor of art history, that they were duds, she'd be more likely to acquiesce.'

'But it didn't work?'

'No.' His voice shook slightly, and glancing across at him I realised he was angry; angry that she'd had the temerity to stand up to him. 'She still wanted to hang onto them. But of course the die was cast as far as I was concerned.' His grip on my shoulder tightened as he thought back. 'Once I'd seen them, I knew I'd have to have them. Whatever it took.'

His voice made me shiver. I remembered Seb had always been fascinated by his desire for works of art whilst he was at university. 'That's my future,' he'd said once. 'I could make a lot of money out of people like him.'

I struggled again to loosen the cord tying my wrists, bracing my fists against each other, but it was no good.

Maxwell-Evans felt me tense and realised what I was doing. 'The knots don't have to last much longer,' he said. 'I'm quite sure I've made them strong enough for what remains of your life.' He smiled and I saw quite clearly that he was enjoying this, revelling in the anticipation.

I tried to fight the panic that rose up inside me, and drew in a stuttering breath. 'So how did you get hold of the drawings?'

'I came up here the weekend that Sebastian stayed in London with Mel. I knew it was likely Julia would be on her own, because she'd been expecting to spend the weekend with him. Once I was with her, it was actually quite easy.' The pride was there in his voice again, he couldn't suppress it.

'I presented myself as a fatherly figure. Said I didn't want to cause her pain, but that I felt I must tell her that Mel and Seb were already lovers. I told her I'd looked into her drawings in more detail, and that I was sure now that I'd been mistaken. They were genuine after all, and it was clear that the only reason Sebastian hadn't finished with her was that he was still hoping he might be able to get his hands on them. I made it seem as though I'd specifically come up to warn her, because she seemed vulnerable, and in need of a friend.'

'You got her to trust you,' I said, the full horror and tragedy of Julia's situation sinking in.

'Yes,' he said. 'I was much more successful with her then than I had been the first time around, when Sebastian was there to muddy the waters. She was understandably upset, but that helped; it knocked down her defences. I made her promise to keep the drawings safe, and get them to a proper expert the very next week. I think she would have done that already – she had some contact that Farron had given her – only she didn't have transport and she lacked the confidence to call someone in to see her. Then we had a few drinks, and popped a few pills too, only I didn't really take mine of course, I just appeared to, to seem companionable. Seb had already introduced her to the calming effects of barbiturates and I think she was forming a bit of a habit. It was hardly responsible of him to let her near them, considering her mental state, but it played to my advantage anyway.'

'Why didn't she see you for what you were?' I couldn't believe how he had treated her.

'It was just psychology. I presented myself as being entirely on her side, and then, when it was really late, I said I thought she needed some air, and so we went for a walk round the lake.'

'To the place where she was found.'

'That's right. And by that stage she was so far gone that it was easy to sort out the drowning. There was very little struggling even, because of the way I managed to hold her, and I left her body without a mark. Do you know, I got the impression she wasn't sorry to let go? Then I simply went back to the house, wiped the few things I'd had to touch clean of my prints and removed my glass. I was back in London with the pictures by morning.'

We had reached the drive of End House.

'Of course,' he said, 'she'd been in no fit state to remember to lock her house, so I didn't have any trouble in that direction. Her key was still in her pocket when she was found.'

It was hard to push away the images he was planting in my mind. They were threatening to banish all other thought, but I knew it was essential to keep him talking. I struggled to focus and managed to find my voice. 'Seb told me Julia never even admitted she had the drawings.'

'Well,' Maxwell-Evans said, 'what would you have done in his place? He knew all right. And when Julia died and that aunt of hers invited him up to look through her things, he was able to see that they were missing. If she had been a bit less thoughtful he might never have found me out. As it was, he suddenly had a very good idea what had really happened to Julia. A little more investigating, and he was in a position to come knocking at my door.'

'He's been blackmailing you?' Again a shiver ran down my spine. Seb's face – a face I'd once loved – swam before my eyes, and I felt sick.

'Of course. What did you think? He wanted the money he would have got from me if he'd been able to sell me the pictures. Hardly fair, I thought, given that Julia would still have had them if it hadn't been for me. Anyway, I couldn't afford to pay the whole lot up front, but I gave him a fat lump sum to set up at the gallery, and then paid the rest in instalments.'

'So he's pretty keen not to have you caught.'

'Naturally. I'd report him. He'd do years in prison, and lose everything he's ever worked for.'

'So he tried to put me off the scent, with his theory about Darrick's guilt.'

'Yes,' Maxwell-Evans said. 'Not a bad plan, but I said when we last met that I didn't think it would work for long. Sex got in the way. It's so often the case. It was quite clear to me that you were in too deep.'

We'd reached the house now. I was almost immobile with fear, my legs wobbling under me. Time was running out.

He unlocked the door. 'Through you go,' he said, and then followed, switching on a table lamp.

The fire I'd lit had burnt down in the grate, the last embers letting out a feeble glow.

'How nice of you to make it cosy for us,' Maxwell-Evans said. He locked the front door and bolted it behind us. 'Move over towards that back wall now, Anna,' he said. 'Face away from me.'

His voice had a finality about it. It wouldn't be long. I was about six inches from the wall. And now Maxwell-Evans was pressing the knife to my back, so I could just feel the force of it, without the point actually cutting through my coat. My mind was blank, fear had taken over, and no words came.

'You needn't worry if you don't like the thought of the knife,' Maxwell-Evans said. 'I don't want your blood all over me. The ligature I used on Toby Mason will do much better. It's time, Anna.'

And as he spoke I saw the glint of the knife he still held in his right hand as he raised the cord and pulled it down, tightening it around my neck.

Chapter Forty-Eight

I moved in the only direction left open to me, dipping sharply to the left and knocking my head against the wall. Maxwell-Evans gave a gasp of surprise as his hands were yanked sideways. The knife wobbled and I heard it catch on the plaster. He struggled to keep control, attempting to regain his grip whilst still clutching the cord, but it was too much. He stumbled, and I heard the knife crash to the floor and skitter sideways. Then he plummeted down with me, yelling out as his left knee made contact with the quarry tiles. I was still facing the wall, and partly underneath him, unable to see what was going on. It wouldn't be enough, but I kicked behind me wildly, using every vestige of strength I had. Within seconds he had his right leg clamped round both of mine and my kicking became a twitching. It was inevitable that soon he would make sure even that movement was impossible.

I was aware of him turning the top half of his body away from me, perhaps to reach for whichever weapon came to hand to finish the job he was bent on. Maybe he would have to use the knife after all ...

I made one last desperate effort to throw him off, turning to the wall and trying to jam my feet against it for some purchase, when I heard a sickening crack and felt some unseen force, pushing me onto the tiles.

'Nice work, Anna Morris,' Darrick's voice said, as the weight of Maxwell-Evans lifted off me. 'I must admit your methods did have me just a tiny bit worried there for a moment, but forcing him to drop the knife like that was a sound move; even if you did leave it until the last minute.'

Maxwell-Evans was lying on the tiles next to me, pale and still.

I wriggled round to sit up and Darrick reached for the knife to sort out the rope that had been tying my hands. My head spun and I felt sick. 'He's not dead?'

'No such luck,' Darrick said. 'A bit of a missed opportunity really. I would probably have got away with it, under the circumstances.' He took Maxwell-Evans's scarf off and began to tie his hands with it. 'As it is, he might not be out for that long, so I won't take any chances.'

The police wanted to ask questions then and there, which, to be fair, wasn't exactly surprising. Once I'd said my bit, I multi-tasked by letting a doctor peer at my head and throat whilst I waited for Darrick to finish his explanations.

At last we were allowed to go, with the proviso that we stuck around to make longer statements the following day.

Darrick took a couple of bags, including my own, out to his car and then came back. 'I'm taking you into Keswick,' he said, putting an arm round my shoulders. 'We'll go and stay at the George.'

It was odd, sitting there in the car with him. I'd wanted to know he was innocent for so long, and just for us to be together again. Now here we were, but I felt detached from reality. It was as though someone had wrapped a thick layer of cotton wool around me that left everything muffled.

I watched him as he drove, his jaw set, eyes fixed on the dark road ahead.

A myriad of questions flowed through my mind – I still had absolutely no idea how he'd found me – but, just at that moment, I couldn't form any of the words I needed to voice them. I suppose it must have been the shock. I was utterly exhausted. The painful realisation that, in the end, I had actually believed Darrick capable of murder, and that he knew it, also held me back.

After a while I stopped feeling I ought to be saying something and my mind felt strangely blank. It was as though I was in a waking dream and when we finally arrived Darrick had to open the passenger door before I realised it was time to get out.

'What time were you up this morning?' he asked.

'I think I started getting ready at five.'

'Hmm. A five o'clock start and a standoff with a homicidal maniac. Not exactly your average day at the office.'

We went up to the front desk and he leant forward, talking to the receptionist. After a moment she handed back two keys.

He put an arm through mine as we walked up the wide stairs. 'Our rooms are next to each other,' he said, 'with a connecting door. They normally use them for families. I'll be listening out for you if you need anything. For now, I'll come and help you get sorted out.' He opened up the room and put my case down. 'They're going to bring you up a tray of food in case you get hungry.'

I made a face.

'I know,' he said, 'but reaction to shock's weird. I once ate three pizzas straight after narrowly surviving a knife attack.'

So, he hadn't got over the habit of saying things that filled me with the gravest misgivings.

I looked at my watch. It was already half-past ten. In my zombie-like state I went and had a bath whilst Darrick sorted out his own things.

I felt slightly more human, and a lot warmer, by the time I'd had a soak. I longed to stay cocooned in the fluffy hotel towel forever, but at last I got dry and dressed. Back in the bedroom, a tray of food had appeared. I presumed Darrick must have taken delivery. It was only a moment before he knocked on the connecting door between our rooms.

'Darrick, I need to know things,' I said, as he walked in. 'My brain is filled with stuff I don't understand.'

'I know,' he said, stopping me, 'but it's a long story and you need to sleep. In the morning we'll talk, but for now I've got these.' He brought out some sleeping pills that the doctor had left for me.

I gave him a look.

'Don't tell me,' he said, before I'd opened my mouth. 'Funnily enough, having narrowly escaped death earlier this evening, you have no desire to plunge yourself into a helpless, drug-induced sleep.' He chucked the pills into the wastepaper basket and smiled. 'A woman after my own heart.'

Despite my decision, it seemed there was no way I was going to drop off without the aid of the doctor's pills. My mind kept drifting back to the dark lane leading to End House. I saw Maxwell-Evans' car headlights sweeping over the tall grassy banks, the hulk of expensive metal hemming me in. Nowhere to run. I felt as though I'd got a fever. Under the covers I became hot as panic washed over me, but if I strode about the room I was shivering violently within seconds. In the end I put the kettle on to make a drink. After a couple of minutes there was a knock at the door, and Darrick stuck his head round.

'I came to check up on you. I sort of got the impression you'd been awake for a while, and there was always the danger you'd finally give in and resort to watching the 3 a.m. showing of Ice Road Truckers.'

'I was getting perilously close to that desperate remedy. Hot drink?'

'Although I applaud your idea of keeping your wits about you, I was wondering whether this might be better than a dose of caffeine.' He came right into the room and I saw he was carrying a bottle of brandy.

'Do you always keep some handy? Just in case you get into rescue situations?'

'Yes. There's nothing between me and a St. Bernard dog.' He went to the bathroom for the tooth mugs and poured us each a generous measure.

We stood opposite one another, I in what now felt like a rather thin nightdress, and he still fully clothed. The drink burnt my throat, though it didn't stop me taking another gulp. He took a step closer, standing inches away from me.

'I'm sure I can't sleep because I don't understand how everything happened,' I said, shifting back a little.

'I'm sure you can't sleep because you haven't managed to unwind yet,' he said, moving another step closer.

I forgot the problem of the burning again, and took another large swig of my drink.

'I don't think it would help you to relax if we started going over everything now,' Darrick said, putting his empty mug down on my bedside table. 'Other methods of unwinding are likely to be far more effective ...'

I found I'd finished my drink too, and as he took the mug out of my hand our fingers touched. I leant forward for a split second, and all of a sudden he was kissing me fiercely, tugging me towards him, and my consciousness of the room fell away. The feeling of urgency and then, afterwards, of pure elation was overwhelming.

He didn't leave me again that night and by the time I woke it was broad daylight and, in spite of the season, the sun had found its way in through a crack in the curtains.

But when I turned towards him his expression was serious.

I felt a twist inside me. 'What is it?'

'I'm worried that when you've heard what I've got to say, you'll regret what we just did.'

Chapter Forty-Nine

We were late down to breakfast and the restaurant wasn't crowded. At a table for two, tucked away in a corner, we started off with toast and some proper marmalade, with the promise of an enormous Lakeland breakfast to follow. Only now my hunger had deserted me.

'So why might I possibly regret last night?' I asked, taking a sip of orange juice.

'I'm guessing you'd like to know how I tracked you down at End House,' he said.

'The question had crossed my mind.'

Darrick sat back in his chair and met my gaze steadily. 'I'd installed spyware on your phone,' he said.

'You did what?' I put my glass down with a start.

He nodded.

'When?'

He sighed. 'When you came to my flat,' he said. 'It's quite a simple process. I only needed access to your phone for about fifteen minutes, and that was easy once you were asleep.'

After we'd had sex, and I'd been on an emotional high. 'You didn't trust me? You wanted me on home ground so you could arrange to hack my calls …'

His gaze was still unflinching. 'Twenty-four hours ago you thought I was a murderer.' He shrugged. 'I didn't know what I was dealing with. I'm effectively a PI for the arts world, and I used the tools of my trade. I was already falling for you, that's for sure, but I couldn't let that cloud my judgement. I didn't think you knew what had really happened to Julia, but you still seemed to have a soft spot for Seb. And that made me all the more keen to keep tabs on you.'

I raised my eyebrows.

'I was sure Seb was guilty, and that he knew what I was up to, even if you didn't. And there he was, drawing you closer and closer to him, trying to persuade you not to see me. He was watching you, checking to make sure you hadn't found anything out.'

He took a sip of his coffee. 'Although I was wrong about the nature of his involvement, I was right about that. And at the same time, I knew that the closer you got to him, the more likely he was to give something away, and that that knowledge would put you in danger. The phone hacking was a way of making sure I could always track you down, if things got out of hand.

'I'm sorry,' he added. 'It was rather unorthodox, I know. But it ended up having its uses.'

It was hard to argue that point. A thought occurred to me. 'Is that how you knew where I was when you caught me at the tube station?'

'That and a conversation I'd had with Lawrence Conran. That really put the wind up me. You working with Seb I could just about cope with, but you and him as a couple was way beyond that. The thought of him having you at his side, ready to dispose of if you ever guessed the truth …'

I looked at him.

A faint smile crossed his lips. 'And as for jealousy,' he said, 'don't even go there.'

'You could have told me what you were up to.'

'Like I said, you still seemed keen on Seb. I thought if I was honest, you might not believe me, or even that you might be stung into telling him what I thought. And then, when Lawrence saw you both arm in arm, heading for an evening out, that seemed to confirm my worst fears.'

He registered my expression. 'I almost called you after Terry told you I'd approached Jez for information,' he said.

'Almost?'

'I was worried what he'd told you would convince you I was the murderer Seb said I was. I thought that if I rang you he might be the first person you told, once you'd put down the phone.'

'But I sent you that text just before, asking to meet up.'

He looked at me. 'Yes, but don't forget I was under the impression you and Seb were an item by then. It did occur to me that he might have put you up to getting in touch.'

I looked down for a moment, rapidly running through all the conversations he must have overheard. 'So after I'd talked to Seb, you knew I'd be at End House.'

Darrick looked at me. 'Yes,' he said. 'And what's more I knew you were being set up. I'd been convinced that Seb was a murderer, but at the same time I couldn't break his alibi. When I went to see Mel, she was absolutely insistent that he'd been with her the night Julia died.'

I thought back to the evening I'd seen Darrick visiting Seb's ex. 'I was there.'

'What?'

'When you went to question Mel. I'd gone to her place with the same idea. She'd been refusing to see me and I wanted answers. At first I thought maybe it was because I'd started working for Seb; he said she'd always been a bit jealous. But it was weird. Her reaction was so extreme. I still don't really know what to make of it.'

Darrick looked thoughtful. 'She was very uncomfortable when I went to talk to her. I came to the conclusion that she was telling the truth about being with Seb when Julia died, but all the same, she was clearly hiding something.'

'So what's your bet?'

He shrugged. 'My bet is she always knew it was odd that Seb suddenly had enough cash to help her rent the gallery. And she probably connected it with Julia's death. Who knows, if she saw Seb and Maxwell-Evans meet up, she might even have had an inkling of what was going on between them. And if she had any suspicion at all, and ignored it, that makes her tacitly culpable.'

He sat back in his seat. 'Meanwhile, Seb was on high alert, knowing his past secrets were under threat, and wanting to cover all the bases. He could have let slip you might come asking questions, without ever openly acknowledging the real truth. He'd have known she'd effectively agreed to be an accessory once she accepted his money without asking where it came from. If she was living with years of pent up guilt, that would be a good reason for cutting you dead. She was probably worried as hell you'd say something that would make her feel obliged to come clean. Being able to lie to herself must have kept her sane over the last fourteen years; break that ability, and she'd be broken too.'

That did make a lot more sense than her avoiding me out of jealousy. 'So what happened next, once you'd decided Seb's alibi was probably sound?'

'As soon as I heard Toby Mason had been killed I got a mate to check up on his whereabouts, just to be absolutely sure he wasn't responsible. It didn't take long to confirm that he was still at home in London. I reassessed the situation. Suddenly it looked as though he wasn't guilty of either murder. But he was clearly working hand in glove with whoever was.

'The moment you ended the first half of your conversation with Seb, I called you. God, you were suddenly so vulnerable, Anna. I guessed he wanted you dead and there you were, in the middle of nowhere in a state of shock, ready to do anything he told you. When you answered I thought I was going to be able to warn you, but I assume as soon as you realised it was me you threw the phone down.'

'I'm sorry,' I said, putting my head in my hands. 'I thought you wanted to get me to talk so that you could try to work out where I was.'

He took my hand. 'Yes, just a little more trust wouldn't have gone amiss ...'

I gave him a look. 'Faults on both sides I'd say. So if you knew I was being set up, did you also know who would be waiting for me?'

'I had a pretty good idea,' he said. 'When we had dinner at The Midnight Hour you mentioned one of Seb's tutors had collected art.'

I nodded. 'I remember.'

'I started to dig around to find out who that might have been and it wasn't long before I had Maxwell-Evans' name. At the very least, I reckoned he might have taken the artworks off Seb's hands. As soon as I knew Seb wasn't our killer, he went to the top of my list.'

'So when did you arrive at the cottage?'

'Just after you and Maxwell-Evans did. But I couldn't intervene straight away. I had to be certain I could overpower him in one hit; otherwise you'd have been as good as dead anyway.' He gave me a look. 'It was you forcing him to drop the knife that gave me my opportunity. I'd have gone for it at that point anyway of course; there was nothing else for it, but the outcome would have been a lot less certain. One false move and I knew he could have stuck a blade into you.'

'But how did you get in?'

'The back door,' Darrick said. 'I was wondering how the hell I would be able to reach you in time, but for some reason it was unlocked.'

It suddenly came back to me. Of course. 'I'd left it unlocked myself, after I'd been outside to fetch some coal. I suppose it would never have occurred to Maxwell-Evans to check it.' It seemed so odd now to think that at that point in the evening I'd been devoting my time to anything as mundane as getting warm.

He looked at me. 'Anna, I know I've behaved like a devious, lying bastard ever since we first met, but I can assure you that's totally out of character. At least, when I'm dealing with lovers ...'

'Hmm.'

'Would you be prepared to put it down to unfortunate circumstances, and start all over again?'

I thought for a moment. 'On one condition,' I said.

He raised his eyebrows.

'That you take whatever it is you put on my phone off again before our relationship goes any further.'

'It's already done,' he said, with a small smile. 'I did it last night while you were in the bath.'

After breakfast we had to see the police, and then we sat in a coffee shop, peering out at the passers-by on Main Street.

I disrupted the pretty pattern the waitress had made in the cream on top of my mocha. 'I still don't understand why all this happened now, so many years after Julia's death,' I said.

He sighed. 'Complete chance. I'd been abroad for

a while and when I came back I went for a drink with Lawrence. There'd been a sale of three of Goya's lost drawings recently and he mentioned it, which made me think of Julia. I wondered aloud what had happened to her, and whether she'd ever done anything more about the drawings she'd had.'

'God how awful! You didn't even know she was dead?'

He shook his head. 'We were never in regular contact. I met her at my cousin's wedding where she'd been doing some waitressing for the catering company they'd used. We got chatting and found we got on.

'She was attractive and, when I took the picture you must have found, I managed to get her in. I suppose I hoped I might see her again.'

In spite of myself I felt a twinge of jealousy.

Darrick went on, 'It was actually at the wedding that she told me about the drawings.'

'So did you see her again after that?' I asked, taking a sip of my drink and trying to keep my tone light.

He stared down into his cup. 'Just once. I took her out to dinner.' His eyes came up to meet mine for a moment. 'She seemed so sad, Anna. We talked more about the drawings, and she said how her boyfriend, who knew about these things, had rubbished her ideas about them. I didn't know who the guy was, but she didn't sound happy with him. Before we finished the meal, I arranged to go back home with her that night, look at the pictures, and give her my opinion.'

He sighed. 'We had a few drinks, and when we left the restaurant, whilst we waited for a taxi, we ended up in each other's arms.' He shook his head. 'I was bang out of order there. I knew she was with someone, and vulnerable, and I was several years older than her.'

My insides were taut – a weird mixture of sorrow for Julia, and a pang of something I didn't want to acknowledge.

'Things got quite passionate. She kissed me back; she was drunk too. But then after a minute or two she pulled away and said she couldn't, because of her boyfriend. And then when the taxi turned up she changed her mind about me going back that night to look at the pictures. I got the driver to drop her home first. There were tears in her eyes as she got out, and that's my last memory of her.'

'You never saw the drawings?'

He shook his head, his face ashen. 'We made contact by phone and set up a provisional date, but then I got called away on a job.

'I emailed her, though, recommending an expert who'd be able to help.' He turned to me. 'And apologising for the way I'd behaved. It was six months before I was back again, and although I wondered periodically how she'd got on, I was involved with other things and I never took the trouble to find out.'

'And then when Lawrence said she'd died?' I prompted.

'When Lawrence said she'd died, he mentioned in the same breath that, at the time, she'd been going out with Seb Rice, who we all know so well now – by reputation if nothing else. I was stunned. I remembered reading about his girlfriend in some magazine article, but I had no idea it was the Julia I'd known. Once the two sides of the story came together, I began to wonder what had happened to those drawings.'

I shivered and we sat in silence for a moment.

'I did some investigating,' Darrick said, 'and found there'd been a sale of Julia's belongings after she'd died, but that there were no records of any lots that matched the artworks she'd told me about.

'It seemed so likely that Seb had taken them, and more and more probable that he'd killed her in order to do so.

'I felt awful. I'd taken advantage of her vulnerability, and then walked away, just when I might have been able to help. If I hadn't made that pass at her, I'd have gone home with her that evening, identified the drawings, and she'd be alive now. Once I knew what had happened I had to find out the truth. It was the only thing I could do. Talk about too little, too late.'

I reached forward and touched his hand, and he met my eyes for a moment.

'When I got to work,' he went on, 'I found Seb's alibi was weak. For the crucial part of the day the woman who'd proved his innocence was the woman he'd ended up marrying. I imagined he'd taken the risk that Julia, who knew almost no one, had told very few people about the drawings.

'Of course, I didn't know whether Julia had told Seb she'd met me, or if she'd mentioned that we'd discussed their possible worth. It was Radley's reaction to my presence at the private view that convinced me she must have.'

'How do you mean?'

'That business of her saying she'd seen me take your photograph was an outright lie,' he said. 'And why make that claim? The only reason I could think of was if Seb had already worked out who I was, and was determined that you and I shouldn't go pooling our knowledge. I suspect he told Radley to say whatever she liked, so long as it put you off seeing me again.'

'So between you coming into the gallery and Radley coming to find me he'd tracked down your real identity?'

Darrick nodded. 'I think so. It wouldn't take long to flash my picture round a few of his contacts and come up with a result.'

'And yet they let me believe they couldn't identify you until much later.'

Darrick nodded. 'Seb spent his whole time judging what information it would be helpful to let you have: what would be most likely to put you off me and what would act as the best smokescreen to disguise his real involvement.'

'And what made you decide to go to the private view in the first place?'

'I wanted to know more about Seb.' He paused. 'And there was always the chance that I might meet the woman of my dreams, obviously.'

'It was pretty risky.'

He gave me a crooked smile. 'I like risky.'

We left Keswick on Tuesday. My car wouldn't start, so I got it relayed home and Darrick drove me.

It was a peculiar feeling, heading back to London, like coming out of a darkened cinema into the daylight again. I was blinded by normality: the M6 traffic and the closing gap between me and Hampstead. I suddenly realised it was less than two weeks until Christmas. I'd hardly given it a thought.

'I'm due to meet a woman about a handbag tomorrow,' I told Darrick, suddenly thinking it might be handy to sell some after all, given my impending drop in income.

He raised an eyebrow.

'I've taken to making them in a small way, and this person runs a crafts gallery. She said she'd like to put them on show.'

'Sounds good,' Darrick said. 'Who is she?'

'Someone called Nadine Constantin.'

'Nadine! I know her from years back. I used to lodge with her sister when I first came to London. You're in for fun in that case, and she's got great taste. Of course,' he said, 'they might still want you at the gallery.'

I shook my head. 'It's like you said. Seb only got me in there because he wanted to keep an eye on me. I thought the atmosphere was pretty odd when I started, and now I know why. No one else had any idea why he'd brought me in.

'I think he must have coerced Radley into being nice to me, at least at first, so that I wasn't put off. But she was obviously starting to get fed up with him bossing her around. I suppose she'll take charge now.' We'd already heard that Seb had been arrested, and that morning it had been front-page news too. Photographs of him being led away from the gallery in handcuffs were set alongside the picture of Maxwell-Evans with the royals that I'd found on the internet previously. Seb was looking at the ground, trying to avoid the cameras. One of the headlines read, 'How the mighty have fallen.'

I shook my head at the thought. The past, and the friendship I'd imagined I'd shared with him, made me ache inside.

Darrick glanced at me and must have read my expression. 'I think people with criminal minds are born with a bit missing. They can form relationships with people but then drop them in an instant if they become a threat.'

I nodded. I knew he was trying to make me feel better. And he didn't officially know that Seb and I had once been lovers, though I reckoned he'd guessed.

By the time we reached the outskirts of London it was gone five o'clock.

'So where now?' Darrick said, as we joined the North Circular.

'Home I suppose,' I replied. I realised I'd sighed as I'd said it. I was conscious that, in spite of all the horrors of the weekend, I didn't want this time to end. Leaving the knife-wielding maniac behind was obviously a plus, but I'd enjoyed the bit afterwards: it being just us, cut off from the rest of the world.

There was a momentary pause as Darrick changed lanes.

'Hampstead home, or Primrose Hill home?' he asked, looking ahead at the traffic.

I glanced quickly across at him.

'I love my flat,' he went on, still looking ahead as a motorbike cut in in front of us, 'but I think I'd like it a whole lot better if you stayed over more often.' He grinned, glancing round at me for a second. 'I like the idea of knowing where you are. Any time you visit, I swear I'll do my utmost to keep the place free of psychopaths.'

'That's certainly a persuasive argument.'

'I'm full of those,' he said, and suddenly his tone was serious. 'Especially when I'm after something that really matters.' And then he glanced at me again, and the look in his eye set off a whole new wave of emotion.

We were both silent for a moment.

'In any case,' he added at last, 'what would happen if you went back to Hampstead now?'

I watched his hands on the steering wheel. 'Well Sally would want a full-scale rundown of my exploits for a start,' I said.

'Which I'm sure you'll want to give her at some point, but possibly not tonight. And your cousin?'

'Alicia? Oh, I expect she'd content herself with giving me a blow-by-blow account of every mistake I've made since deciding to drive up to Cumbria.'

He gave me a sidelong glance. 'Primrose Hill?'

'Primrose Hill,' I agreed.

About the Author

Clare writes fast-paced romantic mysteries, using London and Cambridge as settings. Her influences include JD Robb, Janet Evanovich, Mary Stewart and Sue Grafton. Brought up in the Midlands, she went on to read English at London University, then worked in book and author promotion in venues as diverse as schools, pubs and prisons. More recently she's exercised her creative writing muscles in the world of PR, and also worked for the University of Cambridge. Her current day job is at the Royal Society of Chemistry.

Her writing is inspired by what makes people tick, and how strong emotions can occasionally turn everyday incidents into the stuff of crime novels. It would be impossible not to mix these topics with romance and relationships; they're central to life and drive all forms of drama.

When she's not reading or writing, Clare enjoys drawing, cooking and trips to the Lake District. Closer to home, she loves wandering round the pubs, restaurants and galleries of Cambridge, where she lives with her husband and two teenage daughters.

You Think You Know Me is Clare's debut novel.

www.twitter.com/ClareChase_
www.clarechase.com
www.facebook.com/ClareChaseAuthor

More from Choc Lit

If you enjoyed Clare's story, you'll enjoy the
rest of our selection. Here's a sample:

The Elephant Girl
Henriette Gyland

Peek-a-boo I see you …

When five-year-old Helen
Stephens witnesses her
mother's murder, her whole
world comes crumbling down.
Rejected by her extended
family, Helen is handed over
to child services and learns
to trust no-one but herself.
Twenty years later, her
mother's killer is let out of jail,
and Helen swears vengeance.

Jason Moody runs a halfway house, desperate to distance
himself from his father's gangster dealings. But when Helen
shows up on his doorstep, he decides to dig into her past,
and risks upsetting some very dangerous people.

As Helen begins to question what really happened to her
mother, Jason is determined to protect her. But Helen is
getting too close to someone who'll stop at nothing to keep
the truth hidden …

Visit www.choc-lit.com for more details
including the first two chapters and
reviews, or simply scan barcode using
your mobile phone QR reader.

Never Coming Home
Evonne Wareham

**Winner of the Joan Hessayon
New Writers' Award**

All she has left is hope.

When Kaz Elmore is told her
five-year-old daughter Jamie
has died in a car crash, she
struggles to accept that she'll
never see her little girl again.
Then a stranger comes into her
life offering the most dangerous
substance in the world: hope.

Devlin, a security consultant and witness to the terrible
accident scene, inadvertently reveals that Kaz's daughter
might not have been the girl in the car after all.

What if Jamie is still alive? With no evidence, the police
aren't interested, so Devlin and Kaz have little choice but to
investigate themselves.

Devlin never gets involved with a client. Never. But the more
time he spends with Kaz, the more he desires her – and the more
his carefully constructed ice-man persona starts to unravel.

The desperate search for Jamie leads down dangerous paths
– to a murderous acquaintance from Devlin's dark past, and
all across Europe, to Italy, where deadly secrets await. But as
long as Kaz has hope, she can't stop looking …

Visit www.choc-lit.com for more details
including the first two chapters and
reviews, or simply scan barcode using
your mobile phone QR reader.

The Silent Touch of Shadows

Christina Courtenay

Book 1 in the Shadows from the Past series

Winner of the 2012 Best Historical Read from the Festival of Romance

What will it take to put the past to rest?

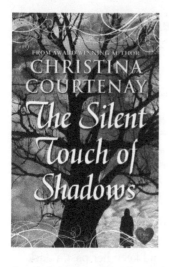

Professional genealogist Melissa Grantham receives an invitation to visit her family's ancestral home, Ashleigh Manor. From the moment she arrives, life-like dreams and visions haunt her. The spiritual connection to a medieval young woman and her forbidden lover have her questioning her sanity, but Melissa is determined to solve the mystery.

Jake Precy, owner of a nearby cottage, has disturbing dreams too, but it's not until he meets Melissa that they begin to make sense. He hires her to research his family's history, unaware their lives are already entwined. Is the mutual attraction real or the result of ghostly interference?

A haunting love story set partly in the present and partly in fifteenth century Kent.

Visit www.choc-lit.com for more details including the first two chapters and reviews, or simply scan barcode using your mobile phone QR reader.

Please don't stop the music

Jane Lovering

Book 1 in the Yorkshire Romances

Winner of the 2012 Best Romantic Comedy Novel of the Year

Winner of the 2012 Romantic Novel of the Year

How much can you hide?

Jemima Hutton is determined to build a successful new life and keep her past a dark secret. Trouble is, her jewellery business looks set to fail – until enigmatic Ben Davies offers to stock her handmade belt buckles in his guitar shop and things start looking up, on all fronts.

But Ben has secrets too. When Jemima finds out he used to be the front man of hugely successful Indie rock band Willow Down, she wants to know more. Why did he desert the band on their US tour? Why is he now a semi-recluse?

And the curiosity is mutual – which means that her own secret is no longer safe …

Visit www.choc-lit.com for more details including the first two chapters and reviews, or simply scan barcode using your mobile phone QR reader.

Follow me follow you
Laura E James

Book 2 in the Chesil series

You save me and I'll save you

Victoria Noble has pulled the plug on romance. As director of the number one social networking site, EweSpeak, and single mother to four-year-old Seth, she wrestles with the work–life balance.

Enter Chris Frampton, Hollywood action hero and Victoria's first love. His return from LA has sparked a powder keg of media attention, and with secrets threatening to fuel the fire, he's desperate to escape. But finding a way forward is never simple. Although his connection with Victoria has lasted the test of time, has he been adrift too long to know how to move on?

With the risk of them breaking, will either #follow their heart?

Visit www.choc-lit.com for more details including the first two chapters and reviews, or simply scan barcode using your mobile phone QR reader.

Introducing Choc Lit

We're an independent publisher creating
a delicious selection of fiction.
Where heroes are like chocolate – irresistible!
Quality stories with a romance at the heart.

See our selection here:
www.choc-lit.com

We'd love to hear how you enjoyed *You Think You
Know Me*. Please leave a review where you purchased the
novel or visit: **www.choc-lit.com** and give your feedback.

Choc Lit novels are selected by genuine readers like yourself.
We only publish stories our Choc Lit Tasting Panel want to
see in print. Our reviews and awards speak for themselves.

Could you be a Star Selector and join our Tasting Panel?
Would you like to play a role in choosing which novels we
decide to publish? Do you enjoy reading romance novels?
Then you could be perfect for our Choc Lit Tasting Panel.

Visit here for more details...
www.choc-lit.com/join-the-choc-lit-tasting-panel

Keep in touch:
Sign up for our monthly newsletter Choc Lit Spread for
all the latest news and offers: www.spread.choc-lit.com.
Follow us on Twitter: @ChocLituk and Facebook: Choc Lit.

Or simply scan barcode using your mobile phone QR reader:

*Choc Lit
Spread*

Twitter

Facebook